Praise for Elmer Kelton

Storytelling as ripe as a bank ripe for robbing. Its quietly knifelike sentences will skin you alive."
—*Kirkus Reviews* on *Texas Vendetta*

Elmer Kelton is a splendid writer. *The Way of the Coyote* is . . . another terrific book."
—*The Dallas Morning News*

Elmer Kelton writes of early Texas with unerring authority. . . . The fate of Texas is at hand, and Kelton will have readers eager to find out what happens."
—*Fort Worth Star-Telegram*

Kelton is a master storyteller who offers more than just blood and gunsmoke. The right blend of action, drama, humor, and suspense makes this a handsome edition to his ongoing saga of the Old West."
—*Publishers Weekly* (starred review) on *Ranger's Trail*

One thing is certain: as long as there are writers as skillful as Elmer Kelton, Western literature will never die."
—*True West* magazine

Forge Books by Elmer Kelton

ELMER KELTON

TEXAS
VENDETTA

FORGE®

A TOM DOHERTY ASSOCIATES BOOK
NEW YORK

This is a work of fiction. All the characters, organizations, and events portrayed in this novel are either products of the author's imagination or are used fictitiously.

TEXAS VENDETTA

Copyright © 2003 by Elmer Kelton

A Forge Book
Published by Tom Doherty Associates, LLC
175 Fifth Avenue
New York, NY 10010

www.tor-forge.com

Forge® is a registered trademark of Tom Doherty Associates, LLC.

ISBN 978-0-7653-4480-9

First Edition: November 2003
First Mass Market Edition: February 2005

Printed in the United States of America

0 9 8 7 6 5 4

To Felton Cochran,
bookseller extraordinaire

1

FOR THE LAST TWELVE OR FIFTEEN MILES ANDY Pickard and Farley Brackett had ridden in almost total silence. One ignored his partner, and the other tried to. They talked no more than the surefooted little Mexican pack mule that followed them across the Texas hill country's rocky ground. That suited Andy fine, for Farley was unlikely to say anything he wanted to listen to.

Andy speculated that the Ranger captain might have been sore at him for some reason, detailing him with dour Farley Brackett on this locate-and-arrest mission. The captain had said, "Brackett's a man I'd like to have beside me in a fight, but be damned if I'd want him for company before and after."

Farley usually looked as if he had just come back from a funeral. The captain had probably been glad to get him out of camp for two or three days and let the sunshine in.

Andy had to squint, riding directly into the setting sun. "Fixin' to be sundown pretty quick."

Farley grunted as if to say he could see that for himself and he resented the break in silence.

Night was going to catch them before they reached the Leach place. That was all right with Andy. He liked a little low-level excitement, but he had no interest in getting killed. He said, "We'd make too good a target ridin' up in broad daylight anyway. Captain told us those folks are apt to put up a fight if we don't catch them off guard."

Farley's eyes were as grim as the muzzle of a shotgun. "Anybody is liable to put up a fight when they're lookin' at a stretch in the penitentiary. These people ain't bright, but even a fool can sight down a gun barrel and kill you."

Andy and Farley carried a warrant for the arrest of one Joseph Bransford on a charge of robbery and attempted murder. He had ambushed a stock farmer back in Colorado County, leaving him for dead after taking money the farmer had collected for selling a team of mules. The captain had received a tip that Bransford was hiding out north of the Llano River on a hardscrabble homestead operated by his sister and her husband, Abner Leach. Leach claimed to be a farmer, but he was suspected of operating a way station for stolen livestock. No one had been able to prove it to the satisfaction of a jury.

So far as the captain could determine, Leach was not currently wanted by the law despite his shady reputation. However, it was probably only a matter of time before he was caught knee-deep in some ill-conceived activity that would put his name on the Rangers' fugitive list.

Farley said, "If we was to shoot them both, the taxpayers wouldn't have to foot the cost of a trial."

Coming from some people, that would be considered idle talk. In Farley's case, Andy doubted it was idle. "There's no charges out against Leach."

"There will be sooner or later. Shoot him now and we'll save some squatter from gettin' his livestock stolen."

Andy could see a certain twisted logic in Farley's view of summary justice, but it went against many stern lectures peace officers like Rusty Shannon had preached to him about the importance of law, about the presumption of innocence until guilt was proven. He wished he had Rusty with him now instead of Farley. "Rangers don't go around shootin' prisoners."

"Wake up and look around you, boy. Sometimes justice gets served out in the brush, where there's no witnesses. No petty-foggin' lawyers, no bought-off jury. Time you get a few more years on you, you'll know what I mean."

Farley had touched a sore spot. Andy was evidently the youngest man in the company, though nobody knew his age. The best guess was twenty years or a little more. Indians had killed his father and mother when he was small and had carried him off to raise as their own. Circumstances had thrust him back into Texan hands about the time his voice began to change. He had had to learn English all over again and stumble along on the white man's road, learning the hard way by trial and error—lots of error. Even with Rusty Shannon's guidance, it had been a rough road to follow after knowing only the ways of the Comanche.

He was keenly aware that he still looked young to be riding with the Rangers. He had recently tried growing a mustache in an effort to appear older. He had shaved it off after three weeks because it looked pathetically thin and weak.

Farley had remarked, "Old men try to look young, and young men try to look like their daddies. They're all lyin' to theirselves."

Andy was aware that an element of truth existed behind Farley's talk about shooting prisoners. He had heard whispered stories about outlaws shot "trying to escape." If a man was considered dangerous, it was safer to carry him in dead. And a quick burial was cheaper on the county. No criminal ever climbed out of the grave to file an appeal.

Many people were afraid of Farley Brackett, with cause. He had come home from the Yankee war with a long scar on his face and a deeper one etched into his soul. During Reconstruction years he had become a scourge to the federally backed authorities. The unionist state police had chased him often but had learned from bitter experience not to get close enough to catch him.

Once the old-time Texans regained political control of their state, transgressions against the former government had been forgiven, even applauded. The reorganized Rangers had been glad to have Farley join their ranks. He knew how men on the dodge thought and acted because he had been one. Andy thought he still had the shifty wolf eyes of a fugitive.

In the fading light of dusk Andy could make out a dim wagon trail. "You sure these tracks lead to the Leach place?"

Farley grumped, "Of course I'm sure. I'm always sure. I came this way before, huntin' a pal of Leach's that stuck up a Dutchman over in Friedrichsburg.

Leach tried to point me onto the wrong trail. I ought to've shot him when I had the chance. We wouldn't have anybody to worry about now but Bransford."

They followed the wagon tracks until Andy saw lamplight ahead. "Looks like we've found the cabin."

"It never was lost. I knew where it was at."

"I guess we'll wait till they're asleep, then bust in?"

Farley assumed command by right of seniority and age. He looked at Andy as if the suggestion were the dumbest thing he had ever heard. "No, we'll make a dry camp and wait for mornin'. Bust in now and we'd have Bransford and Leach both to fight. That ain't countin' the woman, but I expect she'll just scream, faint, and fall down."

Andy argued, "In the mornin' they'll all be awake."

"We'll wait till the men are separated so we can handle them one at a time. Last time I was here, Leach came out about daylight to milk. We'll surprise him at the cow lot."

"And Bransford?"

"He'll give up when he sees we're fixin' to burn the cabin down around him."

"Or he'll come out shootin'."

"Good. We can finish him off legal and proper."

Andy protested, "We can't burn a cabin with a woman in it."

"She'll come out soon as her skirts start smokin'. With people like them, you don't ask permission or beg their pardon."

"I doubt the adjutant general would approve of it."

"The adjutant general!" Farley snorted. "Sittin' comfortable at a desk in Austin, writin' rules like he was dealin' with law-abidin' citizens. Out here the owl hoots in the daytime same as at night, and things look a lot different."

They moved back to the far side of a cedar-crowned hill where they could build a small fire without its being seen from the cabin. Farley commanded, "Cook us somethin' fit to eat."

Andy started to say, *You're a private same as me,* but changed his mind. The day might come when he had a showdown with Farley, but it would have to be over something more important than this. He took a pack from the back of the mule while Farley coaxed a small pile of dead wood into a blaze. Andy wished he had some of the dried buffalo meat that Comanches carried on long rides or the pemmican they made by pounding dried meat, berries, and nuts together. He preferred it over fatback broiled on the end of a stick. But he would settle for fatback because that was what he and Farley had brought, that and cold biscuits dried hard enough to drive a nail.

He knew no fat Rangers.

Water from their canteens yielded a cup of coffee apiece. Farley sat back, stretching his long legs, and slowly sipped his coffee as he might nurse a shot of whiskey. He seemed to withdraw into some private part of his mind, as distant as if he were back in the company headquarters camp on the San Saba River.

Andy broke a long silence. "I wish Rusty was with us." Rusty Shannon had taken charge of Andy when he was separated from the Comanches. He had become like an older brother.

"What's the matter, Badger Boy? You need a nurse-maid?"

Farley took perverse pleasure in using the English

version of the name by which the Comanches had known Andy. He was like some malevolent shaman who could summon up a dark and rumbling cloud from a bright and sunny sky.

Andy said, "Rusty always knows what to do."

"He's not a Ranger anymore, and it's probably a good thing. He always allowed the other feller too much of an edge. Sooner or later he'd get himself killed takin' pity on people that have got no pity comin' to them."

That was one thing Farley could never be accused of, Andy thought. "Rusty had pity on *me* when I needed help. And God knows I caused him trouble enough for a while."

Rusty had taken Andy into his log-cabin home on the Colorado River. He had managed to maintain his patience while Andy made the slow and painful transition from Comanche life. Andy had run away more than once, trying to return to his adoptive Indian family. He had fistfought boys for miles around when they ridiculed him for the Indian braids he refused to cut and the moccasins he wore instead of shoes.

The braids were gone now, and so were the moccasins. He wanted to fit in, to be the kind of Ranger Rusty had been. But he retained a remnant of Indian upbringing. It would probably always be there.

Drinking his bitter coffee, he lapsed into silence, pondering tomorrow and wishing he were as sure of himself as Farley seemed to be.

MORNING WAS A LONG time in coming. Andy lay awake most of the night, visualizing the expected confrontation, imagining the worst that might happen. He pictured Leach's woman lying dead after the smoke cleared, much as he had seen his white mother dead years ago. It was one of his earliest memories, long suppressed because it was so terrible. The image still returned from time to time like a nightmare that would not wait for the night.

Farley seemed to harbor no misgivings. Andy listened to him snoring peacefully.

The stars still glittered when Farley came out from beneath his blanket. He looked up at them to get a rough notion of time. "We'd better be gettin' ourselves in position before daylight. Leach wakes up the rooster."

Andy was hungry. "Hadn't we ought to fix some breakfast first?"

"When we're done we'll make Leach's woman cook us a proper meal."

"Thought you were goin' to burn her cabin down."

"They raise pigs. We'll catch us a juicy shoat and have her roast it over the coals."

Andy started to pack the mule. Farley stopped him. "Don't you know a stupid mule is liable to smell feed and go in there brayin' his head off? We'll leave him here and pick him up when the job is done."

Chastened, Andy tied the mule.

The cabin was still dark as the two Rangers circled around to come in behind the milk shed. They left their horses in a clump of trees. The cow stood outside the gate, waiting in bovine patience for the grain that awaited her in the stanchion. She turned her head to watch the men approach on foot. She seemed to know they were strangers and drew away. She did not go far because she had not yet nursed her calf or had her morning feed. Hogs in a nearby pen grunted but quickly settled back down. Andy's nose pinched. He never had gotten used to the smell of pigs. Horses disliked them, and so did Comanches.

Presently he saw lamplight in the cabin window. A man came out carrying a bucket.

Farley said, "That's Leach. He's meaner than a boar hog with the hives. Be ready for real trouble."

"You don't figure on shootin' him, do you?"

"Not without he gives me cause. But if he gives me cause I sure won't take a chance with him."

Andy's hands were tense on his rifle. He could handle a pistol, but a rifle felt steadier and seemed to carry more authority. He could not see if Leach was armed. The man's face was featureless in the dim light of early dawn, but Andy could see that his body was broad and muscular. He looked as if he would be hard to handle in a fight.

Farley whispered, "He's got a six-shooter in his boot. Get set. It's liable to be a hell of a scrap."

Farley waited until Leach opened the gate for the cow to enter the lot. He stepped out into the open and said, "Hands up. We're Rangers." He shoved a pistol forward, almost in Leach's face.

Leach wilted and raised trembling hands. "Don't shoot. For God's sake, Ranger, don't shoot."

Farley seemed let down by the lack of resistance. "You're harborin' a fugitive. We got a warrant for Joseph Bransford's arrest."

"Go help yourself," Leach said in a quavering voice. "He's in the cabin. Only please don't shoot. I'm a married man. My wife depends on me."

Disgusted, Farley told Andy, "Cuff this cowardly son of a bitch to the fence post." He turned back to

Leach, waving the pistol in his face. "If you holler I'll blow a hole in your brisket."

Fear gave Leach's voice a high pitch. "I won't make a peep."

Andy said, "That was easy."

Farley did not hide his disappointment. "Bransford is apt to come at us like a mad bull. Be ready to shoot him."

"What about the woman?"

"Don't worry none about her. She'll wilt like bluebonnets in June."

A wagon stood in front of the cabin. Farley placed himself behind it. He motioned for Andy to take cover behind a dug well ringed by a circular rock structure about three feet high, with windlass and wooden bucket on top.

Andy thought it would be more effective to burst into the cabin and take Bransford by surprise, giving him no time to put up resistance. But Farley preferred confrontation in broad daylight, where he could see his target and have plenty of room to move around.

Farley shouted, "Joseph Bransford, listen to me. We're the Rangers. There's ten of us, and we've got this cabin surrounded. Come out with your hands up or we'll burn the place and roast you like a pig."

Andy heard a woman's angry shout from inside.

For emphasis Farley fired a shot that showered splinters from the upper part of the door. He called, "Let the woman come out first. We got no paper on her."

The woman came out waving a heavy chunk of firewood. She made straight for Farley, cursing him for twelve kinds of egg-sucking dog. She was tall and broad and looked as if she could wrestle a mule to its knees. As Farley raised his arms for defense, she struck him twice. Startled, then stunned, Farley almost went to his knees. He raised his arms, trying to fend off her blows.

"Damn you, Badger Boy, do somethin'."

Farley's hat rolled on the ground. His head was bleeding.

Andy twisted the firewood from her hand and cast it away, but she closed in enough to leave deep tracks of her fingernails upon Farley's whiskered cheek.

"Get this civit cat off of me."

Andy got an arm around the woman's wide waist and dragged her away from Farley, only to have her turn on him instead. He managed to grab her strong hands and pull them behind her back. He handcuffed her to one of the posts that supported the windlass. She cursed until her voice went hoarse.

Both men struggled for breath. Farley raised a hand to his head and then looked at it. He saw blood. "Damn you, boy, how come it took you so long?"

"I thought you said she was goin' to scream, faint, and fall down."

Farley gave him a look that would wither weeds. He dragged a sleeve across his sweating face and fired a shot through the open door. "You comin' out, Bransford, or do you want to fry like a slab of bacon?"

A shaken man appeared in the doorway, hands above his head. "I give up. You don't need to shoot no more."

The woman turned her fury on him. "You ain't no brother of mine, you snivelin' coward. There ain't but two of them. You could've got them both." She looked around with wide eyes. "Where's my husband? What you done with my man?"

Farley was too choked with anger and embarrassment to answer. Andy said, "He's down at the shed, holdin' on to a fence post. Ain't done his milkin' yet."

The Rangers had just one set of handcuffs apiece, and those were both in use. Andy tied Bransford's hands with a leather string cut from his saddle. He drew the binding down tightly enough that Bransford complained about the circulation being cut off.

Farley said, "Ain't near as tight as a noose around your neck. You're lucky that farmer didn't die. Now, where's the money you took off of him?"

The woman said, "Don't you tell them nothin', Joseph. That money's ours if you'll just keep your damn-fool mouth shut."

Farley tapped the muzzle of his pistol smartly against Bransford's upper teeth. "Bad advice can get a man killed. Tell me where that money's at or I'll scatter your brains for the chickens to peck on."

Andy hoped the prisoner would see that Farley was not bluffing.

Bransford was eager to tell. "It's in there," he said, pointing to the cabin. "Come and I'll show you." Andy followed him while Farley remained outside, wiping blood from his forehead. Bransford pointed his chin toward a wooden box beside the iron stove. "It's at the bottom."

Andy said, "Stand back yonder and keep your hands high in the air." He dug the stove wood out of the box until he found a canvas sack. He could tell by the feel that it was full of paper. Coins clinked together in the bottom when he shook it.

He demanded, "Is it all there?"

Bransford was trying not to cry. All that effort and

nothing left to show for it. "Just spent a little on whiskey. And I left a few dollars with a woman over to Fort McKavett." He was trembling with fright. "What you Rangers goin' to do with me?"

Andy said, "Farley is plumb sore that you didn't put up a fight. But if I can keep him from killin' you, we'll take you to camp. Then I expect they'll send you to Colorado County to stand trial."

"What you reckon they'll give me?"

"Ten to twenty years, the captain said."

Bransford mumbled, "Ten to twenty years. Seems like an awful long time for no more money than I got."

"You shot the man you took it off of."

"I wouldn't have if he'd given it to me right off like I told him to."

Andy motioned for Bransford to walk outside ahead of him. The prisoner avoided his sister's smoldering eyes. He stared at the sack, his expression solemn. "Looks like by rights that money ought to be mine, seein' as I'm goin' to give up ten to twenty years payin' for it."

Farley shook his bleeding head in disbelief. "We sure got a sorry class of criminals these days. At least the Indians gave us an honest fight."

Andy said, "I'm takin' that as a compliment."

It was as much of one as he expected to receive from Farley.

A couple of horses grazed a few hundred yards away. Andy rode out and brought back the better of the two, a grulla gelding, for Bransford to ride. The woman fought the cuffs that held her against the well. "That's my husband's horse." She resumed cursing as the three men went down to the shed.

Bransford pointed out his saddle, and Andy put it on the horse for him. "Mount up." When Bransford was in the saddle, Andy fetched up his own and Farley's horses. He unlocked Leach's cuffs and transferred them to Bransford.

Leach rubbed his raw wrists, his face twisting. "You damned Rangers think you run the world."

Farley said, "We do, and we'll be back to get you the first time you let your foot slip."

"That's my horse you put Joseph on. His is that jug-headed bay out yonder."

Farley had no sympathy. "You just traded. They're probably all stolen anyway." He mounted his horse and poked the muzzle of the pistol in Leach's direction. "Come on back up to the cabin. We ain't plumb finished with you."

When they reached the dwelling Andy leaned down from the saddle and handed Leach the key to the handcuffs that restrained his wife. "Turn her a-loose, then give me the cuffs and the key."

Farley argued, "We ought to just leave her thataway. While her man filed those cuffs off of her, she'd have time to study on a woman's proper place."

"You want to pay the captain for the cuffs?"

"I reckon not. But watch her close when you turn her loose."

Fortunately the woman seemed to have used up most of her fight as well as all the profanity she knew. She stood in fuming silence, trying to kill Andy and Farley with the hatred in her eyes. Leach handed Andy the cuffs and key.

As the three rode away the woman shouted, "Our old daddy's turnin' over in his grave, Joseph, you givin' up so easy. You better ride way around this place when you come back."

Farley turned in the saddle. "Lady, he ain't comin' back."

Andy said, "Some lady."

Farley took a final glance at the cabin. "That place would look a hell of a lot better if we'd left it in ashes."

Bransford said, "You'd really burn it down with me in it?"

"I had the matches in my hand."

Andy remarked, "Thought we were goin' to have her fix us some breakfast."

Farley shook his head. "She'd poison us."

They fixed their own when they got back to where they had left the pack mule tied.

Andy asked Farley, "How's your head?"

"If she didn't break my skull, she bent the hell out of it. And you just stood there watchin'."

"I jumped in as fast as I could." Andy saw that Farley had no interest in his side of the story. "First water we come to, we'd better wash the blood off of your face. I've seen butchered hogs that bled less."

Farley gingerly felt of his head. "Look, it's enough that we bring the prisoner in like the captain told us to. There's no reason we've got to tell him about that woman."

2

NEARING CAMP, THE THREE RIDERS CAME UPON THE company horses scattered to graze on an open flat. They were watched over by two Rangers taking refuge from the sun's heat by shading up under a live-oak tree. The end of the long ride lifted Andy's spirits. Fatigue seemed to slip from his shoulders. The prisoner had been sullen and quiet, slouching in the saddle. Andy could understand, given the likelihood that he faced a long prison sentence. Farley had spoken little. He carried his hat on his saddlehorn, for it had been painful to wear over the knot swollen on his head.

The sound of gunshots made Bransford sit up in alarm.

Andy tried to calm him. "Just some of the boys at target practice." The captain provided an ample supply of cartridges, encouraging his men to sharpen their marksmanship. Cartridges were one of the few things besides food that the Rangers were not obliged to furnish for themselves. Even food was supplemented by whatever game they could shoot or fish they could catch.

The company camp had been established on the bank of the wide, clear San Saba River. Tall pecan trees sent roots deep into the mud and cast a cool shade over a row of canvas tents. To this company of Rangers it was home. It was an easily movable home, its location subject to the region's changeable law enforcement needs.

Earlier, the frontier batallion had busied itself primarily with keeping hostile Indians out of the settlements or chasing those who managed to get in despite the long picket line of Ranger outposts. Now that task had been largely eliminated by a relentless army push against the warring Plains tribes. A concentrated military offensive, moving in from three directions, had forced most of the Indians to give up the fight and repair to the questionable mercies of the reservation. Except for occasional limited outbreaks, the Comanches, Kiowas, and Cheyennes had been put out of action.

Apaches still roamed the far western part of the state and prowled rough hills down along the Rio Frio and upper Nueces, but the most destructive of the Indian raids were over. Of late the Rangers had turned their attention to the criminals who infested the state, especially its less settled portions, where escape was often fast and easy. Nowhere were they worse than in the limestone hills west of San Antonio, where dense cedar brakes and deep, rugged canyons offered sanctuary, where water and game were plentiful and a man could live off the land if the climate elsewhere became too hot.

Thus the principal Ranger mission had shifted from

Indian fighting to domestic law enforcement, to chasing murderers and thieves and border-jumping bandits, to breaking up feuds that broke out occasionally among a prideful, independent people hardened to violence and easily stirred to deadly force.

Protocol demanded that Andy and Farley deliver their report and their prisoner to the captain before they did anything else. Bransford cast anxious eyes at the camp as if he expected someone to step out of a tent and gun him down. He sweated more than the summer heat called for.

Several Rangers emerged from the tents or from under the shady trees to observe the three men coming in. Bransford's expression became even bleaker.

Andy said, "They won't shoot you in the middle of camp, not without you give them reason to."

Farley had transferred to Bransford most of the blame for his injury. "Even if they did, who's to tell? One Ranger ain't goin' to call down the law on another. We're decent people."

Bransford cast a fearful glance at him. He had probably expected a bullet in the back all the way from the Leach farm. Andy had said nothing to disabuse him of the notion, hoping fear would have a positive effect on his behavior.

Len Tanner's clothes were always too large for him except for the trouser legs. They were a little short. The lanky Ranger walked up and stared at the prisoner. "This the gink that goes around robbin' farmers?"

Andy said, "That's the charge, but he ain't been tried yet."

Farley studied Bransford like a hungry wolf eyeing an orphaned calf. "He's guilty, all right. You can tell by lookin' at him."

Andy said, "If that was the case, we wouldn't need judges and juries."

"Far as I'm concerned, we don't. If we shot them where we find them we'd save a lot of bother."

Sergeant Bill Holloway ducked to step out of the headquarters tent, then straightened his tall frame. He squinted against the sun. Deep turkey tracks pinched around bleached blue eyes. "I see you got your man."

Farley took offense. "We wasn't sent out there to *not* get him. We've come to turn him over to the captain."

"I'll take charge of him. Captain's busy right now."

Andy could hear the captain's angry voice through the canvas. Holloway jerked his head as a signal for the men to move away from the headquarters tent. He followed them far enough that they could no longer hear the voice.

He said, "Captain doesn't like to be disturbed when he's bawlin' a man out. Dick Landon put away too much bad whiskey last night over at Fort McKavett. Got into a cuss fight and tried to bend the barrel of his six-shooter over a citizen's skull. Lucky it was one of them hardheaded Dutchmen."

It was a seldom-discussed fact of Ranger life that isolation, boredom, and frustration led some men to drink heavily when off duty, and occasionally even on duty. This could result in unjustified confrontations with civilians unlucky enough to get crossways with them. Those men who became a frequent problem to their commanders were likely to be discharged quietly and encouraged to move on lest they taint the reputation of the service.

Landon had caused disturbances before. The captain had kept him on because he was a good Ranger when

sober, bold when the occasion called for it, a crack
shot with pistol or rifle. Drunk, he tended to create
trouble where there had been none. It was said he
came from a fighting family.

Farley grumbled, "Dick ought to never drink.
Whiskey makes him mean."

Andy said, "Some people don't need whiskey for
that."

Farley gave him a cold stare. "If you mean me,
don't go huntin' trouble. But if it comes, I don't run."

Farley had gone out of his way during Reconstruction times to antagonize the state police, who were
easily aroused. But Andy saw no point in pressing the
issue. Farley would never concede defeat.

Farley said, "I never shot a man that didn't need
killin'. The only regrets I've got are over some I
ought've shot but didn't."

Holloway said, "I reckon Dick had reason enough to
get drunk. He helped bring his own brother in yester-
day on a murder charge."

Puzzled, Andy asked, "How could he do that?"

"He's a Ranger. Dick joined to get away from a feud
back in his home county. Seems like his brother Jayce
killed a man on the other side and came out hopin' for
Dick to give him protection."

"Instead, he brought him in?"

"Rangers do their duty or they quit."

"I don't know if I could do what Dick did."

"I think you would if the chips were down." Holloway led them around the cook tent and pointed.
"We'll take your man down there."

The camp had no jail. For temporary confinement

prisoners were handcuffed to a chain locked around the thick trunk of a pecan tree a few steps up from the river. Most were removed to a regular jail as soon as possible.

Holloway said, "We'll throw your man in with Jayce Landon."

Landon sat on the ground, one arm locked to a sturdy chain. A big man, he stared resentfully at the officers and did not attempt to stand up. Andy untied a leather thong that had secured Bransford's handcuffs to the horn of his saddle. "Get down."

Bransford's legs were wobbly. Andy unlocked one side of the cuffs. He was aware that Farley watched closely, a hand on the butt of his pistol in case Bransford decided to make a break. Andy relocked the open cuff around the chain. This allowed movement up and down the chain but not away from it. Bransford tugged at the chain and found it heavy. "I've seen dogs treated better than this."

Farley said, "Dogs don't go around shootin' the taxpayers."

Holloway intervened. "There's no need to taunt the prisoner. Farley, you and Private Pickard go get yourselves some grub. I can hear your bellies growlin' all the way over here."

Bransford asked, "What about me? I'm starved half to death."

Holloway had no patience for complaining prisoners. "You'll eat when we're good and ready to feed you. Till then an empty belly will help you contemplate your sins." He walked off with Farley toward the mess tent. Andy remained a minute, studying Jayce

Landon. His face bore a striking resemblance to that of his Ranger brother. At a little distance he might mistake Jayce for Dick.

Andy had been trying to discern if there was any way to recognize a criminal on sight. So far he had not come upon any common denominator. Bransford looked the part, at least as Andy visualized the outlaw type. He would have taken Landon for a preacher. Or perhaps a Ranger.

Bransford looked up at the open sky. "What if it comes a rain? We'll drown out here."

Andy had not observed a decent cloud in two weeks. "You can climb the tree and drag the chain with you."

Bransford groused until his fellow prisoner turned on him irritably. "Don't go rilin' them up or we won't get any supper. Some of these Rangers would throw their own brother in jail and lose the key."

Bransford shivered involuntarily. "That Farley Brackett kept starin' at me like I had a target painted on my back."

Landon showed no sympathy. "You're lucky if jail is all you're facin'. I'm lookin' at a rope. Gettin' shot might be the better way out." The prisoner rubbed his raw knuckles. Evidently his capture had not been without incident.

The black cook grinned at the Rangers as they approached. Andy grinned back in anticipation. He had rather eat Bo's high-rising sourdough biscuits than cobbler pie. Bo could make sowbelly seem like beefsteak. Somebody had been out hunting, so Bo was able to fry up some venison backstrap to go with Andy's and Farley's red beans. Andy believed in the Comanche adage that one should eat all he could hold when he could get it because it might be a while before he had it again.

Farley, for all his complaining nature, was normally a hearty eater. Today he nibbled tentatively at what Bo offered. By that, Andy knew he still had a considerable headache.

Bransford *was* lucky he had not been shot.

A towheaded boy brought a blackened coffeepot. He gave a glad shout at the sight of Andy sitting there. "Hey, Andy, did you get your man?"

"We always get our man." That was a shameful stretch of the truth, but the boy had begun taking pride in his loose association with the Ranger company. Andy wanted to encourage that feeling, for Scooter Tennyson had been headed down the slippery road to an outlaw life when the Rangers took him in.

Andy held out his empty tin cup. "You been stayin' out of trouble?"

The boy glanced at the black cook. "I ain't been allowed time enough to get in trouble. Give a darky a chance to give orders to a white man and he'll work him to death." He smiled at the cook to indicate he did not really mean it.

The cook smiled back, but his dark eyes showed he knew Scooter *did* mean it. "You finish washin' them dishes, boy, then fetch me up some firewood. After that you can go fishin' if you're of a mind to."

Scooter's mother was dead. His father was in the penitentiary. The boy had been riding with some of his father's outlaw friends until the Rangers captured him. Finding no relatives, they had more or less adopted him to steer him away from a pathway already blazed for him by his father. Andy had taken a special interest because of parallels with his own boyhood experience.

Scooter had been skinny and hungry-eyed when the Rangers first found him. He was filling out now, putting on weight. Andy said, "Looks like Bo's cookin' is good for you."

"I just wisht he didn't make me work so hard for it."

The boy was earning his keep by doing light chores around the kitchen tent and fetching wood, nothing that would cause him undue strain.

In a severe voice Farley said, "Work'll make a better man of you. Maybe you won't follow your daddy into the pen."

Stung, the boy took the coffeepot back to the fire.

Andy frowned. "You didn't have to say that."

"It's the truth. That kid was far gone before you got ahold of him. It'll be a wonder on earth if he doesn't wind up lookin' out through the bars just like his daddy."

"It doesn't have to happen that way if we give him a chance."

"*You* give him a chance. I ain't got the time or the patience."

The captain came along soon after Andy and Farley finished eating. Andy wanted to ask if he had discharged Dick Landon, but he knew it was not his business. He would know in due time.

The captain had regained his composure after dressing down the wayward Ranger. He said, "You-all did a good job."

Farley shrugged, then paid for it as pain stabbed him. "It's what we get paid so high for."

"Did you have much trouble?"

Farley did not answer, so Andy put in, "Not with the prisoner." He was tempted to tell about Leach's woman but chose not to rub salt into Farley's wound.

The captain bent to look at Farley's face. "You look like you tangled with a wildcat."

Farley looked into Andy's eyes with a silent warning. "Horse fell with me."

The captain studied him thoughtfully. "At least it didn't cripple you. I have another job for you and Private Pickard."

Farley went defensive. "To do what?"

"You two will deliver the prisoners back east to where they're wanted."

Farley was not pleased. "Handlin' two prisoners is a big responsibility. I'd rather take somebody older. This young'un is green as grass."

"Pickard is young, but he's not inexperienced. You were with him when he took an arrow wound."

"Delivered by one of his redskinned cousins. Gettin' wounded ain't no accomplishment. Anybody can do it."

"You two are the only men I can spare. If you don't feel that you can go, I will regretfully accept your resignation."

Farley glared at Andy. "I can put up with him if I have to."

Andy asked, "Where are we takin' the prisoners?"

"Southeast Texas. You'll deliver Bransford to the sheriff of Colorado County. Jayce Landon is wanted over the other side of Columbus. It seems an old feud has fired up again." The captain looked back to see if anyone could hear. "Dick helped bring his brother in, then went off on a drinking binge."

Andy said, "I can see why he would."

"Discipline has to be maintained or everything comes apart."

Andy studied the chained prisoners. "It's hard to figure people. Bransford looks like a hard case, but Landon looks like he ought to be preachin' Sunday services."

The captain shook his head. "You can't judge by appearances. Sometimes the men who seem the meekest and mildest have the bloodiest hands. And I've seen some ugly-looking preachers."

Andy saw a bright spot in the assignment. "If we take Bransford to Colorado County, I'll have a chance to stop by Rusty Shannon's farm." He looked at Farley. "And you could visit your mother and sister."

Farley grunted. "They don't want to see me. I brought too much grief down on them."

Andy was strongly conscious of family ties, having none of his own. He could not understand anyone rejecting family or being rejected by them. "That was a long time ago."

"Not long enough." Farley turned away. "If you're done with us, Captain, I'll go see after my horse."

"You're dismissed." Watching Farley retreat, the captain said, "He ought to be a sergeant by now, but he has a dark streak in him that confounds me. What's this about his mother and sister not wanting to see him?"

The memory still made anger rise in Andy. "It was back in the time of the state police. They mistook his daddy for Farley and killed him. Wounded his mother so bad she almost died. Farley figures his family blames him for all the trouble they had."

"Do they?"

"I doubt they do anymore. They know the war twisted him up inside."

"He's unpredictable, even a little dangerous. In some ways that makes him an effective Ranger. It also makes him risky to be around."

"He's like a bear I saw on a chain. Even when he acts quiet, he's liable to turn on you and bite your arm off."

"It's obvious I can't send Dick Landon on this mission. It would put him in an impossible situation. So it's up to you and Farley."

Andy shrugged. "At least I'll have a chance to see Rusty."

The captain nodded. "Tell Shannon that anytime he wants to be a Ranger again, he just needs to let me know. He's welcome in this company."

"I'll tell him, but he's had more than his share of trouble. I think now he just wants to be a farmer."

Scooter was carrying wood and dropping it into a pile near the cook's fire pit. Andy pitched in to help him. Scooter did not thank him verbally, but his eyes showed he was pleased. He said, "Soon as I get done fetchin' wood, I'm goin' fishin'. I never got to do no fishin' till I come to this camp."

"You like fishin', do you?"

"It's about the most fun thing I ever done." The boy had never been given much chance for fun, riding with a criminal father and his father's lawless companions. When he tried to read he followed the lines with his finger, mouthed the words slowly, and often gave up in frustration. What little writing he could do was in block letters, the words so badly misspelled that it was a struggle to decipher their meaning.

Andy said, "I never did any fishin' either before I went to live with Rusty Shannon. The Comanches leaned to buffalo meat."

"Somethin' else I'd like to do someday is hunt buffalo. I'll bet that'd be fun."

"I was too young to ride with the hunters. They made me stay with the women and children. We skinned out the meat after the hunters got through. That was the work part, not the fun part."

"I ever get the chance, I'm goin' to kill me a buffalo."

Andy shook his head. "You may never get the chance. They say hunters have scattered all over the Plains, killin' for nothin' but the hides. Pretty soon there won't be any buffalo left."

"How come the Indians don't stop them?"

"They've tried, but there's too many hunters. The army has driven most of the Indians to reservations. Tryin' to teach them to farm and eat beef." Sadness fell over him. "The ones I knew are too proud to take to the plow. I don't know what'll become of them."

"You ever think about goin' up yonder to see them?"

Andy dropped an armful of wood and looked northward past the river. "Sometimes. I've got lots of friends there. But I've got a few enemies, too."

"Take me with you. I'll help you fight your enemies."

"Maybe someday." Andy dusted himself off. "I'd best go see after my horse."

Scooter grinned. "I'll catch a fish for your supper."

Andy tousled the boy's unkempt hair. "Just what I've been hopin' for."

Farley was brushing his horse's back. He frowned as Andy approached. "You're wastin' your time tryin' to reform that dogie kid. He's got a taint in his blood. It's waitin' for a chance to bust out like a boil on the butt."

"It doesn't have to. If we treat him right . . ."

"I knew some folks who tried to make a pet out of a coyote pup. The wild blood always showed through. They finally had to shoot it."

"People told Rusty the same thing about me."

ESCORTING PRISONERS CARRIED A degree of risk. The more severe the crime and the probable punishment, the more the risk. Andy had little concern over Bransford, who had shown his fearsome reputation to be all smoke and no fire. However, he had misgivings about Landon. The captain's information was that Landon and his kin were carrying on a blood feud with a family named Hopper. Family feuds in Texas could be long-lasting, and deadly as a den of snakes. Landon had waited for and shot one Ned Hopper on a lonely country road. Cornered by the Hopper-controlled law, he had wounded a deputy sheriff and made his escape, traveling west to seek help from his brother Dick. He had not considered that the telegraph was faster than the horse.

"You-all watch him," the captain warned as they prepared to leave early the next morning. "Don't give him any slack just because he's Dick Landon's brother."

Farley showed no concern. "If he makes a false move, it'll be his last one."

"Don't shoot him unless you absolutely have to. They want him alive back there."

Farley checked to be sure the two prisoners' hands

were securely cuffed and the cuffs tied to their saddles. "Either of you makes a break, you're dead," he warned.

Ranger Dick Landon had watched from the front of the tent in which he slept. He came forward, his eyes full of pain. His face and his halting walk showed the lingering effects of his drinking spree. He said, "Jayce, I'd give all I've got if I could've kept it from comin' to this. I came out here to get away from the feud. I wish to hell you'd brought Flora and done the same."

Jayce Landon turned his head away, not looking at his brother. He stared into the distance. His voice stung. "You went off and left the family. I done what needed doin'."

"When's it goin' to stop?"

"When we've filled up the graveyard with Hoppers."

Ranger Landon turned toward Andy and Farley. "I know he's wanted for murder, but he's still my brother. Don't mistreat him."

Farley said, "If anything happens to him it'll be of his own doin'." He jerked his head as a signal to start. Bransford led off. Farley followed closely behind the prisoners. Andy brought up the rear, leading a little pack mule.

Looking back, he saw Ranger Landon hunched in an attitude of misery. Andy told Farley, "I feel real bad about Dick."

"I've got my own worries. I ain't takin' on none of his. Dick had best watch out for himself and let the rest of his family go to hell."

"That's a cold way of lookin' at it."

Farley turned on him. "Don't be botherin' me with

other people's troubles. Or yours either. Else I'm liable to leave you afoot and take the prisoners by myself."

Anger warmed Andy's face. "Looks like we understand one another."

"The important thing is that you understand *me*."

People who had known Farley as a boy said he had been a kindly youngster who enjoyed hunting and fishing and had sung in church. The war and the angry years that followed seemed to have burned all kindness out of him.

Once clear of camp, Andy turned the mule loose. It followed without having to be led. The morning sun was in their faces. The captain had suggested that they push hard to reach Friedrichsburg before dark so they could lodge the prisoners in a secure jail. That way both Rangers could get a good night's sleep without having to stand guard.

The day passed without notable incident, though Andy sensed that Landon was on edge, watching, wishing for a chance to escape. No such chance presented itself. Farley was always close by, a dark and brooding presence. They occasionally met travelers on the trail. Farley scrutinized them suspiciously and kept his hand on the butt of his pistol while they were within range.

"Landon was mixed up in a feud," he told Andy, "so we've got to watch out for both sides. His own people will look for a chance to free him and the other bunch will be lookin' to kill him. Both sides see me and you as enemies. Us bein' Rangers won't make a particle of difference."

Andy began to fear that night would catch them before they reached Friedrichsburg. Darkness would increase the danger in traveling with prisoners. He was relieved when they came into a wide valley and saw the German settlement. Though the town was relatively young, as were most along the western fringes of the state, its broad dirt streets were already lined with sturdy stone and brick structures built in a style brought from the Old World. They were a sign that its citizens were not transient. They had established deep roots and intended to stay.

A deputy received the Rangers at the jail. His English was heavily accented, his manner efficiently professional. He locked the prisoners in separate cells and suggested that the Rangers would be comfortable in the Nimitz Hotel.

Farley demurred. "I'm never comfortable spendin' my money foolishly. I'll sleep in the wagon yard."

Andy suspected the captain would have chosen the hotel, but the captain was better paid. Privates rode for thirty dollars a month. At least nowadays they actually received it. Rusty had told him that in earlier times they often went unpaid for long stretches while the state struggled with a thin and leaky treasury.

Andy followed Farley from the jail to the wagon yard, each carrying his rolled blankets. Farley turned on him and pointed up the street. "You don't have to copy after me. Go to the hotel if you're of a mind to."

"They don't pay me any more than they pay you." He knew it would look awkward if he, the junior of the two, took better accommodations. Farley was sure to let the other Rangers know. Some would take it as a sign that Andy was being uppity. Among proud Texans, that was a cardinal sin.

Andy let Farley stay a few steps ahead, befitting

Farley's seniority. Anyway, he could do without Farley's company.

He thought about how pleasant it would be to order supper in the hotel, where they served meals on a white tablecloth. Maybe someday, when he had more money in his pocket. A working cowboy earned as much as a Ranger and seldom if ever had to face somebody with a gun and criminal intentions.

He bought a loaf of freshly baked bread and a spicy sausage to share with Farley. Farley bought a bottle but did not offer to share it. Nor did he bother to thank Andy for the supper. The man and his contradictions intrigued Andy as much as they offended him.

The darkness was compromised only slightly by a lighted lantern at the open front doors of the stable. Andy sat on a wooden bench, watching Farley tip the bottle. He broke a long silence. "I heard you say some people oughtn't to ever drink."

"I don't drink enough to let it get in my way."

Andy watched a match flare after Farley rolled a cigarette. He said, "Not that I give a damn, but I wonder what makes you itch so bad. You've never liked me from the time we first met."

The observation caught Farley off guard. "I never thought much about it. Didn't seem important. But now that you mention it, I *don't* like you. You stole a horse from me once."

"He never was yours in the first place." On the run from the state police, Farley had abandoned a worn-out horse and had taken one from Rusty. Farley's father gave Rusty a sorrel in return. Rusty turned the animal over to Andy, who named him Long Red.

Farley said, "I'd told my daddy I wanted that horse.

Figured I'd earned him for all the work I did for nothin' on that man-killin' old farm."

"Guess he didn't see it like you did."

"Lots of things he didn't see like I did. Got to where I couldn't stay around him anymore. But those damned state police had no call to kill him." Farley's voice was bitter.

"You gave the carpetbaggers a lot of trouble. Don't you think you came out about even?"

"I tried to give them back as good as what they gave me."

"Why, then, did you wind up joinin' the Rangers?"

"The state police was mostly scallywags. The Rangers are *us,* the old-timey Texans. You think after all I went through in the war and with the carpetbaggers that I could ever settle down on the farm again? You think *you* could, after livin' with the Comanches?"

"If I set my mind to it. I just got a little restless, so I joined the Rangers. Wanted to see if I could ever be as good as Rusty Shannon."

On that question he was still undecided. He knew he was not yet. He wondered if he ever would be.

Farley asked, "What do you think of the service, now that you've been in it awhile?"

"I didn't look for it to be fun. Mostly it's been long days in camp standin' horse guard or out followin' long trails that fade away before we find anybody. I can see why men like Dick Landon slip off and get drunk."

"Excitement is considerable overrated. Now you'd better go to sleep. We'll try and make Austin by tomorrow night if the horses hold up."

Farley had put his finger on one problem Andy saw with the Rangers. Not much consideration was given to how well the men held up. They were expected to perform regardless of circumstances. But allowances had to be made for the horses. A horse couldn't tell an outlaw from a Baptist preacher.

On reflection, Andy realized that he couldn't either.

They got an early start on what was going to be a long day's ride. Bransford griped about being rousted out before sunup. Landon said nothing, but his eyes were constantly at work, searching for a chance to get away. The same deputy who had checked the prisoners in checked them out and had Farley sign a release absolving Gillespie County of any blame should either prisoner make a break after leaving the jail.

"You watch that man," he warned, pointing at Landon. "All night his eyes are open. Look away from him this long"—he snapped his fingers—"and he will be gone from you."

As a precaution the deputy had put a set of leg irons on Landon. Fumbling with the key, Andy bent to unlock them so Landon could mount his horse. Landon brought his handcuffs and his fists down on the back of Andy's head, knocking him to his knees. Landon grabbed at the pistol on Andy's hip. Andy twisted away, falling on his side so Landon could not reach the weapon.

Farley shouted a curse and slammed the butt of his rifle against Landon's head. Landon staggered. Farley grabbed the back of the prisoner's collar and shoved him up against his fidgeting horse. "I've made allowances for you because you're a Ranger's brother. Next time I'll bust your head like a watermelon."

Andy pushed to his feet, his head aching.

Farley said, "See what comes of bein' reckless?

Didn't the Comanches teach you to watch out for yourself?"

"My hat took the worst of it."

The deputy had observed the incident but had not been close enough to help. He told Farley, "Like I said, better you watch that man. The devil looks from his eyes out."

"I've got three men to watch after, and one of them is a careless kid who's supposed to be helpin' me. You want a Ranger job?"

The man smiled thinly. "I am better paid being a deputy only."

They rode out of town, the prisoners securely handcuffed to their saddles. Bransford glared at Farley. "You could've broke that man's head like an egg."

"He had it comin', and so will you if you keep exercisin' that jaw."

Andy's head drummed with pain. That was Landon's fault, but he could not condemn the prisoner for it. In Landon's position, standing in the shadow of the gallows, he thought he too would probably grab at any straw, no matter how flimsy.

By pushing hard they reached Austin at sundown. Andy worried about the horses' ability to stand the pace. Farley assured him, "They'll make it. The tireder we keep the prisoners, the less trouble they're apt to give us."

Once Bransford and Landon were secured in jail, Farley and Andy reported to Ranger headquarters at the state capitol. It was a matter of form. Farley said he hoped local Rangers would be assigned to finish delivering the prisoners, but the officer in charge simply wished him an uneventful trip.

Andy was pleased, for he had counted on a visit to Rusty's farm. "Like it or not, Farley, you ought to see your mother and sister. They'll be disappointed if they find out you got so close and didn't stop."

"Mind your own business."

They left town on borrowed horses, for two hard days' travel had exhausted their own. Toward the end of the second day out of Austin they turned Bransford over to Sheriff Tom Blessing as ordered. Blessing, a large, blocky man built like a blacksmith, had known Andy since he had returned from his life with the Comanches. Andy asked him about Rusty and black Shanty York and others he knew around the county.

"Rusty's got thin enough to hide behind a fence post. He don't sleep enough and don't eat right. Still grievin' over that girl he lost. He's got a good crop in the field, though. As for Shanty, you know how it is with them darkies: you can't tell their age by lookin'. That black skin hides the lines."

Andy said, "I'll be goin' by to see Rusty once we've delivered this other prisoner."

Blessing frowned. "The word's already out that you're on the way with Jayce Landon. There's liable to be people waitin' for you. If I was you I'd deliver him in the dark of the night."

Farley had been listening to the conversation. "And act like we're afraid of his friends?"

"He's got more enemies than friends. If I was you, I'd be afraid of them all."

3

RUSTY SHANNON LEANED ON HIS HOE AND LOOKED beyond the waving green corn toward a dark cloud boiling on the horizon. One more soaking rain should finish bringing the corn and his other crops to maturity.

I wish Josie could have been here to see this, he thought. But the prospect of rain brought no real pleasure. Very little did anymore, not since Josie had died.

A rider approached him, mounted on a mule. Rusty recognized Old Shanty's slight, bent form and walked out to the edge of the field to meet him. He removed his hat to wipe sweat from his brow and the reddish hair that had given him his nickname. Sprinkled with gray, it was uncut and shaggy because he'd lost interest in his appearance. He had not shaved in a week.

He lifted his hand in what he meant to be a welcoming wave, though it fell short. "Get down, neighbor, and give that old mule a rest."

Many white men would not shake hands with a

black. Rusty did so without thought. Shanty had been a friend too long for racial proprieties to stand in the way.

"How do, Mr. Rusty. Kind of hot. Buildin' up to a summertime shower, looks like."

Shanty always addressed him as *Mister*. He had spent a major part of his seventy or so years as a slave, and old habits died hard, if at all. He had inherited a small farm from his former owner. For a time he had had to struggle to hold it in the face of opposition from some in the community who resented his being an owner of property. That battle had been fought to a standstill with help from Rusty, Andy, and others like Sheriff Tom Blessing who had kindly feelings toward him.

Since losing Josie, Rusty had found it difficult to arouse much interest in his own farm. He frequently rode over to Shanty's place to help him with heavy work that had become too much for the old man to handle alone. In return Shanty felt obliged to repay in kind, whether Rusty needed his help or not. He had spent more time in Rusty's garden than Rusty had.

Rusty said, "I judge by the direction that you're not comin' from your own place."

"I been over to Mr. Fowler Gaskin's, helpin' him work his vegetable patch. Hoed his weeds. Picked him some squash and beans and tomatoes so he's got somethin' to eat. He's a sick man, Mr. Gaskin is."

Rusty snorted. "Sick of work, mostly. That old reprobate has enjoyed bad health ever since I can remember."

Gaskin was notorious for sloth, feigning illness and using his age as a crutch. He had made an art of chiseling others into doing for him the work he did not want to do for himself. His neighbors had long since learned to watch their property when he came around because he was likely to leave with some of it.

Rusty said, "You've done a lot of work for him, and I'll bet he hasn't paid you a dollar."

Shanty shrugged. "Mr. Gaskin's a poor man. Besides, the Book says I am my neighbor's keeper."

"He never was *your* keeper. He did his damndest to run you out of this country. He was one of them that burned your cabin down."

"We never did know that for certain sure. We just supposed. Anyway, I can't be grudgin' agin a sick old man. He says it won't be long till he's knockin' on them Pearly Gates."

Rusty could think of few things that would improve the community more than a funeral service for Fowler Gaskin. People would come from miles around to attend, just to be sure he was gone. No hog pen or chicken house was safe so long as he drew breath.

Shanty said, "He's been speakin' remorseful about all the wrong things he's done. Cries when he talks about his two boys that was killed in the war."

For years Gaskin had been using his sons' death in an effort to arouse sympathy. Most people around here had learned the truth long ago, that his sons had not died in battle. They had been killed in a New Orleans bawdy-house brawl.

"That's just to get you to do his work for him, and do it for nothin'. He still hates you, but that doesn't mean he won't use you."

Shanty shrugged. "I'm just tryin' to serve the Lord any which way I can. Someday I may be old and sick myself. Maybe Mr. Gaskin will come and help *me*."

Perhaps, when cows fly over the moon, Rusty thought.

It was pointless to continue the argument. Shanty was of a trusting nature. Freedom had not come to him until well into his middle age. Up to then it would have been considered presumptuous of him, even dangerous, to pass judgment on anyone white. Now he did not know how.

Rusty made up his mind to ride over to Fowler Gaskin's soon and read the gospel to him.

Shanty gave Rusty a quiet appraisal. "You're lookin' kind of lank, Mr. Rusty. Ain't you been eatin'?"

"It's been too hot to eat."

"It don't ever get *that* hot. That girl's still heavy on your mind, ain't she?"

"Some things ain't easy forgot."

"You don't have to forget. Just take the things that trouble you and set them on a high shelf where you won't be lookin' at them all the time."

"I've tried, but life has sort of lost its flavor around here."

"Maybe supper would taste better to you if somebody else cooked it. I could stay and fix you somethin'."

"Thanks, but by the looks of that cloud, you'd better be goin' home before you get soaked. I'll fix for myself if I get hungry."

Shanty soon left. Rusty knew it was too late to visit Gaskin. Tomorrow would be soon enough, or the next day. The extra time would allow him to think of more shortcomings to call to Gaskin's attention.

He was about ready to quit the field and do the evening milking when another visitor appeared. Rusty had counted Tom Blessing as a friend as far back as he could remember. Tom was a contemporary of Daddy Mike Shannon, who had been a foster father to Rusty.

As a small boy more than thirty years ago, Rusty had been carried away by Indians after they killed his parents. Unlike Andy Pickard, he had been rescued a few days later. Because of Daddy Mike and Tom Blessing and several others, he had not spent years among the Comanches as Andy had.

After howdying and shaking, Rusty said, "Follow me up to the cabin, Tom. I'll fix us some coffee and warm up the beans."

"Beans." Tom gave Rusty the same critical study that Shanty had. "You don't look like you've been eatin' regular, not beans or anything else."

"It don't taste all that good when you're by yourself."

"You oughtn't to be by yourself."

Tom had been arguing that Rusty needed a wife. He even had one picked for him. But the suggestion stirred up painful memories Rusty was still struggling to cope with. He sidestepped the subject. "I could fry up some bacon."

"Sorry, but I ain't got time. Need to get home and do the chores before it rains." Tom pointed with his chin. "I happened into Shanty on the road. Said he'd been by here."

"He was over at Gaskin's, doin' work Fowler ought to do for himself. Fowler needs a load of fire and brimstone dropped on him."

Blessing smiled. "If you do it, just don't kill him. The court docket's already full enough." He looked toward the building cloud. "I'd best get into a high lope."

The cloud had grown considerably since Rusty had last paid attention to it. "And I'd better get the cow milked. Need to carry some dry wood into the house too."

The cow was waiting at the milk-pen gate. Her calf was penned inside so that the two were separated all day. Rusty allowed the calf to nurse long enough that the cow let down her milk, then penned the cow and took the milk he needed for his own use. Done, he let the calf in again to finish what remained.

The cloud was coming up rapidly. Rusty hurried to the cabin with the bucket of milk, set it on the kitchen table, and went outside to fetch in a couple of days' supply of dry wood for the fireplace. He had barely finished when the rain started. The drops were large and in the first moments struck the ground with force enough that they raised dust.

He became aware of a roaring noise, rapidly growing louder. He knew immediately that it was hail.

"Oh damn," he said under his breath.

The air, so warm earlier, quickly chilled. The initial stones were no larger than the first joint of his little finger. Quickly, however, they became much larger, hammering the ground. Though he stood in the shelter of the open dog run, some of the hailstones bounced up and rolled against his feet. He stepped back into the kitchen door. The impact of ice pellets against the roof was loud as thunder. Soon the ground was white as if a heavy snow had fallen.

He shivered, but some of the cold came from within. An hour ago he had every prospect of a good crop. Now he wondered if a stalk remained standing.

As quickly as it had come, the hailstorm was gone. A slow, steady rain followed, the kind of rain he had needed in the first place. Water dripped down into the cabin from holes in the roof. He would have to replace a lot of shingles, perhaps all of them.

He pulled a slicker over his shoulders and stepped out to survey the damage. He did not have to walk all the way to the field. He could see it through the rain. Everything in it was beaten to the ground.

He had known people who worked off their frustrations with a burst of profanity. He stood in stony silence, shivering from the cold wind that had come with the hail. Rain rolled off the brim of his hat and spilled down his shoulders.

He saw a couple of dead chickens on their backs, their legs in the air. They had not made it to the shelter of the crude henhouse. Hailstones floated in the spreading puddles of rainwater.

Feeling as if a horse had kicked him in the belly, he trudged back to the cabin, mud clinging to his boots. He had to move the bucket of milk because water was dripping into it. He brewed a pot of coffee and slumped into a chair, holding a framed photograph from the mantel over the fireplace. His throat tightened as he studied the face that smiled at him from the picture.

His shoulders were strong. They could bear this new burden; they had to. But they would bear it better if Josie could have been here.

He imagined what old Preacher Webb would say: *The Lord giveth, and the Lord taketh away.*

Rusty bowed his head. He sure as hell took it all, he thought.

THE LIGHT OF DAY brought no comfort. The rain was gone, and the morning sun was bright through breaking clouds. He walked first to the garden, where his tomato and okra vines looked as if a herd of cattle had trampled them. He had not removed the two dead hens. The other chickens pecked around them, oblivious to their sisters' fate. Some were half-naked, feathers stripped away.

His field was a muddy ruin. The only salvage he could see was to turn cattle in on it when the ground dried enough. They might find a few days' forage. But he would have nothing to put in his corncrib, much less to haul to town and sell.

He was well aware that a farmer's life was a constant gamble. Each year he bet his land, labor, and personal welfare against the threats of drought, excessive rainfall, heat, and untimely cold as well as insects and various orders of blight. Every so often the farmer would lose his bet, and the best he could hope for was a better next year.

Next year seemed a long way off, for this was still summer.

Rusty returned to the cabin and fixed breakfast, though he could bring himself to eat but little.

Tom Blessing rode up and hollered. His eyes were sympathetic as Rusty walked out to meet him. "Just ridin' around checkin' on my neighbors," Tom said. "Looks like that hail knocked the whey out of you."

Rusty could only shrug. "What about your place?"

"Not enough to break an egg, hardly. Looks like there was just one strip of heavy stuff, and it hit you the hardest of anybody. Missed Shanty's place altogether."

Rusty was gratified to hear that. "I may have to move in with Shanty this winter. What about Fowler Gaskin?"

Blessing shook his head. "I haven't been over there yet, but it doesn't look like the hail went that far."

Rusty felt regret. If Providence was even half-fair,

Fowler's place should have been beaten into nothing but a puddle of mud.

Blessing said, "Preacher Webb always claimed everything happens for a reason. Said no matter how cold and cloudy the day, the sun is still shinin' someplace. Maybe you can replant."

"Garden stuff, maybe, but it's too late for corn. I won't be puttin' away any fresh money for a while."

Blessing faced the cabin. "Looks like your roofs got beat real bad. Want me to have a load of shingles sent out from town?"

"Can't afford to buy what I can make for myself. I've got plenty of timber down on the river. Tell you what you *can* do, though: see if you can find me a job."

"I'll try, but I'm afraid there's not much to choose from around here. Times are slow."

Rusty had not inventoried his toolshed in a while. He found his saw was missing. So were the froe and mallet he used to split shingles the time he had helped rebuild Shanty's burned cabin. He was certain he had brought them home after that job was done.

He knew where he was most likely to find them, at Fowler Gaskin's. That scoundrel had a habit of borrowing without asking. Stealing, most people would call it, for he brought nothing back except under duress. Rusty had never liked going to Gaskin's place, but he had already decided to raise Cain with the old heathen over his abuse of Shanty. He hitched his team to the wagon. The tools would be unhandy to carry home on horseback. He had no way of knowing what-all of his property he might find, things he had not yet missed.

For years Gaskin's cabin had leaned to one side,

away from the prevailing winds. Logs had been propped at an angle against it to keep it from falling over. Trash and debris littered the premises around it. Gaskin sat on a bench in the shade at the front of the cabin, a jug within easy reach on the ground. He was rail-thin, his skin sallow. His ragged beard was mostly gray, laced with rusty streaks left by tobacco juice dribbling down his chin. He squinted bleary eyes in an effort to bring Rusty into focus.

"What the hell you doin' here?" he demanded. "I ran you off of this place, didn't I?"

Rusty climbed down from the wagon. "You've never run me anyplace that I didn't want to go. I believe you've got some tools that belong to me."

"No such of a thing. Ain't nothin' of yours here." Gaskin arose on wobbly legs, then dropped back onto the bench. "You've got no cause to come accusin' me. I'll sic my dogs on you."

Gaskin's two dogs had barked once, then had slunk away at the wagon's approach. They had much in common with their master.

Rusty did not wait to hear any more of Gaskin's protests. He walked out to a half-collapsed shed and began to dig through tools and implements piled there in a heap. He found his froe and mallet. They bore the initials *RS,* which he had burned onto the wooden handles with a steel rod heated to a red glow. He also found his timber saw and a sledgehammer that belonged to him. He carried them back and placed them in the bed of the wagon.

Gaskin protested, "You got no right to carry a man's tools away. I'm liable to need them."

"Not unless you can get somebody else to use them

for you. It's too bad you don't have four hands, Fowler. You could steal twice as much."

Gaskin stood up again, bracing one hand against his cabin. Rusty thought it was a toss-up as to which might fall first. Gaskin said, "You come on my land, you steal my tools, then you insult me to my face. If I wasn't old and sick I'd whup you good and proper."

"Speakin' of bein' old, you've been playin' on Shanty's sympathy when the truth is that you're younger and stronger than he is. I'm tellin' you to stop it or else."

"Or else what? You goin' to hit a poor old man?"

Rusty clenched his fists. "I might. I sure as hell might."

He climbed into the wagon and clucked the team into motion. Gaskin followed in short, shaky steps, shouting his opinion of Rusty and all his ancestors. The dogs came out from hiding and barked from a safe distance.

Gaskin had only a small field, for planting required work. But his corn stood tall, the stalks rustling in the wind. The hail did not seem to have touched him.

Rusty looked up and said, "Lord, next time You send us a storm, I hope You have a better sense of direction."

Reaching home, he carried the tools down to the river. With an ax he cut a deep notch in a tree in the direction he wanted it to fall, then used the saw. When the tree was down, he sawed it into shingle lengths. He dropped several trees before he thought he had enough. Then he began splitting off shingles.

In a couple of days he had a supply of them piled behind the cabin. He was on the roof, removing damaged ones when he saw a wagon and several riders approaching on horseback. He recognized Shanty on his mule. Tom Blessing loped ahead, one of his brothers spurring along behind.

Blessing shouted, "Got a bunch of your neighbors here. We can't do anything about the crop you lost, but we've come to help you put your roofs back on."

Rusty's dark mood lifted. It was a custom in rural Texas communities that neighbors work together. If a man was sick or hurt, his friends came to do whatever work was necessary. If hard luck befell him, the neighbors pitched in to set things as nearly right as possible. No one could guess when his own time might come.

Rusty climbed down the ladder and walked out to greet the visitors, shaking hands with each in his turn.

Blessing smiled broadly. "You need some good news after all that's happened to you. I saw Andy. He'll be by to visit you in a few days."

Rusty grinned. That *was* good news. "His arm wasn't broke, was it? He's written me just one letter since he's been in the Rangers, and it took up only half a page."

"He looked healthy to me. Him and Farley Brackett delivered a prisoner to me and had another they were fixin' to take a little farther. Said he'd see you before he heads back to the Ranger camp."

Rusty's grin faded. "He was with Farley Brackett?"

"I know him and Farley don't gee-haw too good, but I suppose he had no choice. A young man needs to learn how to take orders so he'll know how to give them when his time comes."

Rusty said, "Farley wakes up every mornin' with a dark cloud over his head. And he's got a wild hair in him that pops out every now and then."

"Andy can think for himself. It's good for him to

learn how to get along with all kinds of people. Even somebody like Farley."

Two women rode on the wagon seat, the younger one driving. The older of the pair was Tom Blessing's wife. Rusty had to look a second time before he realized the other was Bethel Brackett, Farley Brackett's sister.

Mrs. Blessing said, "Bethel and me are goin' to fix dinner for the workin' crew. Mind helpin' us carry some vittles into your kitchen? Looks to me like you need a good square meal."

"Been livin' on my own cookin', such as it is."

"What you need here is a woman." Mrs. Blessing quickly had second thoughts about what she had said. "I'm sorry. I wasn't thinkin'."

Rusty's momentary cheer left him. He forced a thin smile, though he did not feel it. "Been a while since I lost Josie. I think I've pretty well got over it."

He had not. He did not know if he ever would.

He turned toward Bethel. He remembered that Andy had shown a considerable interest in her once. Rusty had long wondered how a girl so pleasant-looking could have a brother like Farley. If he did not know her mother to be a woman of stern moral standards, he might wonder if the two had the same father.

He said, "Welcome, Bethel. Been a long time since that day you came here with your daddy, bringin' me a sorrel horse."

"The horse you gave to Andy." She smiled. "Have you heard anything from Andy lately?"

"Andy's not much for writin' letters."

"So I've noticed."

He suspected the sheriff had not told her Andy was

due soon for a short visit. That meant she probably did not know Farley was with him. Perhaps Blessing had a good reason for not telling her. It might be that Farley had said he did not plan to visit his mother and sister. In that case it was just as well they did not know. Farley had caused them pain enough over the years.

Mrs. Blessing followed Rusty into the kitchen with a sack of flour. She looked back to be sure the girl was not within hearing. "Bethel has turned into a right pretty young lady, don't you think?"

Rusty sensed where she was heading. "But too young for me, and I'm sure I'm too old to interest her. She's more Andy's age."

"But Andy's not here. You are."

"I'm just not ready to be thinkin' in that direction."

"If not Bethel, then how about Alice Monahan? Alice is a sweet girl. She was a godsend to me when I was sick for so long. And she *is* a sister to Josie, or was."

Rusty had been in love with two of the Monahan sisters, Geneva and Josie. He had lost them both. He would not allow himself to consider another. "Looks like the Lord intends for me to be an old bachelor."

"It's not for us to say what the Lord intends, but I can't believe He wants you to spend your life alone."

Rusty was grateful for an interruption by Tom Blessing. "Rusty, let's get started on that roof."

Tearing out old shingles, placing new ones where they had been, Rusty told Blessing, "Thanks. You came in at just the right time."

"I know. When my wife takes a notion about somethin', she's like a cold-jawed horse. There's no turnin' her back. I just let her play it out to the end of the

string." He frowned. "But you know, she's right. Tha[
hail didn't leave you much reason to stay around her[
till plantin' time comes again. If I was you I'd take a rid]
up to the Monahan farm. Alice might surprise you."

"I'm not lookin' for surprises. Unless you can sur[
prise me with a good job."

"I've asked around. Haven't found anything."

Rusty felt the bleak mood settling over him agair[
"It's liable to be a long fall and winter."

4

THE TRIP HAD NOT MADE JAYCE LANDON ANY LESS of a puzzle to Andy. In comparison to Bransford, who had been left in Tom Blessing's custody, Landon still looked as if he might be a preacher, or at least a law-abiding storekeeper. But Andy had a sore place on the back of his head from Landon's attack. And Landon had laid in wait to shoot a man. Bransford had never done that so far as Andy knew.

Farley Brackett said, "Don't waste sympathy on him. He's got blood on his hands."

"How about the state policemen *you* killed?"

Farley said, "They was lookin' at me. They could've shot me as easy as I shot them."

"Do they ever keep you awake at night?"

"Dead is dead. They don't come back."

Andy did not like the look of five horsemen riding to meet them from the direction of Hopper's Crossing. He tensed, and again he wished Rusty Shannon were here. "What do you think, Farley?"

"I think *damn it*. I hoped this wouldn't happen." Farley reached across to recheck Landon's handcuff and the rawhide strip that bound them to the saddle horn. "Take a good look at them, Jayce. Are they friends of yours, or enemies?"

For the first time since the trip began, a smile creased Landon's face. "Some of my kin and a couple of my neighbors. They won't like it, seein' me shackled like a runaway slave."

"They'll like it even less if they try and turn you loose because I'll shoot you dead. Badger Boy, you better draw your weapon."

Andy already had. He was not surprised about being met on the road. Tom Blessing had warned that the word had gone out ahead and that it was wise to be prepared for anything.

Thirty feet from the approaching horsemen, Farley stopped. He placed the muzzle of his pistol behind Landon's ear. "You men had better put aside any foolish notions. The only way you'll get this prisoner away from us is if he's dead. And some of you will ride to perdition with him."

Andy's mouth went dry as he tried to read the men's intentions.

One rider pushed his horse a little past the others. His facial features resembled Jayce's so much that Andy guessed they might be brothers. Dick Landon must have come from a large family. "Now, Ranger, we just come to make sure he gets to town alive. The Hoppers would like to see that he don't."

Farley said, "And they'll have their way if you make a move to help him. I want all of you to turn around and ride out ahead of us. Way ahead of us."

The men argued among themselves. Farley brought the conversation to a close by cocking back the hammer. Jayce gasped. Andy held his breath.

Jayce said, "You-all better do what he says, Walter. This Ranger is one mean son of a bitch."

The man called Walter jerked his head as a signal for the rest to comply. He said, "Don't you let your finger get nervous, Ranger. If somethin' happens to Jayce, you'll be dead two seconds after he is."

Andy sensed that whatever intentions the five might have had, had been thwarted by Farley's unyielding stand. They were not likely to try anything unless circumstances changed drastically in their favor.

Farley said, "Take a lesson from this, Badger Boy. Never give an inch or they'll run over you."

"You'd really have shot him, wouldn't you?"

"If it was the last thing I ever did."

Sweat rolled down Jayce's face. He trembled in fear's aftermath. "God, Ranger, but you're cold-blooded."

"I am, and don't you forget it."

"You don't know what kind of a man I shot."

"Makes no difference. Me and Badger Boy are paid to deliver you to the local sheriff. The rest is up to the jury that tries you."

"The judge is old Judd Hopper. He's a direct grandson of the devil himself. Him and the rest of them Hoppers'll do all they can to see me hung."

"You've got a brother who's a Ranger. Have you got one who's a lawyer?"

Landon looked behind him as if expecting pursuit. "This fight goes way back. Why can't the law stand aside and let the families work it out for theirselves?"

"I know how crazy-mean these feuds can get. You

kill an enemy, then one of his family has got to kill one of you. It goes on and on till just about everybody is dead. Better for the law to hang you instead of one of your enemies shootin' you. Maybe that'd put an end to it."

"It won't end till that Hopper bunch is all dead and gone."

Andy shook his head. "I'll bet you don't even remember what started it."

"It commenced over an election for the county seat, but that don't matter anymore. It's a blood thing now."

Farley looked at Andy and shrugged. "No use arguin' with him. You can't talk sense to people like that."

Andy said, "It's a good thing for Dick Landon that he joined the Rangers and got away from the trouble."

Farley grunted. "Even Dick'll bear watchin'. He's got bad blood in him."

Andy could count on one hand the times he had heard Farley speak well of somebody, and he could give back a couple of fingers.

Jayce said, "If you think the Landon blood is bad, wait till you meet the Hoppers."

Hearing hoofbeats behind him, Andy turned in the saddle. He counted six riders. Farley demanded, "Who are they, Jayce?"

Jayce looked back in dismay. "They're Hoppers . . . Hoppers and their kin."

Andy said, "Five Landons in front, six Hoppers behind, and us in the middle."

Farley growled, "Best thing would be for us to pull out of the way and let them settle their stupid feud for good."

Andy considered the situation, then moved his horse toward the six men.

Farley shouted, "What do you think you're doin'?"

Andy did not answer. He drew his rifle from its scabbard, laid it across his lap, and rode almost within touching distance of the horsemen. "Which one of you is in charge of this bunch?"

A big bear of a man with a short, curly beard said, "Ain't nobody in charge. We're workin' together to see justice done."

"And your name?"

"I'm James Hopper. Big'un, they call me." He looked strong enough to wrestle a bull to the ground from a standing start. He was half a head taller and fifty pounds heavier than any of the men who rode with him.

Andy swung the rifle muzzle around to point at the man's belly. He jerked his head. "Come on, Big'un. You're ridin' up there with us. The rest of you stay back. If one of you makes a move against us and our prisoner, I'll blow this gentleman's lights out."

The bearded man protested, "I'll have you know that I'm a deputy sheriff. Appointed by the county judge hisself. What gives you the right to tell me what to do?"

"This rifle does. Are you comin' or do I shoot you right here?"

Hopper did not consider long. "I'm comin'. The rest of you better do like he says."

One of the riders was a smaller man but had the same facial features as Big'un. He said, "He's bluffin'. Say the word and we'll take him."

Big'un declared, "Shut up, Harp. We don't need no blood spilled here. Not mine anyway."

Andy started Big'un moving toward Farley and Jayce. Big'un said, "You look kind of young to pack so much authority."

"A gun makes everybody the same size."

Farley looked the deputy over, then turned critical eyes on Andy. "What did you bring him for?"

"For insurance."

"You think you could really kill him if you had to?"

"You said to never give them an inch."

Farley almost nodded in approval but caught himself. "Lookin' at you right now I'd swear you're a Comanche after all."

Andy took that as a left-handed compliment, the only kind Farley Brackett gave.

Jayce's face hardened, displaying his hatred of the bearded man. "Well, Big'un, looks like they've got you the same as they've got me."

Hopper's eyes burned with malice. "Not quite the same. They'll turn me loose when we get to town. They're already stackin' lumber over by the jailhouse to build your scaffold."

Farley broke in. "I've got half a mind to cut you two coyotes loose and let you go at one another, but there's probably some fool law against it. So both of you shut the hell up."

A mile from town they were met by the county sheriff. Jayce's supporters pulled to one side but did not leave. The Hoppers started to move up, but Andy made a show of pressing the rifle's muzzle against Big'un's midsection. That stopped them.

Big'un complained, "Damn it, Ranger, you got to bruise my ribs?"

A middle-aged man with gray hair and a slight

paunch, the sheriff reacted sharply at the sight of Big'un being held at gunpoint. "What do you think you're doin' with my deputy?"

Andy said, "He was fixin' to get himself in trouble. We're protectin' him."

The sheriff turned his anger on Big'un. "Damn it, I told you to stay home, and keep all the Hoppers there too."

Big'un bristled. "We just come to make sure none of Jayce's kinfolks let him loose."

"That's my job." The lawman turned back to the Rangers, making no secret of his antagonism toward Jayce Landon. "Thank you, Rangers, for deliverin' this murderer. I'll take over from here."

Farley gave Andy a severe look that warned him to be alert. "Our orders are to deliver him safe to your jailhouse. Till then, he's still ours."

Andy watched the Ranger and the sheriff glare at each other. He knew Farley would stand his ground if it took all afternoon. The sheriff evidently came to the same conclusion. He said reluctantly, "All right. Another mile won't make much difference."

Big'un looked back for support. "A trial is goin' to cost us taxpayers money. There's a good, stout tree yonder. I say we drag Jayce over there and hoist him like a fresh beef."

The sheriff's voice crackled, "Shut up, Big'un. The judge crowded me into takin' you and Harp as deputies, but I don't have to listen to you talk like a damn fool." He pointed his thumb toward town. "All right, Rangers, Jayce is still yours till we get him to jail. Let's go before some idiot takes a notion to show how stupid he is." He looked at Big'un again.

A crowd had gathered to watch Jayce being brought to town. Andy had never seen so many angry people. Some supported Jayce, but it appeared that the majority were hostile to him. A couple of fistfights broke out as the horsemen approached the jailhouse door.

Farley muttered, "Keep a close watch. There's no tellin' what some hothead might do." He cut the leather thong that bound Jayce's hands to the saddlehorn, but the cuffs remained on the prisoner's wrists.

Andy stayed in the saddle, holding the rifle in a firm grip. Big'un slipped away from him and rejoined the five who had ridden behind. The sheriff opened the front door of the jailhouse but stood in the middle, blocking it for what seemed to be several minutes.

Giving somebody a good chance to shoot Jayce, Andy thought. He studied the people with anxious eyes.

The long road to justice had many a shortcut.

Farley took a firm grip on Jayce's arm and led him through the doorway, past the sheriff. This time Jayce showed no resistance. Instead, he seemed in a hurry to get inside away from the crowd. Andy dismounted and followed, walking backward, the rifle ready.

Farley said, "Badger Boy, would you mind fetchin' my saddlebags?"

Andy could not remember that Farley had ever asked him to do anything. He had always just told him.

A woman burst through the door and ran to the prisoner, her arms outstretched. "Jayce," she shouted. "Jayce!"

The sheriff tried to restrain her, but she was strong enough to break free. She embraced Jayce, sobbing loudly. Too loudly, Andy thought. He sensed that she was making a show of it. After letting her cry for a bit, Jayce's brother Walter pulled her away. "Come on, Flora, you oughtn't to act like that in front of these Hoppers. They've had too much satisfaction already, just seein' him brought in."

She launched a tearful tirade at the sheriff. "My Jayce is a better man than you, Oscar Truscott." She turned on the crowd. "He's better than the lot of you. All he done was kill a man that needed killin'. There's a whole bunch of you Hoppers needs killin'." She seemed to concentrate particularly on Big'un.

Andy thought he saw a look of satisfaction in her eyes as Walter Landon led her outside. He wondered about it.

Farley withdrew some papers from the saddlebags Andy had brought. He handed them to Sheriff Truscott. "Me and Pickard have done what the captain ordered. Jayce belongs to you, but you'll need to sign this release."

Truscott signed with a flourish, smudging a little ink. "It'll be like havin' a box of dynamite in here, but I'm glad to have him. I hope the trial don't take long."

Big'un grinned. "It won't, not with Uncle Judd on the bench."

The wooden floor trembled as an iron door slammed heavily. The sound made Andy feel cold even though he was not the one being locked away.

Farley told the sheriff, "There's lots of people out yonder that would like to do the prisoner harm."

"You don't have to tell me my business. You Rangers have done your job. I expect you'll want to head west and put some miles behind you before dark." His voice was hopeful.

"Our horses need a rest. We'll bed down at the wagon yard and make a fresh start in the mornin'."

The sheriff shrugged. "Suit yourselves. There's a fair-to-middlin' eatin' joint down the street yonder, run by one of my wife's nephews. Nothin' fancy, but it's cheap."

"Sounds fine to me." Farley beckoned to Andy. "Let's go see to our horses."

Walking outside, Andy sensed the tension. His scalp tingled as if an electrical storm were building. It would take but little to set off a riot. The fight would be one-sided, for the Hopper crowd appeared to outnumber the Landons by a considerable margin.

Farley growled, "Don't look to the left nor the right. Just walk straight ahead. This don't concern us anymore."

"Jayce won't get a fair trial in this town."

"Don't matter. Even a fair trial would end up hangin' him. He's as guilty as sin."

Andy rubbed his throat. The thought of a rope around it gave him a chill.

Farley said, "It would've been better for him if he'd made a break along the way. We would've shot him, and it would already be over with. Now he'll sit in that jail cell broodin' about it. He'll die a thousand times before he ever feels the rope."

They ate a mediocre supper. A good one would have had no more appeal to Andy under the circumstances. He asked, "Doesn't it bother you that we brought Dick Landon's brother here to die?"

"Jayce put the rope around his own neck when he took aim on Ned Hopper. He tripped the trapdoor when he walked up and shot him a second time. It wasn't none of my doin', nor yours."

The stable keeper was a small man with a flushed face that indicated he was a favored customer at some bar up the street. He seemed to fancy the sound of his own voice. "You-all are the Rangers that brought Jayce in, ain't you? Bet you didn't know what a hornet's nest you was fixin' to stir up. Soon as it gets dark and some of the Hoppers get enough liquor in them, you'll see the biggest fireworks we've had around here since the Yankee war."

Farley said, "It's nothin' to us. We just want to get some sleep and head out in the mornin'."

"May not be much sleepin' done in this town tonight. Me, I ain't takin' sides. Their money all looks the same to me. I'll still be here when it's over."

Farley scowled. "It's a smart man who knows how to mind his own business."

"But ain't you Rangers supposed to keep the peace? Looks to me like you'd be out there amongst them, holdin' the lid down."

"Our orders were to deliver Jayce to the sheriff. From now on it's up to him and the court."

"The sheriff's married to a Hopper. He's got some in-laws he ain't real fond of, like Big'un and the judge, but they come with the deal."

Andy said, "It's a cinch there won't be anything fair about Jayce's trial."

The stableman looked around to see if anyone else could hear. "Ain't goin' to be no trial. Talk is that they're goin' to stage a fight and draw the sheriff away after dark. The jailer is a Hopper cousin. When his kinfolks come callin' they won't have to tell him twice to raise his hands."

Andy's jaw dropped. "They're goin' to take Jayce out and hang him?"

"No, they'll shoot him right there in his cell and scatter before the sheriff or the Landons have time to do anything about it."

Farley frowned. "Are you sure about this?"

"I got it from one of the Hopper boys. He was already tanked up on Kentucky courage."

Andy told Farley, "We've got to do somethin'."

Farley shook his head. "What's the use? They'll just keep tryin' till they get him. Feuds are nasty business."

He forked dry hay onto the ground and spread it evenly, then unrolled his blankets on it. "Best thing is to let the damn fools fight it out. Then we can hang the winners or send them to the penitentiary."

"I'll bet that's not in the captain's rule book."

"The book has got blank pages in it so we can write our own rules when we have to."

Andy did not consider long. "I didn't make this ride just to stand back and watch them lynch our prisoner." He drew his rifle from its scabbard on his saddle and dug into his saddlebag for extra cartridges.

Farley arose from his blankets. He gripped Andy's shoulder tightly enough to hurt. "They'll cut you to ribbons, and for what? Jayce is goin' to die anyway. If he doesn't do it tonight, he'll do it when the trial is over. Leave it alone."

"I can't."

"Listen to me, Badger Boy. Even if you *are* half Indian, you're worth more than Jayce Landon."

Andy thought that was an amazing admission for

Farley. He could not think of an adequate response. "Like the man said, we're supposed to keep the peace."

"Ain't goin' to be peace in this town till they've killed enough of one another that they gag on the blood. You'd best look out for your own skin."

"What'll the captain say if we tell him we delivered Jayce and then stood by while a mob shot him to pieces?" Andy cradled the rifle across his left arm and walked out of the stable into the darkness.

The jail was a little more than a block away. He had a strong feeling of being watched, but he could see no one. He heard a horse somewhere behind the buildings, moving into a slow lope.

He pondered whether he should go inside the jail or wait for the Hoppers in front of it. He had heard of mobs burning a jail to get a prisoner. In such an event he could do little from inside. Besides, the jailer was in on the deal. He would probably do whatever he could to put Andy out of the way. He decided to take a stand outside, blocking the door.

The street remained quiet for a while. Andy began to wonder if the hostler's information was overblown. People sometimes made bold talk but did not have the stomach to follow through. Then he saw several men moving up the street toward him. He tightened his grip on the rifle. Though he could not distinguish the faces, he sensed that these were of the Hopper clan.

Sternly he said, "That's close enough."

A gruff voice shouted, "Step out of the way, Ranger."

Andy thought the voice sounded like Big'un's. He said, "I'm tellin' you to disperse."

The men moved closer but stopped when Andy leveled his rifle on them. Big'un declared, "You've got no jurisdiction here. You finished your job when you brought Jayce in."

Andy's throat was too tight for a reply. He hoped silence was more threatening than anything he might say. The men huddled, murmuring among themselves. Several more came up the street, joining them. By Andy's rough count there were fifteen, perhaps more.

One man edged beyond Big'un and the others. He said, "You're just a shirttail kid. You won't really shoot us." He paused a moment, gauging Andy's reaction, then moved forward again with confidence in his step.

Andy aimed the rifle, but he could not bring himself to squeeze the trigger. The blood rose warm in his face.

He sensed a movement on the street. A pistol blazed, and the man went down. He gripped his leg and squalled in pain.

Farley's voice was deadly. "Next shot goes in somebody's gullet." He fired again, kicking up dust in front of the mob.

Andy expelled a pent-up breath. Farley walked up and joined him in front of the door. His stern gaze never left the Hoppers as he muttered, "The graveyards are full of people who wouldn't pull the trigger."

"I tried. I just couldn't."

The wounded man lay on his back, gripping his bleeding leg. He kept hollering.

Farley said with contempt, "Listen to that brave son of a bitch, squealin' like a pig stuck under a gate."

Members of the mob conferred among themselves. Big'un shouted, "You're protectin' a murderer."

Farley said, "He ain't been tried yet."

"We come here to give him all the trial he needs."

Farley muttered, "If they rush us, shoot the foremost. That'd be the one called Big'un. If that doesn't stop them, shoot another."

"You'd do that for Jayce Landon?"

"No, for us. Right this minute we're in worse danger than he is."

Big'un shouted, "You Rangers can't stay here forever. We can wait."

Farley pointed the pistol at him. "You'll have to. Now you-all had better scatter because in one minute I'm goin' to shoot every man I can see." He held up his watch so he could read it in the moonlight.

The men lingered a little, then began to peel away. Some, like Big'un, shouted threats back over their shoulders, but soon all had retreated beyond sight, carrying their wounded man with them.

Farley said, "You have to talk to people in a way they understand, then be ready to back up what you tell them. Remember that and you'll live longer."

Andy shuddered. "You were really set to kill somebody."

"I would, if there'd been a brave man amongst them. But after one shot everybody started thinkin' about home and mother. That's generally the way."

"You told me at the stable that you wasn't comin'."

"I didn't intend to. I don't give a damn about Jayce Landon, but I didn't want to have to tell the captain I stood back and let a mob kill a Ranger. Even an ignorant Comanche Indian."

A stubborn streak would not allow Andy to show his pleasure. He had taken too much abuse from Farley to grant him the satisfaction. He looked down the dark, empty street. "I don't understand why none of the Landon bunch was here. Looks like they'd have turned out to protect Jayce."

"That does strike me a little peculiar. It goes to show that both sides are crazy."

After they had watched for ten or fifteen minutes Farley said, "I don't think they'll be comin' back for a while. I want to do some Dutch talkin' to that jailer."

Andy was not surprised to find that the front door had been left unlocked. He said, "I guess the jailer wanted to make it easy for them. All they had to do was walk in."

Inside, he locked and barred the door in case some of the Hopper people drank enough courage to come back. He did not see the jailer. Farley walked through the door that led back to the cells. He called, "Come here, Badger Boy. This is a sight to tell your children about if you live long enough to have any."

The jailer was handcuffed to the bars of a cell. The cell door was open. Jayce was gone.

Farley snickered at the jailer. "Now ain't you a pretty sight? How did you get yourself into this fix?"

The man's eyes were downcast. "Jayce has escaped."

"I figured that out for myself. What did you do, go to sleep on the job?"

"No such of a thing. The sheriff went to see about a fight. Soon as he was gone, Jayce pulled a gun on me. Just a little derringer, but it could kill a man."

Farley gave Andy a speculative glance. Jayce hadn't had a gun on him when the Rangers brought him into town.

Andy did not have to think about it long. He remembered how Jayce's wife rushed up and hugged him. He would wager a month's pay that she stuck it inside his shirt during the moment of confusion.

He chose not to mention it. The woman had misfortune enough just by being Jayce's wife.

The jailer wailed, "Are you-all goin' to get me out of this mess?"

Farley came dangerously near smiling. "We ain't got the key."

"Look in the top desk drawer out yonder."

Andy rummaged around and found it. Freed, the jailer rubbed his wrist, raw from straining against the handcuff. "I think Jayce went out the back door. I heard a horse lope away. Some of his kin must've been waitin' out there."

Farley grunted. "So now he's took to the tulies."

The jailer wailed, "If the sheriff doesn't murder me, my kinfolks will."

"I've got half a mind to do it myself. On account of you, me and Pickard made a long ride for nothin'. And that mob out yonder could've killed us."

"You got to tell them it wasn't my fault."

Andy suggested, "Might be a good idea if we left town. They're liable to think we had a hand in this."

"Run away?" Farley took offense at the suggestion. "Last time I ran from anybody it was the state police. I swore I'd never run again. No, we'll stay and tell them how it was. Next time maybe they'll hire better help."

Someone began beating against the front door and shouting for the jailer to open it. The jailer appeared about to wilt. "Oh God, that's the judge."

Andy assumed that thwarted mob members had carried their frustration to the Hopper family leader.

Farley said, "Just as well let him in. But nobody else. This place could get crowded in a hurry."

Reluctantly Andy slid back the bar and opened the door just enough for Judge Hopper to enter. Several men were with him, but Andy pushed the door shut and barred it before any of them could bully their way in. Big'un shouted threats from outside.

Judd Hopper was a tall, angular man with gray chin whiskers and angry eyes that cut to the quick. "What are you Rangers doing here? Protecting the prisoner is the sheriff's responsibility."

Farley did not waver under the tirade. "I'm glad you said that. I think your jailkeeper has got a little news for you."

The jailer hung his head. His voice was little more than a thin squeak. "Jayce is gone."

"Gone?" The judge took long strides into the back room. His face reddened as he saw the open cell door and absorbed the full import of Landon's escape. He whirled around, jabbing an arthritic finger at Andy and Farley. "You-all turned him loose. I'll send you both to the pen."

Farley gripped the jailer's wrist so hard that the man cried out. "Tell him the rest before I twist your arm off and beat you to death with it."

Defensively the jailer explained that Landon had produced a pistol and forced him to unlock the cell. "Next thing I knowed he had me handcuffed to the bars. I hollered, but nobody heard me. Wasn't nothin' I could do."

The judge fumed. "I wish he'd killed you. I guess you know you're fired. You'll be lucky if some of my nephews don't flay the hide off of you. How did he get ahold of a pistol?"

Andy and Farley stood silent. The jailer spoke in a subdued voice. "We didn't make him take his boots off. Maybe he had it in one of them."

The judge slammed the cell door shut and then shook it in rage, gripping the bars tightly enough to turn his knuckles white. "I'll make somebody wish he was in the fires of hell instead of in Hopper's Crossing."

Farley beckoned to Andy. "I don't see nothin' more for us to do here."

Hopper demanded, "You're goin' to help us hunt him down, aren't you?"

Farley showed his disdain. "Ain't our fault you-all couldn't hold him. Our assignment was to deliver him to the sheriff. We done that, so now we're leavin'."

Andy slid back the bar and opened the door. As he and Farley left, a dozen Hopper partisans rushed in, bumping one another against the door in their haste.

Andy said, "The judge is liable to tell them it was our fault. Anything to shift the blame. We better get away from here."

"We ain't runnin'. We're walkin'. We'll show this bunch we ain't afraid of nobody."

"Maybe you're not, but I am."

Farley set a slow and deliberate pace toward the wagon yard. They had not gone far before Andy heard someone shout a curse. The voice sounded like Big'un's. A shot was fired. Farley spun half-around, grabbing his right side.

A man stood in lamplight that spilled through the open jailhouse door. He held a pistol. Andy raised his rifle and made a quick shot. The man went down, twisting in the dirt.

Farley swore under his breath. Andy asked, "How bad are you hit?"

"I don't know. It hurts like almighty hell."

"We'd better keep movin'. They didn't get to kill Jayce Landon, and they're fired up to kill *somebody*."

Andy took Farley's left arm to give him support. At the wagon yard he found the stableman standing in the open front doors, staring into the dark street. "Heard some shootin'. What . . ." He seemed to lose his voice when Andy and Farley came into the lantern's light and he saw Farley's bloody shirt.

Andy said, "Saddle our horses for us and throw our pack on that mule. Be quick." He helped Farley to a straight wooden chair and brought the lantern up for a close look. The bullet had struck high up and from behind. "Can you move your arm?"

Farley raised it a little.

Andy said, "Could've busted some of your ribs. You're bleedin' like a stuck hog."

Andy took out his handkerchief and pressed it against the wound. "Feel like you can sit in the saddle?"

"I don't see I've got much choice. Them crazy Hoppers'll be lookin' to finish the job."

The stableman brought their horses and the mule. "If I was you-all—"

Andy interrupted. "Is there a doctor in this town?"

"There is, but you'll be needin' an undertaker instead if you've got yourselves in Dutch with them Hoppers."

The stableman reluctantly gave directions, then helped Andy boost Farley into the saddle. Andy found the doctor's house, but he saw that several of the Hopper people were already there. The doctor would be treating the man Farley had shot. The one Andy had shot would probably be brought along shortly.

He said, "We'd better not stop here."

Farley nodded in painful agreement. "Doctor may be one of them Hoppers anyway. Whole town seems to be infested with them."

"I'm afraid you'll have to tough it out for a while."

Farley grumbled under his breath, "Badger Boy, you're a damned Jonah. You'll get me killed yet."

5

ANDY FEARED HE MIGHT HAVE TO HOLD FARLEY IN the saddle, but Farley hunched over the horn and stubbornly refused help. The horse's every step hurt him.

They rode back down the road they had come on for what Andy thought must have been two or three miles. He saw lamplight in a window. "Farmhouse," he said. "Maybe they'll help us."

Farley's voice choked with pain. "If they ain't Hoppers."

"Even if they are, maybe they don't know what happened in town. No need in us tellin' them."

Andy strode up onto a wooden porch and knocked on the door. He heard a floor squeak as someone walked across it. The door opened, and a woman stood there, a shotgun in her hand. A cold feeling came to Andy's stomach. He recognized Jayce Landon's wife.

Her voice was like ice. "You're one of them Rangers. What do you want here?"

"I've got a hurt man outside. He needs help."

She looked at Farley but offered no sympathy. "You-all brought my husband back and turned him over to them Hoppers. Now you've got the nerve to ask for my help?"

An old man's voice came from a back room. "Who is it, Flora?" He came out carrying a pistol and squinted at Andy in the dim lamplight.

She said, "It's them Rangers, Papa. By rights we ought to shoot the both of them."

The bewhiskered old man poked the muzzle of his pistol toward Andy. "What you got to say for yourself?"

"I need help for my partner. He's been shot."

"By who?"

"By one of the Hoppers."

The pair's hostility began to fade. The old man said, "Thought you was in league with them, fetchin' Jayce in like you done."

"That was our job. But afterwards we stood guard on the jail to keep a mob from bustin' in. We didn't know Jayce had already broke out." He allowed a hint of accusation into his voice. "But I'll bet *you* knew it."

A satisfied look passed between the pair. The woman spoke first. "We ain't ownin' up to nothin'. But if you're lookin' to catch Jayce, you'd better have some damned fast horses. He left town on the best runner in the county."

"Right now I'm just interested in gettin' help for Farley Brackett."

The old man's attitude quickly mellowed. "Brackett, you say? Is he the one that gave them state police so much hell durin' the Yankee occupation?"

"He's the one."

"Lord amighty. Bring him on in here, boy. We'll see what we can do for him."

The woman still seemed reluctant, but she deferred to her father's judgment. Andy helped Farley out of the saddle and up the step.

The old man said, "Any enemy of the Hoppers is a friend of ours."

Farley growled, "I ain't their enemy, and I ain't your friend."

The old man appeared to take no offense. "He's probably half out of his head. Set him in that chair. Let's see how bad he's hurt."

They took off Farley's blood-soaked shirt, then peeled his long underwear down to his waist. Flora Landon held a lamp close and examined the wound, probing with her fingers while Farley ground his teeth. Andy got his first good look at her face. He thought her handsome, at least for a middle-aged woman. He figured her to be about thirty.

She said, "Looks to me like the bullet glanced off of the ribs. Gouged a pretty good hole comin' and goin', but it's a long ways from the heart. If he's got one."

Farley winced against the pain. His face was pale. "Ain't the first hole I ever had shot in me."

She frowned. "If you get blood poisonin' it may be your last. Grit your teeth, because this is fixin' to burn like the hinges of hell's front door." She washed the wound with whiskey. Andy thought for a moment that Farley might faint. She said, "We'll bind them ribs good and tight."

The old man said, "A broken rib is liable to punch a hole in his lung and kill him deader than a skint mule. Be better if he didn't ride horseback for a while."

The woman studied Farley with her first hint of sympathy. "I don't see where he's got a choice. Right now them Hoppers are probably searchin' all over Jayce's and my farm. When they get through there they'll be comin' here. I don't think you Rangers'll want to be around."

Andy said, "I was wonderin' if you folks have got a wagon I could borrow."

Flora looked questioningly at her father. He said, "This man faced up to the Hoppers and led them scallywag state police on a merry chase. You bet he can have my wagon." He jerked his head at Andy. "Come on, boy. Help me catch up my team."

He walked out onto the porch and stopped abruptly. "Daughter, you'd better come and look."

Andy saw flames in the distance. He could not guess how far away they were.

Flora gasped. "They're burnin' down our house, mine and Jayce's."

The old man nodded. "This place'll be next."

Andy heard horses coming. "Sounds like they're already here."

Flora declared, "Be damned if they're goin' to burn my papa's house." She reached inside the door and grabbed her shotgun.

The old man's bony hand pushed the shotgun muzzle down. "This house ain't nothin' but lumber and nails. I can build a new one. But the Lord Hisself can't build a new me or you."

Andy said, "It's too late to run. You-all get back inside and blow out the lamp. I'll talk to them."

Flora said, "I doubt as they're in a listenin' frame of mind."

"They'll listen to me or they'll answer to the state of Texas." He made his voice sound more confident than he felt. He stepped out to where he had tied his and Farley's horses. He lifted his rifle from its scabbard and got Farley's as an afterthought. He stood in the moonlight on the edge of the porch, his own rifle in his hand and Farley's leaning where he could reach it without much of a stretch.

He counted seven horsemen. An eighth followed behind. The deputy Big'un was in front as the riders came to a stop. He recognized Andy. "You Rangers again. Seems like you're everywhere."

"We try to be where we're needed."

"You know who we're after."

"Jayce Landon isn't here. I can vouch for that." He really couldn't. He had not seen anything here except the front room of the house. But the imperious lawman did not need to know that.

Big'un declared, "You Rangers have stepped way over the line. You helped a fugitive get away."

"He didn't escape from *us*. We delivered him like we were ordered to. He was the sheriff's prisoner. It was the sheriff's responsibility to see that he didn't bust out."

"I expect that woman of his knows where he's at. This is her daddy's house, and I'm bettin' she's in there."

Flora came out onto the porch, shotgun in hand. Andy started to tell her to go back inside, but he knew she would not heed him. She looked like a woman who would charge a bear with a willow switch.

She said, "I'm here, Big'un Hopper, and here I'm stayin'. It don't take much of a man to burn my house down, but it'll take a better man than you to run me out of this country. You or any of your other line-bred Tennessee ridge-runner kin."

The deputy moved his horse up closer to the porch. "If we ever find out you helped Jayce get away, you wouldn't be the first woman ever hung in Texas."

Andy shifted his rifle to point at Big'un. "There'll be no more talk about hangin', especially of a woman. You'd better back away if you don't want the whole Ranger force swarmin' this county like a nest of hornets."

"It ain't the Rangers' business to take sides in a local affair."

"It is when it comes to killin'."

Hopper seemed not to hear. "Flora Landon, I'm placin' you under arrest for aidin' and abettin'. You come down here."

She did not move. "You come up here and get me if you don't mind a load of buckshot in your belly."

For a minute Andy was not sure which way the pendulum would swing. Big'un seemed to weigh his chances, and anger appeared stronger than caution.

Farley Brackett walked out to join Andy and the woman on the porch. He held his arm tightly against his ribs, but in his hand was a pistol. He said nothing. He let his eyes deliver his threat.

Looking at Farley, the deputy took fresh stock of his situation. "Somethin' about you seems familiar to me. But I don't recollect that I heard your name."

"I'm Farley Brackett."

The name jarred Big'un. "From down in Colorado County? Somebody told me you was dead."

"I ain't heard about it."

Andy said, "And I am Andy Pickard." That name carried no weight with the deputy, but Farley's had drawn his full attention. Andy thought it was time to try to close the conversation. "You've got no grounds to arrest Mrs. Landon. You're trespassin' here on her daddy's place. You'd best be movin' on, or you're biddin' fair to see inside one of your own cells."

Big'un reluctantly began to cave. "You Rangers won't be stayin'. We can wait till you're gone." He pulled his horse around and started back in the direction of town. The other men followed, some grumbling about not finishing their job.

Flora looked at Farley. "Big'un almost lost his breath when he heard your name. You must've left some deep tracks."

Farley started a shrug but pain stopped it. His face pinched. "Would you have shot him in the belly?"

She replied, "I don't say anything I don't mean."

She went back into the house. Farley was ordinarily sparing with admiration, but he said, "There, Badger Boy, is what I call a woman!"

In the house, Andy said, "That was brave talk outside, but the Hopper bunch has got killin' on their minds. It would be smart if you folks left here for a while."

The old man told his daughter, "Get your stuff together and we'll go with these Rangers."

She resisted until her father said, "There ain't no shame in runnin' when it's the only way out. Jayce has done it. At least we'll live to hit them Hoppers another day."

Andy asked, "Where's Jayce runnin' *to*?"

The old man shook his head. "If I was to tell you that, you'd go after him."

"We would if it was our orders."

"Jayce ain't an easy man to warm up to, but he's the only son-in-law I've got. That's why I ain't tellin' you. Let's get that team hitched up. I don't fancy bein' around to entertain that bunch when they swaller a little more panther juice and come back."

ANDY DID NOT ASK at first where Flora Landon and her father wanted to go. He simply turned the team away from the direction of town and the fire still burning in the distance. He and Flora sat on the wagonseat. Farley lay on blankets in the bed of the wagon. Flora's father rode Andy's horse. Farley's was tied on behind, trailed by the little pack mule. They traveled a couple of miles in silence, though Andy stopped the wagon several times to listen for sounds of pursuit.

He saw a new fire and knew the house they had left was burning. The old man cursed under his breath. "I'll build it back, and I'll bury a couple of Hoppers in the backyard for good luck."

Flora said, "I'll help you dig the hole."

Andy asked, "You-all got kinfolks you'd like to go to?"

Flora said, "Not till things die down some. We'd bring more trouble on them, and they've got trouble enough just bein' Landons and kin. Where are you headin'?"

"To Colorado County, to some folks that will take care of Farley."

"Mind takin' us with you? Papa and me need to be scarce for a while."

"What about your husband? He won't know where you're at."

"We'll come back when the Hoppers ain't lookin'. They'll find out that their houses can burn just as easy as ours did."

The bitterness in her voice reminded Andy of what Farley had said about feuds. Often starting over some trivial incident, they tended to grow out of all proportion into a senseless succession of brutal killings. Andy had heard of one bloody vendetta that began over nothing more than mistaken accusations about a few missing hogs.

He doubted that Flora knew the origin of the Landon-Hopper feud, but he asked anyway. That started a mild argument between her and her father.

She said, "It was when Old Man Hopper shot at Jayce's daddy and took a chunk out of his shoulder."

"No," the old man countered, "that come later, after one of them Hopper boys and his cousin tried to beat up on Jayce's granddaddy. That old man whipped the britches off of them all by hisself, then whittled a swallow fork in the Hopper boy's ear."

The talk left Andy with a feeling of futility. Families killed one another though they could not agree on what had started the fight. It was a process with no foreseeable end.

Farley became feverish, drifting in and out of reality. From time to time he mumbled incoherently. At other times he was lucid enough to ask, "Where we goin'?"

Andy would tell him, "You'll see." He feared that a better answer would touch off an argument.

Flora occasionally checked the bandage while Andy stopped the wagon. She asked, "How'd he get that scar on his face?"

Andy told her he had brought that home from the war.

She said, "I have a feelin' he's got other scars on him that don't show. He must be a hell-bender in a fight."

Andy admitted, "He takes care of himself."

"Didn't do so good this time, did he?"

"Somebody shot him from out of the dark. He didn't have a chance."

Seeing the Brackett farm took Andy back to a terrible night when Reconstruction state police had shot up the house in the mistaken belief that Farley was there. They killed Farley's father, Jeremiah, and wounded his mother. Ironically, Farley was miles away at the time.

Lying in the wagon, Farley was unaware of Andy's destination until they were within a hundred yards of the house. He pulled himself up to look over the sideboards. Sight of the place jarred him out of his dreamy state. "Damn you, Badger Boy, I didn't want to come here."

"You need lookin' after. Who'll do it better than your mother and your sister?"

"They won't want to see me." Farley made a feeble try at getting up, but he hurt too much to do it on his own. He managed to say, "I'll whup you, boy, soon as I get my strength back."

"You can try. Right now you couldn't whip a sick kitten."

Andy shouted as soon as he thought he was within earshot. "Hello, the house."

A young woman stepped out onto the porch, shading her eyes with her hand. "Andy?"

"I've got Farley here, Bethel. He's hurt."

She hurried toward the wagon. Her flaring skirts startled the team, and Andy had to draw hard on the reins. Bethel gave Flora and the old man only a glance. She looked anxiously over the wagon's sideboards. "What happened to him?"

Andy said, "He's been shot."

Flora said, "He lost a right smart of blood."

Elnora Brackett and a black woman came onto the porch. Farley's mother watched anxiously as Andy and Flora helped Farley climb the steps. Color drained from her face. She said, "Bring him in. We'll put him in his own bed."

This was a large house in comparison to most Andy knew. Jeremiah Brackett had been a prosperous farmer before the war and before confiscatory Reconstruction taxes had stolen much of his property.

The black woman led the way down the hall and into a spartan room devoid of furniture except for a bed and a chair. Farley had not spent much time in this house after going off to war and later coming home to the desperate life of a fugitive, defying the occupation authorities.

His mother said, "That bandage is soaked. It needs changing." She held her son's hand as Andy cut through the bloodied cloth. "Is Farley in trouble again?"

She had reason to ask, for her son had led a reckless life after returning from the war. Andy told her, "No,

he got this in the line of duty." He explained about delivering Jayce Landon, about standing off a mob, and
about shots fired on a dark street. He said, "I brought
Farley here because I thought his family would take
better care of him than anybody."

Bethel touched Andy's arm. "You did the right thing."

"He didn't want to come. He thinks you-all still hold
it against him for his daddy gettin' killed."

Bethel seemed surprised. "We got over that a long
time ago."

Mrs. Brackett had lost two sons in the war and her
husband in its aftermath. She said, "He's the only son I
have left. He should know we'd stand by him."

"That's what I told him. Maybe he'll believe it,
comin' from you." Andy doubted Farley was in any
condition to follow the conversation. His eyes were vacant, staring at nothing.

The wound looked angry around the edges. Elnora
fretted about the possibility of blood poisoning. She
cleansed the opening and replaced the bandage with
help from Bethel and the black woman.

Only then was there time for Andy to introduce Flora
and her father and explain why they were with him.

Bethel said, "Thank you-all for your help. You're
welcome to stay here as long as you want to."

Flora said, "It won't be long. Soon as I think them
Hoppers are lookin' the other way . . ."

Andy said, "I'll go over to town and fetch the doctor. We don't want to take any chances with Farley."

Bethel asked, "Have you had anything to eat?"

"I guess I did, but I don't remember when it was."

"I'll fix you something before you go. Maybe we
can get Farley to take some broth."

In the interest of time Andy settled for warming up some beans and smearing a heavy load of butter on cold biscuits. He was aware of Bethel's eyes. She stared at him while he ate.

She said, "You quit coming around to see me."

"I've been tied up with the Rangers."

"Before that, though. I hope I didn't say or do anything . . ."

"You didn't. I just got real busy. Anyway, it seemed to me like you were havin' company enough without me. And I had a notion that I reminded you of the night the state police came."

The memory darkened her expression. "I would remember that anyway, with or without you. I kept hoping you'd come around. You will come back, won't you, with the doctor?"

"Yes, I'll want to see what he thinks about Farley and how long he'll be laid up. Then I'll visit with Rusty before I report back to the captain."

She touched his hand. "If what happened to my brother is any measure of life with the Rangers, I don't want to see either one of you go back."

He did not pull his hand away. In the past he had wondered how a girl like her could have a brother like Farley. He stared at her, trying to find any facial resemblance. He said, "It's a pretty good life most of the time. There's more boredom than excitement. The food's good when we're not out on patrol."

"The pay isn't much, is it?"

"I don't need much. They feed me. Rusty Shannon never let me pick up any wasteful habits."

"Maybe you could use some. Maybe you could come and see a girl once in a while."

"You mean that?"

"If I say it, I mean it."

He had heard that statement from Farley several times. Farley and his sister might not look alike, but they thought alike in some ways.

Bethel came outside to watch Andy get on his horse. He said, "Looks like you-all have had a good rain." The ground was muddy, and water stood in the fields.

"A storm passed through here a few days ago. All we got was rain, but your friend Rusty caught a terrible hail. It just about wiped him out."

"Sorry to hear that." Andy paused a moment, feeling a rush of sympathy for Rusty. "I'll be back with the doctor soon as I can."

6

ANDY WAS NOT PREPARED FOR THE RUIN THAT HAD been Rusty's field. A maturing crop of corn had been battered into nothing more than stalks, standing bare and broken. Leaves and half-developed ears were pounded into the muddy ground. The devastation was complete.

Approaching the cabin, he saw that its roof was newly shingled, as was the roof of a smaller cabin Rusty had built for Andy when he had expected to bring Josie Monahan home as a bride. Several chickens pecked about the yard. Some had lost many of their feathers. Patches of bare skin showed through.

Andy called out. He heard an answer and reined his horse toward the shed where Rusty kept his farming implements and tools. Rusty stepped out into the open, leather harness in his hand. Recognizing Andy, he forced a smile, though Andy knew smiling must come hard to him these days.

"Hey, Andy, I'll put this stuff away, then we'll go up

to the house." Rusty went into the shed, emerging without the harness. The smile was gone. He looked haggard. "Tom Blessing told me you'd be comin'. I suppose you got your prisoner delivered."

Andy dismounted to shake Rusty's hand. "For what it was worth." Andy would tell him about it later. Right now he was having difficulty absorbing the damage he saw around him. "Looks like you had a buffalo stampede."

Rusty had always stood tall and straight. Now his shoulders sagged. His voice was weary. "You can put up a fight against most things that come at you. You can whip down a fire or dam up against a flood. But a storm like this, all you can do is hunker down and watch it happen."

"I see you got new roofs."

"Neighbors." Rusty led Andy into the kitchen. "Had anything to eat?"

"Ate dinner with the Bracketts."

For a moment Rusty's eyes seemed to light up. "I'm glad you went by to see that Bethel girl. She's been askin' about you."

"It wasn't on account of her." Andy explained about the Jayce Landon affair and Farley's being wounded.

Rusty frowned. "Farley always did draw lightnin'." He and Farley had had their differences. "Lots of young men around here think Bethel Brackett is the best-lookin' thing in a hundred miles."

"She looks all right."

"Just all right?"

Andy was aware that Rusty had been trying a long time to promote a romance between Andy and Bethel. "Why don't you pay court to her yourself?"

Pain came into Rusty's eyes. "You know the luck I've had when it comes to women."

Andy wished he could take back what he had said. It had slipped out. "I'm sorry."

"No matter. I've halfway come to accept things like they are. I didn't need that hailstorm, though."

Rusty turned away, but not before Andy saw grief rekindled in his eyes. On the mantel stood a tintype of Josie Monahan. Andy could only imagine how many times a day Rusty must look at that picture.

He asked, "Ever hear anything from Alice?" Alice was Josie's younger sister.

"Not directly. Got a letter from her mother. Clemmie said the boy Billy keeps askin' about you."

"Nothin' from Alice herself?"

"I've got no reason to expect anything. There's nothin' between us. Never was."

Andy had hoped there might be.

Rusty poked at coals banked in the fireplace until they glowed red. "I'll boil us some coffee. It'll tide us over till suppertime."

Andy placed small sticks of dry wood atop the coals. "What're you goin' to do, Rusty? You've lost the year's work. It's too late in the summer to replant your field."

"I've got meat in the smokehouse and hogs runnin' loose on the river. I won't starve."

"You're not one for sittin' around idle."

"There's always work to do if I feel like lookin' for it. But lately I've been askin' myself what's the use?"

Rusty's dark mood made Andy uneasy. He said, "How about gettin' away from this place for a while? Come back to camp with me. You could sign up with the Rangers for three months or six months, however long you want to. The captain said he'd be tickled to have you."

Rusty toyed with the idea but resisted at first. "Rangerin' is for young men like you."

"There's older men than you in the force. Len Tanner is about your age. The Morris boys ain't far behind."

"I'll admit it'd be good to ride with them again." Rusty walked to the door. He looked out past the dog run to his ruined field. "The thing is, I'm gettin' to where when night comes I want a real bed, not a blanket on the hard ground."

Rusty was thin and drawn. Andy wondered how many meals he had cooked, then not eaten. "I always thought you enjoyed your time with the Rangers."

Rusty nodded. "I did, even with the long trips and the days I didn't eat. There's a lot of satisfaction in ridin' with a bunch of men you like and respect."

"Then come along with me. I guarantee that the captain will be pleased to see you."

"I'll admit I'm a little tempted."

"It might do you good to see some fresh country. This farm could pretty well take care of itself from now till spring plantin'."

Rusty gradually warmed to the idea. "I could turn the milk cow and her calf out together. I could take the chickens over to Shanty so the coyotes don't get them."

Perhaps later, when more healing time had passed, Andy could talk Rusty into traveling up north to visit the Monahans. If he spent time close to Alice, he might finally see what everybody around him already knew.

* * *

BETHEL BRACKETT STOOD ON the porch watching as Andy and Rusty dismounted in front of her house. She spoke first to Rusty, then to Andy. "Going back to camp already? I hoped you might stay awhile longer."

Andy said, "It's time I reported for duty. Just came to see about Farley so I'll know what to tell the captain."

He caught a moment's disappointed look before she hid it. She said, "Farley's stubborn and hard to get along with, but he always was. He's raisin' a ruckus about wantin' to go back to camp."

"He can't be ready yet."

"No, but he thinks he is. Nothing counts with him except what he thinks."

"What about Flora Landon and her daddy?"

"They're still here. Farley actually smiles when Flora comes into his room. I think he's a little taken with her."

Guess he's got some human feelings after all, Andy thought. "Reckon they know where Jayce is at?"

"I make it a point not to ask questions. If anybody comes around hunting for information, I won't have to lie to them." She managed a weak smile. "You-all are not in too much of a hurry to stay and eat dinner with us, are you?"

Rusty took the decision out of Andy's hands. "We'd be much obliged."

That was how it had always been, Andy thought. He never got to make a decision of his own unless he was by himself. He was always in Rusty's shadow, or someone else's.

He remembered how to reach Farley's room, but he chose to follow Bethel anyway. He enjoyed looking at her, though he would not tell her so, or Rusty.

Farley lay on his bed, atop the covers. Pale, unshaven, he was fully dressed, even to his boots. His shirt was only partially buttoned because of a bulky bandage wrapped around his ribs. He grunted at the visitors, either a halfhearted greeting or a dismissal. He had always lacked confidence in Andy, and he had only a strained tolerance for Rusty. Both had gotten in his way more than once.

Farley said, "I hope you're ready to ride, because I sure am. I may just beat you back to camp."

Andy saw worry in Bethel's eyes. She said, "You wouldn't get ten miles from home before you fell off of your horse. You'd lie there and bleed to death."

Farley said, "I got hurt worse than this in a skirmish with the Yankees and still rode thirty miles before dark."

Bethel shrugged. "How can you talk sense to a man like that?"

Andy saw no reason to tell her it was useless to try. She knew it better than he did. But he sensed that Farley understood the truth. Despite his blustering, he was not ready to ride, nor would he be for a while.

Rusty said, "Farley, I hear you and Andy turned back a mob."

Farley grunted. "It was a damn-fool thing to do, seein' as the man they was after had already lit out."

"You didn't know that at the time."

"This Badger Boy of yours was all set to try it by himself. When he takes it in his head to do somethin', you couldn't beat it out of him with a club."

Rusty nodded. "I've got no quarrel with that."

"Fool kid could've got us both killed." Farley glowered at Andy. "Look what happened to me. I deserve it for takin' pity on him."

Rusty said, "You got it for doin' the right thing."

"That Jayce Landon is a knot-headed idiot. The only reason I'd give a damn what happens to him is that he's got a wife who ought to've done better for herself. And a good-hearted daddy-in-law. Do you know he's out in the field right now, workin' like a hired hand? And her with him."

Andy took that for a sign Farley might be mellowing. The Bracketts still had the help of a black woman who once had been their slave. She now worked for her keep and received a modest wage when Elnora and Bethel had any money to pay her. When they did not, she stayed anyway. She had nowhere else to go. Andy could hear her clanging pots and pans in the kitchen. It reminded him he was hungry.

Farley tried to get out of bed but gave up. "I'm damned tired of takin' my meals in bed like a baby."

The black woman brought him his meal, but he ate only a little of it. He stared at the window and offered no more conversation.

Flora Landon and her father came in for dinner. Andy noticed that the first thing she did was go to Farley's room to see about him. She came back shortly, grinning. She said, "I thought Jayce knew every cuss word in the language, but I believe Farley could teach him some. When he finally gets up he's liable to drag that bed outside and burn it."

Her father asked Andy, "Seen any more of Sheriff Truscott or Big'un?"

"No, but I ain't been lookin' for them."

"Watch out. They're liable to come lookin' for *you.*"

The meal finished, Andy felt reluctant to leave. For one thing, visiting with Bethel and her mother seemed to have brought some life back into Rusty's eyes. But duty's call was loud. Andy jerked his head at Rusty. "It's a long way to the San Saba."

Farley shouted from his bedroom, "Saddle my horse for me. I'm goin' too."

Bethel cast a sad glance at Andy.

Rusty said, "Farley knows he can't. It just gets under his skin to have to depend on other people."

Andy and Rusty said their good-byes to Elnora and the Landons. Bethel followed them out onto the porch. She told Andy, "Write me a letter once in a while. Let a body know you're still among the living."

"I'm not much of a hand with pencil and paper. But I'll try."

Rusty said, "I'll see that he does."

Riding away, Andy looked back. Bethel remained on the porch, watching them.

Rusty said, "One word from you and she would follow you anywhere."

"To a Ranger camp? What could she do there?"

"You won't stay with the Rangers all your life. Nobody does."

They rode awhile before Andy said, "I'm tempted to go back up the river and see if there's any news about Jayce. Dick Landon would want to know about his brother."

Rusty threw cold water on the idea. "I've heard stories about the Hoppers and the Landons. Especially the Hoppers. I'd as soon see you stick your head into a rattlesnake den."

"I wish there was somethin' we could do about that double-dealin' Big'un."

"Time has a way of payin' off his kind of people. Chances are that some Landon will clean his plow or he'll get caught dippin' his hands into the county trea-sury."

"I hate to ride away and leave things hangin'."

"If trouble is lookin' for you it'll find you without you huntin' it. Let the Landons and the Hoppers fight it out amongst theirselves."

THE NEXT MORNING THEY rode for several miles in brooding silence. Andy was thinking about the unfin-ished business with Big'un Hopper and his kin. He suspected Rusty was thinking about his farm and Josie Monahan.

At length Andy said, "Folks holler about savage In-dians, but I don't see that they're any more savage than people that go feudin' and killin' one another. Most of them don't even know anymore what the fightin' is about."

Rusty pointed out, "Comanches kill Apaches any time they can. And Apaches kill Comanches the same way."

"That's different. They're blood enemies."

"Why? What started it?"

Andy tried in vain to remember if anybody had ever told him. "I'd guess it might've commenced over horses a long time ago. Somebody stole them and somebody else wanted them back. Or maybe some-body insulted somebody. With Apaches, who cares?"

"See, you ain't got past all of your Comanche raisin'. You hate Apaches without knowin' why. Co-manche or Apache, they're all Indians. It's a family feud just like with the Landons and the Hoppers. And it doesn't make a lick of sense."

That stung, although Andy could not quite reconcile

himself to Rusty's viewpoint. Every Comanche knew
that Apaches were like rattlesnakes, to be killed wherever they were found. Children were taught that lesson
as soon as they were able to learn. "It's the People's
way," he said.

"Killin' one another is the Hoppers' and the Landons' way. The Lord never made any perfect humans,
Indian or white."

WEST OF AUSTIN THE rugged topography always lifted
Andy's spirit. It seemed to lift Rusty's too, for his eyes
brightened as he surveyed the rough terrain, the live-
oak flats, the limestone layers that were like broken
stair steps up the sides of the hills. He said, "I never
spent much time out in this part of the country. I wish I
had. It's pretty."

"Pretty wild."

"If I was just startin' out and didn't already have my
farm, I think I'd find me a place out here. I'd set my
roots deep and never leave it the rest of my life."

Andy was gratified to see Rusty beginning to come
out of the darkness. "I've studied on it some myself."

He remembered older Comanches' accounts of long
hunting trips down into this land rich in water and
grass and game. By the time he was with them they
never ventured this far south anymore except to raid.
The Texans had made it too dangerous for them to
stay. In Andy's view the hill country had not yet been
spoiled by civilization. Most of it was too rough to be
violated by the plow except for narrow valleys where
soil had washed down from the steep hillsides to accu-
mulate deep and rich. In springtime it was like a

boundless garden exploding in color with bluebonnets and other wildflowers. Now in summer the season of blooming was gone and the maturing grass was more brown than green. Spring was short, but the memory was long.

It was a perfect haven for grazers and browsers, wild and domestic. Now and then Andy glimpsed white-tailed deer. Alert to danger, they bounded into the cedar thickets and live-oak mottes long before the horsemen reached them. A hunter needed stealth and steady nerves to stalk them with a rifle. How much harder it would be, he thought, to stalk them with a bow and arrow as the Indians traditionally did.

He saw wild turkeys too. He brought one down with a well-aimed shot to the head.

"What did you do that for?" Rusty asked. "It's hard to strip off the feathers without boilin' water to scald the bird."

"I'll skin him like a squirrel. He'll make a nice supper." Andy was proud of his shot. Bringing down a turkey with a rifle was a test of marksmanship. Rusty had taught him so well in the use of the rifle that Andy was now the better shot. In fact, when he gave it any thought he realized that Rusty had taught him most of what he knew about living in the white man's world.

Having finished all he wanted of the turkey, he sat on the ground a little way from the dwindling campfire. The night was warm enough that he did not need the heat. He said, "You're studyin' me awful hard."

Rusty said, "I was wonderin' with your Indian raisin' why you ever decided to be a Ranger. Rangers and Comanches have fought one another ever since Stephen F. Austin's time."

"It's more like the life I had with the Comanches than the life I had on your farm."

"But it's not a job you'd want to spend the rest of your years at. Even if you could depend on it, which you can't. The state is always runnin' out of money. You never know from one month to the next if you'll get paid."

"Money's not the main thing."

"It's easy to say money's not important when you've got a little in your pocket. It looks different when you don't have any. First time the state's money gets tight they'll cut the Rangers again. Folks back in East Texas will say the Indian fightin' is done so there's no use spendin' that tax money. But let a bank get robbed or somebody get killed and they'll holler, 'Where's the Rangers?'"

An owl hooted. Andy felt a chill. "Hear that?"

"It's just an owl in the tree yonder. He's probably lonesome for company."

"I don't like owls. They bring nothin' but bad luck."

"That's just an old Comanche notion."

"Some Comanche notions are real. Owls are bad medicine."

Andy lost himself awhile in memories of his Comanche life. He was shaken back to reality by the sound of a horse's hoofs striking against the limestone rocks. He reached for his rifle.

A voice called from the darkness, "Hello, the camp. All right if I come in?"

Rusty shouted, "Come ahead." He was watchful but did not seem worried. Andy's instincts told him to keep his hand on a gun.

The rider dismounted at the edge of the firelight and

tied his horse where it would not kick dust into the cook fire. He appeared to be of middle age. He had several days' growth of whiskers, though his hair was cut short. If he carried a weapon it was hidden. "Glad I seen your fire. I was about to make a cold camp, and a hungry one."

Rusty said, "You're welcome to what's left of a skinny turkey. You've traveled a ways by the looks of you."

"Several days, but I think I'm gettin' close to what I'm lookin' for. You-all know anything about a Ranger camp out thisaway?"

Rusty said, "Reckon we do. You thinkin' about joinin' up?"

"Me join the Rangers? Not hardly." The visitor seemed to find dark humor in the thought. "But I've got business with them."

Andy was still tense, trying to gauge the stranger's tone of voice. "You got a quarrel with the Rangers?"

"No, I stay away from the law and hope it stays away from me. Took me a long time to learn that, and I've got the gray hair to show for it. You say you know where the camp is at?"

Rusty said, "We're headed that way ourselves."

The stranger stiffened. "You're Rangers?"

Andy did not like the reaction. "I am. Rusty's fixin' to be. Is there somethin' we can do for you?"

"The Rangers been keepin' somethin' of mine."

Andy burned to ask for more details, but he considered it ill manners to be inquisitive without a clear reason. The visitor attacked the remnant of turkey as if he had not eaten in two days. Andy boiled a can of fresh coffee. The stranger blew steam from a cupful and drank it without waiting for it to cool.

Rusty said, "It ain't much, but it's the best we can do travelin' across country."

The stranger made a gesture of approval. "It's mighty fine. Where I been they don't know nothin' about makin' coffee, or much of anything else."

Andy itched to ask him where that was, but if it was important he would know in time. If it wasn't, it made no difference.

The stranger rubbed his stomach with satisfaction. "Couldn't be no better if you'd served it on golden plates. I'm obliged." He poured the last of the coffee. "Be all right with you fellers if I spread my roll here tonight and ride along with you tomorrow?"

Andy had doubts. But Rusty said, "I don't see any reason not to."

"I ought to let you know right off. I just come from a stretch in the penitentiary. You might not be comfortable with the likes of me around."

Andy's suspicions were confirmed. "If you escaped, we'll be honor-bound to take you in."

"No, I served my time and got out legal. They gave me a few dollars and a suit of clothes. Said they didn't want to see my ugly face no more, and I promised them they wouldn't."

Rusty said, "As long as you've paid up fair and square, I don't see where we've got any kick comin'. I'm Rusty Shannon. This is Andy Pickard."

The stranger nodded but did not offer to shake hands. "My name's Tennyson. Lige Tennyson."

Tennyson. Andy's pulse quickened. "Have you got a boy that goes by the name of Scooter?"

The stranger spilled some of his coffee. "You know him?"

Andy stared into the fire, his stomach uneasy. "I know him."

He was sure now why Lige Tennyson had come looking for the Rangers.

7

TENNYSON WALKED OFF INTO THE DARKNESS TO TAKE care of necessities. Andy said, "We can't let him take Scooter away."

"He's the boy's daddy."

"But he's an outlaw. He's been in the pen."

"He's served his time."

"What if he goes back to his old ways and drags Scooter along with him? We can't let that happen."

Rusty was sympathetic but offered little comfort. "If his mind is set, the only thing apt to stop him would be the court. You know a good judge?"

"I don't even know a bad judge. Well, Judd Hopper. I just know that kid was on the road to hell before me and some of the others took him by the scruff of the neck. We may not be able to rescue him the next time."

"Maybe Tennyson has decided to walk a straight line. I've known men that slipped once but never did it again."

"An old horse doesn't change his color. I've got a bad feelin' way down in my gut."

Though he knew it was unlikely, Andy could not shake a suspicion that Tennyson might steal their horses and make off with them in the dark. He dozed fitfully, never falling into deep sleep.

Tennyson snored all night.

Frying bacon for breakfast, Rusty noticed the droop of Andy's shoulders. "It won't help for you to lay awake frettin'. If the boy's daddy wants him there's not much you can do."

"Maybe the captain can."

Andy studied Scooter's father as they rode. It had long seemed to him that there should be something in a criminal face that marked it as different. He could find nothing unusual in Tennyson's unless it was the restless eyes, constantly searching. He had seen the same characteristic in frontiersmen used to being in Indian country, ever on the lookout for danger. Watchfulness was not necessarily a sign of a criminal mind.

Tennyson asked many questions about his son. "I'll bet he's growed up to be a man, almost. It's hard to picture him that way. Last time I seen him he stood about waist-high to a tumbleweed."

Andy looked for any sign of hope. "You may not know him, and he may not know you. You might've grown too far apart to fit back together again."

"Give us a little time. Blood will always tell."

Blood. That was what Andy worried about. Lige Tennyson's blood ran in Scooter's veins. It was an outlaw strain.

Andy said, "Scooter's come a long way. Sergeant Holloway's been schoolin' him in readin' and writin' and figures. It'd be a shame to take him away from that."

"I studied a few books while I was boardin' with the state, and I was always pretty good at figurin' up sums. I'll teach him all I know."

That was the problem, Andy thought. Lige knew too many of the wrong things.

They rode into camp at midafternoon and reined up in front of the headquarters tent. Sergeant Holloway stepped out, his turkey-tracked eyes pinched against the sunshine. Holloway gave Tennyson a glance, then turned to Andy and Rusty. "Rusty Shannon! It's good to see you back. You figurin' to stay awhile?"

"If you-all will have me."

Holloway asked Andy, "Where's Farley? Don't tell me he decided to resign." He looked a bit hopeful.

"Farley got shot up a little. I left him with his family till he heals up enough to ride."

Andy was about to give Holloway the details when the captain emerged from his tent. He acknowledged Rusty and told him he would be glad to have him sign up for whatever period Rusty might choose. Then he diverted his attention to Andy. "I received a wire saying you and Brackett delivered your prisoners all right."

"Delivered and signed for. But Jayce Landon didn't stay a prisoner for long."

"So I understand."

Andy explained about Jayce's escape from jail. He omitted his belief that Jayce's wife had slipped him the derringer, for she was in enough trouble with the local law. She didn't need the Rangers hounding her as well.

Dick Landon came up in time to hear most of it. He

smiled broadly as he listened to the account of his brother's flight. "I figured he'd get away if he had even a ghost of a chance."

"Got away slicker than wagon grease. My guess is that he put the county line behind him as fast as his horse could run. He left a bunch of disappointed Hoppers, not to mention the county judge."

"Judd Hopper!" Dick spat the name as if it were a wad of bitter tobacco. "The old son of a bitch has stolen half of the county."

Andy said, "Sheriff Truscott seemed like a decent sort, considerin' what-all he's got to deal with."

"But he's got Judd Hopper's leash around his neck."

Tennyson listened intently, saying nothing as his eyes cut from Andy to Dick to the captain.

The captain impatiently changed the subject. "Tell me again how Brackett got wounded. The wire was much too sketchy."

Andy repeated the account. The captain asked, "And you're sure you shot whoever did it?"

"I saw him fall and grab his leg."

The thought seemed to please the captain. "There's nothing so stupid as a feud, and Texas seems to be suffering an epidemic of them. The trouble isn't over just because you-all managed to ride away. It may follow you out here."

That thought was not new to Andy. "Any shots we fired were in self-defense, plain and simple."

The captain said, "From what I know of that county, the court belongs to the Hoppers. If they take a notion you've thrown in with the Landons, your testimony in court wouldn't be worth a Continental." His face indicated concern. "I'll need you to write a full report at your first convenience. Perhaps I can get it to Austin ahead of any protests from the judge or the sheriff."

The captain turned his attention to the visitor. "You say your name is Lige Tennyson? Somehow that has a familiar ring."

Tennyson shrugged apologetically. "I'm sorry to say that too many people used to know my name. Five years down at the state hotel has taught me that the outlaw road is all uphill, through flint rocks and cactus. But I've wrestled with the devil, and I've finally pinned him to the floor."

"Well and good, but what brings you to this camp?"

"I've come to claim my son. He's the boy called Scooter."

The captain's brow wrinkled. He gave Tennyson a more intense scrutiny. "I believe I see a family resemblance."

"The Tennyson blood has always showed out strong. Ain't goin' to be no trouble about me takin' my boy, is there?"

"I'll have to satisfy myself that it's the right thing to do. I'll want to see what the boy says."

"He's his daddy's son. He'll want to go."

"That I shall determine for myself. Follow me, Mr. Tennyson." The captain strode toward the cook tent. Tennyson took long steps to catch up with him. Andy trailed along. Rusty stayed behind, talking to Holloway.

The black cook looked up from his Dutch ovens, puzzled by the crowd converging on him. "Howdy, Captain. A little early for supper. Got coffee ready, though."

"We're looking for Scooter."

"He's out draggin' up firewood. Ought to be back

right soon." Bo's forehead creased with worry. "He ain't got in no trouble, has he?"

"No trouble. His father has come to see him."

Bo seemed at a loss for words. He started to extend his hand but reconsidered and drew it back. He would not expect a white stranger to shake with him. "You're Scooter's daddy?" His voice hinted at the same misgivings Andy felt. "You and him been away from one another a long time."

"Too long, but I'm fixin' to make it up."

Bo looked at the captain and at Andy, a silent pleading in his eyes. "I hope you ain't fixin' to take him away. That boy's been a right smart of help to me."

Instead of replying to Bo, Tennyson turned to the captain. "You got him takin' orders from a nigger?"

The captain stiffened. "He listens to all of us. That's how a boy learns."

"Not a boy of mine. I want him growin' up proud and strong. He's got no business playin' servant to anybody, least of all a nigger."

The captain's face flushed as he struggled for an answer. Andy knotted his fists.

They were distracted by a scraping sound. Scooter approached on horseback, dragging several long, dead tree branches at the end of a rawhide rope. He brought them up even with a remnant of woodpile and jumped to the ground. He retrieved the rope and coiled it. "That ought to last a couple of days, Bo. You want me to chop it up?"

Bo's eyes were troubled. He did not answer.

Tennyson said, "You're through doin' chores around here, son."

Scooter noticed the visitor for the first time. He blinked in confusion.

Tennyson bent down. "Don't you recognize your old daddy?"

Scooter appeared at first to disbelieve what his eyes told him. "Pa?"

"Son, I've come to fetch you away from this place. It's time me and you was partners again." He opened his arms.

Scooter hesitated another moment, then accepted his father's hug. "Pa, I didn't know who you was."

"Five years make a lot of changes in a man. But not as many as in a boy." He pushed his son off to arm's length and gave him a long study. "You've growed a sight bigger than I expected. You're might near a man."

"Might near."

"Have you missed me?"

"I didn't think I'd ever see you again."

"There was times I wondered too, but you'll see a lot of me from now on. We've got places to go and things to do."

"Where we goin'?"

"We'll talk about that. How long before you're ready?"

Scooter looked to the officer for an answer. "Is it all right with you, Captain?"

The captain was slow to answer. "Son, you're free to do whatever you want to. Just be sure you know your mind."

"This is my daddy." Scooter looked at Bo. "You're always talkin' about Scripture. Don't it say in the Book that I'm supposed to obey my daddy?"

The cook's words came reluctantly. "It ain't for me to tell you what you should do. All I know is that you've been a changed young'un since you've been with us."

Scooter turned back to his father. "These Rangers have treated me real good."

Tennyson said, "But they ain't your kin. Blood is what matters most in this world."

Scooter pondered his dilemma, his freckled face twisting. "I guess I belong with my daddy."

The captain nodded gravely. "If that's your choice."

Andy protested, "Scooter, you were ridin' with outlaws when we found you. You don't want to be doin' that again."

"I'll be ridin' with my daddy."

Andy wanted to grab the boy and shake him until he changed his mind, but he could not bring himself to lay a hand on Scooter. He said, "You're makin' a mistake."

The captain said, "Leave him alone, Pickard. I told him the choice was his."

"But he's makin' the wrong one."

Tennyson said, "Keepin' a boy away from his kin is like cuttin' off the roots to a tree. It ain't right. He needs to know who he is and who his people are."

Scooter asked, "We don't have to leave today, do we?"

Bo put in, "Stay a little longer and I'll fix this boy a supper like he ain't never had before."

Tennyson considered. "Supper? Sounds all right to me. My horse is about give out anyway."

Andy had found that tired horses were always a logical excuse for inaction.

Rusty had come up by then. Taking him aside Andy

told him, "Maybe this'll give me time to talk Scooter out of the notion."

Rusty frowned. "Careful. If you push him into a decision he comes to regret, he'll resent you the rest of his life."

"If he makes the wrong decision, he'll resent me for not advisin' him better."

Rusty shrugged. "Looks like you're rimfired either way you go."

Bo joined them. He seemed unable to conceive of the boy going away. He said, "When he first come here I felt like skinnin' him alive. But us all workin' together, we've made a pretty good kid out of him. Maybe he'll still decide not to go with his daddy."

Andy said glumly, "Maybe. But if *my* real daddy was to show up, I guess I'd want to go with him. Kin is kin."

"There's a difference. Your real daddy was a peaceful farmer, so they say. He wasn't no outlaw."

Andy noticed that Tennyson sought out Dick Landon and talked with him at length. Later, when he had a chance, Andy asked Dick what Tennyson had been so interested in.

Dick said, "He asked a lot of questions. Told me he heard talk in the pen about the fight between the Landons and the Hoppers. I told him I've been tryin' to stay out of it, but it's hard when so many people are tryin' to hunt down my brother."

"Maybe Jayce has got to Mexico by now."

"I doubt he'd go there without Flora. No, he'll stay close enough to keep in touch with her and the rest of the family."

"Then he's always in danger of bein' found."

Dick's face darkened. "Them that find him, they'll wish they hadn't."

ANDY HAD EXPECTED TROUBLE to come sooner or later from Sheriff Oscar Truscott or at least his deputy, Big'un Hopper. He had not expected the county judge to show up at the Ranger camp in a buggy, sided by Big'un and another Hopper on horseback. Andy remembered Big'un calling this one Harp. The family resemblance was strong.

Judge Hopper looked to be in the final stages of dyspepsia. He stopped at the headquarters tent first, conferring awhile with the captain. The captain in turn sent for Andy.

The captain's face was sober, but Andy could sense anger simmering beneath the surface. "Private Pickard, Judge Hopper has made grave charges against you and Private Brackett."

Andy stood straight and defiant. "We expected somebody would." He wondered why Sheriff Truscott had not come instead of the judge. He had sensed almost from the first that friction existed between the sheriff and his in-laws.

Big'un poked a thick finger toward Andy's face. "This man and his partner contrived for a prisoner to escape."

The captain maintained a stern attitude. "And how did they do that? Private Pickard brought me a signed release certifying that the prisoner had been delivered into the sheriff's hands. All further responsibility was the sheriff's."

Big'un said, "They claimed they'd searched him, but he had a gun on him. He forced the jailer to turn him aloose."

Andy said, "Didn't you or the sheriff search him too before he went into the jail?"

"We took you-all's word."

"I distinctly remember seein' you feel of Jayce's pockets."

"He must've had it someplace else. In his boot, maybe. We trusted you Rangers to be sure he didn't carry any weapon when you turned him over to us."

"He didn't." Andy was gratified that the Hoppers evidently had not figured out something that seemed obvious to him: Flora Landon had slipped her husband the derringer. He did not want to make their job easier or the woman's life harder than it already was.

Big'un declared, "One of them Rangers wounded a cousin of mine. Took a chunk out of his leg. He'll never walk straight again."

Andy retorted, "The way most of them were liquored up that night, he wasn't walkin' very straight before."

The captain frowned at Andy, a quiet signal for him to tread lightly.

The judge looked up the row of tents. "Where is that other Ranger, the one named Brackett? Why is he not out here?"

Andy did not answer. He decided that was for the captain to do if he so chose.

The captain said, "He is recuperating from a wound some of your people inflicted upon him."

"I asked you where he is."

"And I have chosen not to say. Any business you

have with him, you can take up with me." The captain's firm stance made it plain that he did not intend to tell more than he already had.

Big'un broke in, "We understand you've got a man here by the name of Landon."

The captain said, "Yes. Private Dick Landon."

"Do you know he's a brother to the fugitive?"

"I do, but I've kept Private Landon here in camp or on assignment nearby. You cannot implicate him in this fiasco."

"He didn't have to be there. I'm bettin' that him and Pickard and Brackett were in cahoots. And I'm bettin' he knows where his brother is at. He may even be hidin' him somewhere close to this camp." Big'un's voice rose as he spoke.

The judge said, "I have sworn out a warrant for the arrest of Pickard and Brackett and your Ranger Landon. I intend to bring them before the grand jury." He removed some papers from his vest pocket.

The captain planted his feet a little farther apart. "You are out of your jurisdiction." Nevertheless, he gave the documents a cursory inspection. His voice edged toward the sarcastic. "Signed by Judge Judd Hopper. I wonder why the Hopper name does not surprise me."

"I was duly elected by the voters of the county. Those papers are as legal as if they were signed by Sam Houston himself."

The captain handed back the documents. "I cannot accept these. I do not know if the signature is genuine."

"I just told you."

"I do not know if *you* are genuine. You have shown me no documentation to prove you are who you say you are."

Big'un said, "You can see my badge."

"Any half-sober silversmith can counterfeit a badge. The men you seek are Rangers under my command, duly sworn. You will not have them unless I receive direct orders from the adjutant general."

Big'un said, "He's way to hell over in Austin."

"Probably, if he is not away on an inspection tour somewhere across the state. I suggest you go to Austin and wait for him."

Big'un started to turn his horse away but paused to curse the captain. "We ain't done yet. You'll be wishin' you'd never heard of us Hoppers."

The captain said, "I already do. Leave this camp, or I shall place you under arrest for disturbing the peace. I may come up with another charge or two if I set my mind to it."

Andy watched the judge's face flush a deep red. He thought Hopper might be in some danger of bursting a blood vessel. Big'un gave the judge a cautionary look. "Better ease off, Uncle. You know what the doctor told you about them conniption fits." He turned his eyes to the captain. "Looks to me like he needs a drink."

"We don't keep liquor in camp."

"Some water, then."

The captain offered no sympathy. "There's a whole riverful of it down yonder."

Big'un and the judge rode down toward the river. Harp followed a length behind. He had never spoken. Andy surmised that he simply rode in his kinsmen's shadow.

Sweating heavily, Andy said, "Thanks, Captain. I was afraid you might give them what they asked for."

"The Rangers stand by their own."

"Those Hoppers are a hard bunch. From what I heard, so are the Landons. Dick is an exception."

"Perhaps. Given sufficient provocation, there is no telling what any man might do, including yourself. I gather you have had no experience with a real Texas family feud."

"Not like this one."

"They can be vicious. They can draw in an entire community, including people who are no blood kin. Back in the time of the republic, two groups known as the Regulators and the Moderators went to war against one another. It took Sam Houston and the Texas army to stop the bloodshed."

"I've heard about that one."

"Sometimes it's hard to stay neutral, but we have to. It's our job to keep the peace, even if we have to kill some people to do it."

"Big'un Hopper is a determined man, and so is the judge. Do you think they'll just turn around and go back?"

"I'll see that they do. I'll send Len Tanner as an escort to see the three of them safe from Indian attack the first forty or fifty miles."

"There hasn't been an Indian attack around here in years."

The captain smiled thinly. "And we want to keep it that way."

Andy thought by the time the Hoppers listened to a one-sided conversation from Len for fifty miles, they would not want to come back. He could talk the ears off a dead mule.

8

THE RANGER COMPANY HAD GIVEN SCOOTER AN UN-
claimed fourteen-year-old horse recovered from
a thief, along with an old saddle and a bridle acquired
the same way. He had been as proud as if the rig were
brand-new and the horse a three-year-old. He rode beside his father, who had not told him their destination
but had set out after breakfast in an eastward direction.

A squirrel chattered at them from the limb of a
pecan tree. Lige said, "There's supper." He drew his
pistol and fired. The squirrel toppled, its head gone.

Scooter whistled. "Man! I never even seen a Ranger
shoot like that."

"It ain't nothin' you can't learn to do. Just got to set
your mind to it. I'll learn you."

Lige motioned, and Scooter dismounted to retrieve
the squirrel. Lige said, "Keep watchin' for another. We
can have us a regular feast as good as what that darky's
been fixin'."

"Ain't many can cook like Bo."

Lige frowned. "Them Rangers had no business lettin' you do chores for the likes of him. You're white, and don't you ever forget it."

"Bein' black ain't Bo's fault. He's good people."

"As long as he knows his place."

At dusk they sat before a campfire, watching two squirrels broiling on the ends of long sticks. Scooter said, "Been a long time since we camped together. So long I can barely remember it."

"We'll do it a lot more. We're partners, me and you." Lige leaned forward for a look at the squirrels. "I done a lot of campin' when I was younger. Bet you didn't know I lived for a few years up in the Cherokee nation."

"With the Indians?"

"They was good Indians."

"I didn't know there *was* any good ones. Comanches come awful close to killin' me once. I hid out to where they couldn't find me, but they sure tried. They come so close I swear I could smell their breath."

"The Cherokees are a different breed. I had me some good friends amongst them, and we cut some real shines together. Of course I was a sight younger then." Lige mused for a while, staring into the fire. "I got it in mind to go back up to the nation and find me a Cherokee wife. They each got a head right to some land. Me and you could get us a good little farm that way."

"You'd marry an Indian just to get some land?"

"It ain't easy for a poor man to get ahold of good land these days. Besides, there's other advantages to bein' married. Me and your mama had a pretty good life together. I miss her."

"I don't know how I'd take to havin' an Indian mother. I'd keep thinkin' about them Comanches wantin' to scalp me. I'd wonder if she had the same notion."

"Them Cherokees live like white people. Got their own government. Even got their own newspaper."

"Still, I don't know as I'd like it. I might not go with you up there."

"You'll go where I say." Tennyson's face clouded with anger that came quickly and faded the same way. "The Good Book says to honor your father."

"You've read the Good Book?"

"Parts of it."

"You believe everything it says?"

"The parts I agree with. I heard a lot of preachin' while I was back yonder workin' for the governor. So we'll follow the Book, and you'll go where I go."

Scooter had forgotten how mercurial his father's moods could be. He remembered how hard his father could slap him with an open hand, then hug him tenderly. He decided to step with caution. "And where'll that be?"

"Back where that feud is goin' on. I talked to Dick Landon, and I watched that judge and the deputies. I figure a man good with a gun ought to be able to hire out to one side or the other for high dollars. That'd set us up fine for goin' to the Cherokee nation. But first we need us a little road stake."

"Road stake?"

"Travelin' money. There's a nice little bank over in Kerrville. I think I could talk them into makin' us a loan."

Scooter did not hide his misgivings. "When you say loan, you're really thinkin' robbery."

"Robbery is an ugly word. *Borrowin'* touches softer on the ear."

"I doubt as the Rangers would see the difference."

"You're not with the Rangers anymore. It's time you quit worryin' about what they think."

"I was with Arliss and Brewster and another feller when they held up the bank in Brownwood. Scared me near as bad as them Comanches did."

"There's nothin' to be scared of when you know what you're doin'. Watch me and learn. Every boy needs to master more than one trade."

THE RANGERS HAD TOLD Scooter that Kerrville and several other towns in the hill country had a strong German influence. They explained that in the years before the war, many groups of Europeans—German, Polish, Alsatian, Irish—had immigrated into Texas, usually settling into enclaves among their own kind, where they felt comfortable.

All he knew about Germans was that they talked differently from most people though they looked like just about everybody else. He wondered if the men in the bank would understand Lige's words. But of course they would understand his meaning. Everybody knew what a gun meant when they looked at it from the front end.

He was sure Andy and Bo and everybody else back in camp would be furious at him and Lige both. But he knew he could not talk his father out of the notion. Lige was better at talking than at listening.

Lige gave the bank several minutes' scrutiny. "I was

in there six or seven years ago. Doubt it's changed much."

"You've robbed it before?"

"I looked at it as a loan. Never intended to keep the money permanent. I always figured on payin' it back someday when I could. Just ain't been able to. Besides, it ain't right, some people havin' so much money and some not havin' none. What the government ought to do is take up all the money in the country and divide it equal. When you look at it that way, all I'm doin' is seein' that we get our share. That's what democracy is all about."

Scooter saw three horses tied in front of the bank. He wondered if their riders would stand idle while Lige single-handedly robbed the place. "Hadn't you better go in and look things over first, Pa?"

"They might recognize me from last time. Best thing is to get straight to business. Now you stay in the saddle and hold my horse. I'm liable to be in kind of a hurry when I come out."

Hands shaking, Scooter took the reins his father handed him. "What if things go wrong and you don't come out?"

"Then run like hell. The penitentiary ain't no place for a growin' boy." Lige turned away, carrying his saddlebags over one arm.

Scooter's stomach churned. He tried to ease the tension by pretending that his father was only teasing him, that he actually intended to negotiate a legitimate loan. The fantasy faded like a wisp of smoke. The truth was as solid and forbidding as that stone bank building.

A friendly voice called, causing him to freeze. "Howdy, Scooter. What you doin' so far from camp?"

He turned, trembling. Ranger Johnny Morris walked toward him. Scooter stammered, trying for some kind of answer. He remembered that the captain had sent Johnny on a mission of some kind a few days ago.

"I'm with my pa," Scooter managed. "He came and got me."

"Your pa? I thought he was in . . ." Johnny broke off. "Where's your pa now?"

"He went in the bank."

"The bank!" Johnny turned on his heel, drawing his pistol as he ran. He barely had time to enter the front door before Scooter heard a shot from inside.

Lige rushed out, a smoking pistol in one hand, the saddlebags slung over the other arm. He tossed the bags to Scooter and grabbed the reins from Scooter's hand. "Hang on to them bags. Hold them tight."

He swung into the saddle and fired a shot through the open bank door. Someone stepped quickly back out of sight.

Lige shouted, "Let's go. This town ain't got no friendlier."

Scooter was too frightened to talk until they had cleared the outskirts of town. They galloped eastward alongside the rock-strewn Guadalupe River and its tall cypress trees. Looking back, he could see no one in pursuit, but he reasoned that they would soon be coming. "I hope you didn't kill somebody."

Lige cursed. "Everything was goin' just dandy till some feller come stormin' in with a six-shooter. Wasn't nothin' I could do but shoot him before he could shoot me."

"That was a Ranger. He was a friend of mine."

"When it comes to the law, us Tennysons ain't got no friends."

Scooter wanted to cry but couldn't. "Did you kill him?"

"Things went too fast. I just know I hit him. He ought to've minded his own business. I was mindin' mine."

Scooter felt a measure of relief, but not enough. "That *is* his business, chasin' robbers."

"Don't call me a robber again or I'll take my belt to you. I swear, young'uns these days have got no respect."

Scooter's anger flared, the aftermath to his earlier fear. "If you ain't a robber, what are you?"

"A rebel. They got too many laws in this country, and I've fought against damn near all of them. I was born free. I intend to stay that way."

Scooter thought that might not be easy. "The Rangers will all be after us now, and they don't stop at no county lines."

THE NEWS FROM KERRVILLE brought all the off-duty Rangers to the headquarters tent. The report was that a bank robber had badly wounded Johnny Morris. A boy had been with him. The message did not offer any names, but Andy was sure Lige Tennyson was the culprit. Scooter was a witness at the least, perhaps even an unwilling accomplice.

Andy told the captain, "I had a bad feelin' about Tennyson from the start. I want to go over there."

"I don't think I should let you. You're too close a friend to the boy."

"Everybody in camp was friends with Scooter. He's liable to end up killed if we don't get him away from that outlaw daddy."

The captain's face indicated that he was going to turn Andy down, but he said, "All right. I'm sending Sergeant Holloway and Rusty Shannon. You can accompany them. Saddle up. You'll leave in twenty minutes."

Rusty and Andy were sitting on their horses in front of the headquarters tent when Sergeant Holloway came out carrying his rifle. They had blanket rolls tied to their saddles, grub from Bo's kitchen hanging in cloth sacks. The sergeant walked to where a Ranger had Holloway's horse saddled and waiting. He said nothing. Conversation tended to be sparse on a serious Ranger mission.

The three Rangers rode far into the night, following a wagon road that wound through the valleys and between the hills. Andy judged that it was past midnight when they rode up to the jail in Kerrville. For the last couple of hours he had felt the horse gradually tiring beneath him. He doubted the animal had another hour of travel left.

The sergeant knocked on the door several times before a sleepy-headed deputy sheriff answered, holding a lamp so he could see the faces before he opened the door all the way. He recognized Holloway on sight. "I was sort of expectin' you Rangers, but not at this hour of the night."

Holloway said, "Rangers don't get much sleep when outlaws are on the prowl. How's Johnny Morris?"

"He'll live, but he was hard hit. Goin' to be a long time before he does any Rangerin' again."

Rusty asked, "Where's he at?" He and the two Morris brothers had been friends for years.

"Over at the doctor's house. I wouldn't go beatin' on the door now, though. Him and the doctor both need sleep. You can bunk down here till daylight. I got some empty cells."

Holloway thanked him for his thoughtfulness. "We'll need to put our horses away first. I'll want to talk to witnesses as soon as we can. We're pretty sure we know who the culprit is."

The deputy nodded. "Your Ranger told us the boy's name is Scooter Tennyson. The robber was the boy's daddy."

Andy asked, "Did Scooter help with the robbery?"

"The Ranger said it looked to him like the kid was holdin' the horses. Said he hoped the young'un didn't realize what was goin' on."

The sergeant frowned at Andy. "For the time bein' we'll give Scooter the benefit of the doubt. But if he knew what his daddy was doin', and he helped, we'll have to consider him an accessory."

"He's just a kid."

"A kid can pull a trigger."

Andy found a jail cell a poor place to sleep. The bunk was rock-hard. He had never given much consideration to the comfort of people he helped to arrest. He thought perhaps in the future he might be more conscious of prisoners' rights.

Holloway had little use for a bed after sunup nor was he sympathetic with others who would rather sleep than meet the new day. He hollered, "Daylight!" at the top of his voice. He was not accustomed to saying it twice. Andy had slept in his clothes, all but boots and hat. He donned the hat first, then pulled on his boots.

The deputy soon emerged from his living quarters. "Got water and a wash pan out by the back door. I'll see if I can scramble up some breakfast."

Andy appreciated the fresh eggs, though the deputy cooked them too long and gave them a scorched flavor. The biscuits were soft and warm. He smeared them liberally with fresh butter and dipped them in black-strap molasses. Good biscuits could make up for a lot.

His thoughts ran to Scooter. He wondered where the boy was now. Camped out along a trail somewhere, more than likely, possibly hungry and frightened. He thought of Johnny Morris lying in the doctor's house, in pain from a bullet wound that could easily have killed him.

Damn Lige Tennyson. Andy wished there were a dozen of Tennyson, and every one of them was locked up in the Kerrville jail. Or better, buried at the back side of the Kerrville cemetery.

Andy kept glancing at the sergeant, wanting him to hurry his meal. Holloway took note of his impatience. "In due time. Johnny may still be sleeping."

The deputy said, "The robbers headed east along the river road. We trailed them a ways, but we lost their tracks because they was mixed with so many others. There's no tellin' which way they went once they got plumb clear of the town."

Johnny Morris was awake and propped up in bed. His face was pale, his cheeks drawn in, but his eyes lit up when he saw his fellow Rangers. He said in a thin voice, "I thought for a while I was fixin' to go absent without leave."

The sergeant smiled. "That'd be desertion. You're too good a Ranger for that." He quickly got down to business. "We figure the robber was Lige Tennyson. Are you sure it was Scooter you saw?"

Johnny said, "It was him, all right. I was surprised to see him sittin' there holdin' a second horse. When I asked what he was doin', he said he was waitin' for his daddy. I remembered that his daddy was supposed to be in the pen, so I figured he didn't go in the bank to make a deposit."

"And you set out to stop him?"

"The bank was dark. Comin' in from the daylight, I couldn't see much. The robber shot me before I got a good look at him."

Andy said, "Reckon Scooter knew what his daddy was up to?"

"Maybe there wasn't nothin' he could do about it."

The sergeant said, "He could have ridden away and left his father."

Andy argued, "You couldn't expect him to do that. He hadn't seen his daddy in five years. He wouldn't leave him so soon."

"In the eyes of the law he's old enough to make choices, even the hard ones."

A visit to the bank filled in some extra details but did not change the cardinal fact that the holdup man was almost certainly Lige Tennyson. A quick-thinking teller had filled the saddlebags with low-denomination bills and a stack of blank counter checks so that the bank's loss was minimal. Tennyson must have been sorely disappointed when he stopped to count the fruits of his labor.

Holloway said, "Comin' up short, he'll likely pull

another robbery before long. I'll wire Austin a description, and the adjutant general's office will send it across the state. I doubt that Tennyson has any idea how the telegraph lines have spread durin' the time he was in the pen."

Impatience stung Andy like a case of hives. "Every time he does it he puts Scooter in danger. Sooner or later they'll run into somebody who's a good shot."

"We'll try to pick up his trail. Maybe we'll have better luck than the townfolks did."

Andy burned inside. He wished he had Lige Tennyson in front of him right now. He would gladly shoot him, even if Scooter hated him for it afterward.

LIGE TENNYSON HAD BEEN in a dark mood since he had stopped to open the saddlebags and find out how rich he was. Scooter watched him uneasily, fearful that he might become the whipping boy for his father's frustrations. So far he had not, but Scooter remembered harsh punishment inflicted long ago for minor infractions.

Lige had turned the air blue. "Damned teller with his clean white shirt and necktie. A dirty crook is what he is, cheatin' me thisaway. I wouldn't put it past him to've stuck the real money in his pockets and then claim I got it all."

Scooter considered the implications. "That'd be double robbery, wouldn't it, robbin' you and the bank both? He could go to jail twice."

Lige rumbled on, "I'd go back and blow his lamp out, but the town'll be swarmin' with Rangers by now. We got to keep movin'."

Scooter figured his father was probably right about

the Rangers. He wondered if Andy and the others were on the trail right now. Lige had been careful to stay on the river road at first so their tracks would be difficult to separate from the others. They had turned off at a place where the road crossed a field of gravel deposited by some long-ago flood. They had not left a track that he could see.

He was torn between a wish that the Rangers would catch up with them and a fear that if they did, they might shoot first and discuss consequences later. He had heard enough talk in camp to know that at times it was considered good judgment to bring a prisoner in dead rather than alive. Under stressful circumstances the Rangers were prone to be both judge and jury.

Lige muttered, "We ain't got near as much money as I figured. We're goin' to have to find us another loan."

Scooter said, "We don't have to *borrow* money that way. We could find work and earn it fair and square."

"Doin' what? I never was no good at a town job. Tried clerkin' in a store once. Pretty soon I was talkin' to myself. I done a little work as a ranch hand, but I never saw an outfit that didn't have a bunch of rank horses they expected you to ride. I'm gettin' too old for that. Banks, now, that's somethin' I know a right smart about. You just walk in, get their attention in the right way, and they'll generally loan you anything you ask for."

"Sometimes they've got guards with guns."

"If you want money, you've got to go where the money is at."

They came in sight of a modest frame farmhouse. Lige signaled for Scooter to stop. He studied the place awhile, then observed, "Crops ain't well tended. Weeds look to be doin' better than the corn."

Scooter smelled wood smoke and saw that it was coming from the backyard. A skinny middle-aged woman carried water from a steaming wash pot to a wooden tub, her thin back bending under the strain. She began scrubbing clothes.

Lige speculated, "Widder woman maybe. If she had a man the weeds wouldn't be takin' the field that way."

Scooter worried, "We ain't fixin' to rob her, are we?"

Lige seemed scandalized that his son would think such a thing. "There's no gain in holdin' up poor folks. They've got nothin' to give you anyway. But maybe we can get us a woman-cooked meal. You're lookin' a little drawed."

Scooter had not had much to eat except for squirrel and somebody's young shoat they had caught rooting for acorns. "Whatever you say, Pa."

The woman raised up from her scrub board as they approached the rear of her house. She seemed unconcerned. Scooter supposed she reasoned that a man traveling with a boy at his side presented no threat.

Lige touched fingers to the brim of his misshapen hat. "How do, ma'am. Me and my son are just passin' through. We noticed that your garden stands in need of weedin'. We wondered if we might trade a little service for a good meal. The boy ain't et proper in a while."

Scooter thought the woman looked a little like his mother when she gave them a weary but grateful smile. She said, "That'd be a mighty welcome trade. My husband's laid up with a broke leg, and things around here have got away from me some. Soon as I get these clothes on the line I'll see what I can cook up for you."

Lige nodded. "If you'll kindly direct us to where your husband keeps his workin' tools, me and the boy'll get busy."

She accompanied them to a small frame barn where a hoe, a rake, and smaller tools were neatly arrayed. She said, "You wouldn't see things in this shape if my husband was able to work. Neighbors come now and again to help, but they got needs of their own to see after."

Lige said, "We'll do the best we can."

There was only one hoe. Lige told Scooter, "I'll pull up the big ones by hand. You foller along and cut down the littler ones."

Lige worked faster with his bare hands than Scooter could with the hoe. "Pa, you act like you've done this before."

"I got lots of practice while I was studyin' at the state school. They expect you to earn your keep. When we get that farm of our own up in the territory, we'll be doin' a lot of this. Watch out you don't cut them tater vines instead of the weeds."

Scooter soon worked up a sweat. He was not sure he looked forward to that farm of their own, but maybe it would keep Pa happy enough to give up his forays into the banking business.

Between them they finished most of the garden before the woman called them to supper. The food made up in quantity what it lacked in variety. She said apologetically, "It ain't fancy, but there's nourishment in it for a growin' boy. Lucky we still got ham and fatback and such in the smokehouse from last winter."

Lige said, "It's mighty fine."

The woman's husband had limped to the table, aided by crutches. One leg was immobilized by splints bound securely with strips of cotton cloth. He said, "I'm much obliged to you fellers. As you can see, I been about as much use around here lately as teats on a boar hog."

It was obvious to Scooter that the place had been a long way from prosperity even when the farmer had full use of both legs. The little furniture he saw looked as if its best service would be as kindling to start a blaze in the fireplace. Newspapers had been pasted to the wall in lieu of wallpaper. They might block the wind that pushed between the siding's raw pine boards, but they would do little to shut out summer heat or winter cold.

The woman noticed Scooter's silent appraisal of the room. She said, "It ain't much, but it's ours. We done it all ourselves. Grubbed it out of the ground, me and my husband, with the Lord's help."

Lige said, "Glory be to the Lord."

That startled Scooter. He doubted that his father had given the Lord much thought when he robbed the bank in Kerrville.

The farmer said, "If you-all ain't in too much of a hurry, you're welcome to stay all night. Eat breakfast before you go on your way in the mornin'."

Lige said, "That's kind of you. We couldn't go much farther before dark."

Scooter observed that his father enjoyed other people's cooking far more than his own. That was probably one reason he was eager to find himself a Cherokee woman, beyond the possibility of profiting from her head right to land in the territory. Scooter worried that somebody might have picked up their trail and be following it even as they idled at this farmer's table, but Lige seemed not to share his concern. With a warm and solid meal in his belly, he appeared content to accept the world on its own terms.

There being no sign of rain, Lige elected to spread a little hay on the ground and unroll his blanket on top of it. "Ain't nothin' healthier than the clean outdoors with the stars for your ceilin'," he said. "For five years the only stars I seen was through a high window with bars in it."

"Pa, are you sure a farm is what you want? These folks have got one, and they're as poor as church mice."

"Because they ain't got enough land. Me and you, we ain't goin' to settle for nothin' small like this. We're goin' to have a big farm with a big house and lots of stock. We'll have cornfields stretchin' as far as the eye can see. I've had lots of time to plan it all out. I know just where everything is goin' to be—the house, the barns, the fields."

"All that is goin' to take lots of money."

"The reason most people don't have enough money is that they don't have the guts to go where it's at and get their fair share."

As they finished breakfast Scooter saw his father stick a roll of bills into the sugar bowl when the farmer and his wife were looking away. He said nothing about it until they had put the little farm behind them.

"You said we ain't got much money, but I seen you leave a wad of it for them folks."

"Do good where you see the need and the Lord will reward you. Next time maybe He'll lead us to a bank where the teller ain't a crook like that last one was."

9

SERGEANT HOLLOWAY HELD OUT LITTLE HOPE OF finding Lige's and Scooter's tracks. Too many others had been made along the river road that led eastward from Kerrville, including those of the earlier posse. The sergeant was about ready to give up.

He said, "Anywhere there's a telegraph, the local authorities will be on the lookout for Tennyson and the boy. These modern communications are the wonder of the world. Did you know a man can board a train in New York and get to San Francisco in less time than it takes to ride horseback from Fort Worth to San Antonio?"

Andy argued, "But we're not goin' to San Francisco, and most of Texas doesn't have a railroad yet. Lots of places ain't even got a telegraph."

He chafed with impatience, but he was just a private. It was the sergeant's place to make decisions.

Rusty recognized Andy's anxiety. "We've come this far, Bill. Won't hurt us to try a little longer."

Holloway reconsidered, respecting Rusty's long experience. "Wouldn't want the captain sayin' we quit too quick. Andy, how's your trackin' eye?"

Andy feared his reputation was better than his ability, for most people assumed his Indian background gave him an advantage in following trails. But a show of confidence might keep Holloway from abandoning the search. "Nothin' wrong with my eyes."

He had found long ago that he had better hunches than most people. He wondered if it might come from his association with the Comanches, who put a lot of faith in intuition, visions, and dreams. When the three riders reached a place where a flood had deposited a large bed of gravel at a bend in the river, he had one of those hunches. He said, "If I was wantin' to cover my trail, right here is where I'd quit the road. A buffalo herd wouldn't leave tracks in that gravel."

Holloway said, "It's your hand. Play it."

Andy moved forward while Rusty and the sergeant waited so they would not add their horses' tracks to any already there. He rode along the leading edge of the gravel deposit until he found the trail of two horses. A light shower had created a thin skim of mud. The tracks had dried hard enough to preserve them from the wind's destructive touch. His hunch told him these marked the passage of Lige and the boy. He waved his arm.

"We're on the money," he shouted.

Rusty dismounted and studied the tracks. "One horse's forefoot turns out a little, like he might've been crippled at some time."

Andy said, "That'd be Scooter's. I remember the old brown they gave him had a funny way of walkin'. Kind of paddle-footed." He felt a rising excitement. "What about it, Sergeant?"

Holloway pointed his chin eastward. "We came to catch a bank robber. We're not doin' it sittin' here."

It occurred to Andy after a while that Lige had evidently not put much effort into hiding his trail. He probably thought he had followed the well-traveled road far enough to throw off a posse. Now and then the trail would disappear on hard ground or in thick grass, but Andy would manage to pick it up again a little farther on. Lige's direction seemed well set.

Holloway said, "Looks like he's headed almost due east. We can afford to lope up some. Even if we lose the trail awhile, we ought to be able to cut it again. Maybe we can gain on him."

THE SECOND DAY THEY had not seen the trail in a while but were traveling on faith and hope. Spotting a small frame house, they stopped to water their horses. A gaunt, hard-used farm woman came out to greet them. The sergeant introduced himself. "We're obliged for the water. We'd be glad to pay for it."

She demurred. "I don't see how I can charge you for water. It's a gift from the Lord."

The sergeant smiled. "The Lord didn't dig that well for you, did He?"

"No, sir, me and my husband done that. But the Lord was lookin' on and made sure we found water."

Holloway handed her a silver dollar. "I'll pay the Lord His share next time I get to church. Been any strangers pass this way the last day or two?"

"The only people been by here lately was a man and a boy. Fine folks. They taken time to hoe the garden for me. My husband is laid up and can't work."

Andy stiffened. "Did you hear any names?"

"I don't recall that he ever introduced himself, exactly. And the boy just called him Pa." She frowned, trying to remember. "Seems to me I heard him call the boy by name, but I can't remember what it was."

"Could it have been Scooter?"

Her face brightened. "I believe it was. You know them?"

Holloway said, "We do. Were they still travelin' east when they left here?"

"They was. But I can't imagine what interest you Rangers would have in God-lovin' folks like them. Even after workin' for their keep, they left some money for us."

Kerrville bank money, Andy guessed. Tennyson could afford to be generous with it. It wasn't his.

The sergeant said, "May I be so bold as to ask how much?"

"Close to fifty dollars. I wanted to give it back, but they was gone by the time I found it."

Andy said, "It doesn't make sense, him *givin'* somebody money."

The sergeant said, "It's a waste of time to try and figure out people like Tennyson. They serve the Lord one minute and the devil the next. Tryin' to stay in good with both sides, I guess."

Riding away, Holloway seemed cheered. "He gave those folks most of the little bit he got in Kerrville. He'll be needin' more. We already wired Austin to send a warnin' to all the banks. Next time Tennyson tries to make a withdrawal, he may find himself lookin' down a dozen gun barrels."

Andy felt a dark foreboding. "What about Scooter?"

"Let's hope his daddy thinks enough of him to leave him out of harm's way."

Rusty brooded. "I can't figure Lige. If it was me and I was on the dodge, I'd go west to where law is scarce. I wouldn't go back where there's a badge on every section corner."

Holloway said, "Where law is scarce, there aren't many banks either. A workin' man goes where the work is. Or in Tennyson's case, where the money is."

Rusty said, "If I didn't know better I'd say he's headed almost directly toward my farm."

Andy said, "He'd have no reason to be goin' there."

Holloway said, "You can bet Tennyson knows what he's doin', or thinks he does. He wouldn't be travelin' this direction without he had cause. I'd give a month's pay to know what it is."

The third day Andy lost the trail and could not find it although he crisscrossed several times, returning always to a generally eastward direction. Toward dark the three Rangers came upon a family of movers camping with a tarp-covered wagon and a trail wagon hitched behind. The wagon tongue was pointed west. A young boy herded half a dozen cows and a bull. Andy could only guess at the disappointments that had put these people on the road to new country and a fresh start.

Holloway hailed them in an easy, smiling manner. "How far you-all headed?"

The man was straightening harness. "Pecos River or bust. We hear there's cheap land out there."

Cheap for a good reason, Andy thought. Charles Goodnight had called the Pecos River "the grave of a cowman's hopes." But settlers were starting to drift out that way regardless. So long as there was new land, there was always a chance, or at least the illusion of one, even where it didn't rain enough to grow much more than greasewood and prickly pear.

The Indians were not alone in following dreams.

As he had with everyone else they met, Holloway asked if they had seen a man and a boy traveling east.

The mover said, "We did. They rode into camp just as we was fixin' to have supper last night. Ate with us and rode on. Nice-actin' folks, they was."

The woman said, "Shy kind of a boy, though. Acted like he was scared to talk. I reckon he hasn't been out among strangers much."

Rusty asked, "Did they give any names?"

The man thought about it. "Not that I remember, and we didn't ask. I always figure if a man wants you to know what his name is, he'll tell you. If he doesn't want to, he's probably got a good reason."

Holloway politely turned down an invitation to stay for supper, explaining afterward that the people didn't look as if they had enough that they could afford to share. He said, "At least we're travelin' in the right direction. If we can find where those folks camped last night, maybe we can pick up Lige's tracks again."

The effort proved fruitless. They came across evidence of several campsites where fire pits had been dug and wood burned for cooking. Some were fresh enough to have been used within the last night or two. But Andy found no tracks he could identify as the paddle-footed brown's.

Holloway looked discouraged. Andy feared he might decide to quit. He had another hunch, that they were closer than they had been since they started, even if he could find no trail. But hunches would not carry a lot of weight with the sergeant. He was inclined to believe only what he could see, hear, or feel.

The land became increasingly familiar. Andy realized he had ridden over it with Rusty, looking for strayed cattle. Rusty acknowledged that they were not far from his farm.

Holloway asked, "Do you want to go by and see if everything is all right?"

Rusty said, "I haven't been gone long enough for much to've gone wrong. Unless Fowler Gaskin has come over and carried everything away." He had to explain about Gaskin.

Holloway understood. "I used to have a neighbor like that. He finally threw a conniption fit and died. You never saw so many people smilin' at a funeral."

"I doubt the Lord is anxious for Fowler to show up. He'll probably outlive us all."

Rusty's horse stumbled over a rough spot on the trail. "He's tirin' out. I expect they all are. How about we ride over to Sheriff Tom Blessing's and see if he can get us a change of horses?"

Holloway frowned. "We've already stretched pretty far past our district."

The Rangers did not have to stop at county lines. They were free to operate anywhere in the state. However, efficiency required that they remain within their own appointed areas of responsibility unless in pursuit or on a specific assignment.

They stopped at Rusty's farm. Nobody was there, a relief to Rusty. "I was half-afraid we'd find Fowler takin' up residence while I was gone. He did it once before when I was off chasin' after Indians."

The fields were as desolate as when Andy had last

seen them in the wake of the hailstorm. Some plants were making a feeble try at regrowth, nature's eternal effort at survival, but they were stunted and doomed to be killed by frost before they could mature. In contrast to the fields, the garden showed signs of fresh work, freshly risen greenery.

Rusty said, "Shanty's been over here."

They went into the cabin and cooked a meager dinner. Andy noticed that Josie's photograph was missing from the mantel. Rusty must have carried it with him, though Andy had not seen him looking at it. He probably did that in private. Grief was taking a long time to heal.

Done with the meal, Rusty said, "Let's get on to town. Stoppin' here is like visitin' a graveyard."

They came upon Shanty's cabin. At Rusty's call, Shanty came out grinning. "Mr. Rusty, Andy. You-all ain't already quit bein' Rangers, have you?"

Rusty introduced him to Sergeant Holloway. "We've been trailin' a bank robber. He's got a boy travelin' with him. Anybody like that passed this way the last day or two?"

"Not as I noticed. I see most folks that come along this road. Anyway, what would a bank robber want with me? I don't have nothin' anybody'd want to steal."

"This one might've *given* you money."

"Then he sure ain't been by, because there ain't nobody given me nothin'."

Holloway grimaced. "I'm afraid we've played out our string. Tennyson may not stop till he gets halfway across Louisiana."

Andy clenched a fist in frustration. "You mean we're turnin' back?"

"I'll wire the captain and ask him what he wants us to do."

Andy said, "As long as we're this close, don't you think we ought to go by the Brackett place and see about Farley? He may be healed up enough to go back to camp."

"You and Rusty can do that while I stay in town and wait for the captain's answer."

Andy had a bitter taste in his mouth. He had far rather be taking Scooter back to camp, but he might have to settle for Farley Brackett.

At least he would see Bethel for a little while.

SCOOTER SAT NERVOUSLY ON his horse half a length behind his father's while Lige quietly studied the town that lay before them. He had seen Lige count his money last night and frown.

Lige said, "Can't tell from here if this place is big enough to have a bank. Only way to know is to ride in and see."

Scooter asked, "How many times we got to do this, Pa?"

Lige turned to study him. "You're shakin', boy. Ain't nothin' to be scared of. Your old daddy knows what he's doin'."

"So do the Rangers. How do you know there ain't a bunch of them waitin' for us?"

Lige's eyes narrowed. "I can tell you ain't cut out for this business. That's why we need to travel on up to the territory and get us that farm as soon as we can. But we got to have money first, don't you see?"

"Most people don't get it this way."

"Everybody has got to find out what he's good at. I'm good at the bankin' business. Now come on, let's see what this place has to offer." His spurs jingled against his horse's sides. Scooter hesitated, then followed, his eyes searching for something to be afraid of. There was plenty, most of it imaginary.

They rode down the length of the short street. Lige slumped in disappointment. "This burg ain't big enough to support a bank. I'd settle for a good general store, but the only one I see don't look very prosperous. I wonder when the hard times are goin' to be over with."

"Seems like it's been hard times ever since I can remember."

"That's on account of the war. It's been more than ten years, but Texas ain't got over it. Times was flush before the Yankees started all that trouble. There was money enough for anybody who had the nerve to go and get what was due him. I can remember when I had so much gold that I had to have a packhorse to carry it."

"What went with it, Pa?"

"Money's like water. It dribbles out between your fingers no matter how hard you try to hold on to it. And who knew those good times were fixin' to end? We thought they'd go on and on."

They turned and rode back up the street the way they had come. Lige's attention was fixed on the general store. It was a square-fronted frame building innocent of paint. Farming tools and wooden barrels were displayed on the plank sidewalk, against the wall. A sign in the window advertised chewing tobacco and prickly bitters. Lige said, "I wonder what day it is. Used to be that Saturday was when all the farmers came to town. A good general store would have a lot of cash on hand."

"I think it's Wednesday, Pa. Or Tuesday."

"We can't wait around for Saturday. When you can't have all you want, you settle for what you can get." He dismounted in front of the store, stretching his arms and back. Scooter had heard him complain about rheumatism.

Lige handed over his reins. "Hold them. I'll go see to business. Stay awake, because when I come out I'll be lookin' to travel."

Scooter accepted reluctantly. "I'll be right here."

Lige patted him on the leg. "You're a good boy. You've got the makin's of a good man."

If you don't get me killed, Scooter thought.

A large man with a black mustache and a dark expression blocked Lige's entry into the store. He held up a hand that looked as big as a hindquarter of beef. The other hand rested upon the butt of a pistol high on his hip. "Just a minute, stranger. I need to know your name."

Scooter saw a small silver badge on the man's vest. A chill went all the way to his toes.

"My name?" Lige seemed momentarily taken aback. "What for?"

"I'm a deputy sheriff. We got a wire tellin' us to look out for a man and a boy that robbed a bank out west someplace. You've got a boy with you."

"My son," Lige said. "What do you mean, you got a wire?"

"Ain't you heard about the telegraph?"

"I've heard tell, but I never knew it'd come to a little place like this."

"They're gettin' it just about everywhere. There

ain't a horse alive that can outrun it. Now what's your name and what you doin' here?"

Scooter searched Lige's face for a clue about what his father might do. He wondered if he might shoot this deputy the way he had shot Johnny Morris at the bank in Kerrville. He froze in dread.

Lige tried running a bluff. "My name's Simon Good. That's my boy Willy. We're just poor farmers passin' through on our way to help my baby sister over in Colorado County. Her husband is laid up with a broken leg and can't work his field."

Scooter realized his father was drawing on the experience of the farm couple with whom they had spent a night.

The deputy demanded, "You got any papers to prove you're who you say you are?"

"What would I carry papers for? Ain't got but little money, either. If we'd robbed a bank, don't you think we'd be carryin' a lot of money? You can search us. If you find more than twenty dollars you can keep it."

The deputy had developed a deep and doubting frown. He approached Scooter. "Is that right, kid? Is your name Willy Good?"

Scooter could not bring himself to speak. He could only nod.

The deputy asked, "Is the boy slow-minded that he can't talk?"

Lige said, "He's hardly ever got off of the farm. Ain't used to town. It's natural that he'd get a little scared when a sheriff starts askin' him questions. It never happened to him before."

The deputy softened. "Didn't mean to upset you,

son. Just doin' my duty, is all. You and your daddy have got honest faces. It's plain to see that you ain't the bank robbers they're lookin' for. Besides, their name is Tennyson, not Good."

Lige blinked at the sound of his name, then shook his head. "What would bank robbers come into a little town like this for?"

"Right enough. We ain't even got a bank."

"This town'd probably starve a banker to death. All right if we go on about our business?"

"As long as it ain't bank robbery." The deputy laughed at his own joke. No one else did.

The lawman walked on, ambling toward an ugly stone courthouse that stood two stories tall at the end of the street. It had a cupola with a clock that either was not running or was off by several hours. It was a poor town, Scooter thought, that couldn't afford to fix a clock.

Lige watched the deputy. "Damn. They already know my name. Makes me want to cut down every telegraph line I come across."

"Maybe we ought to forget that road stake and go straight to the Cherokee nation."

"We can't go there broke." Lige considered for a minute before going into the store. To Scooter's surprise he was not in a hurry when he came out. Lige bit a chaw from a plug of tobacco he had just bought.

Scooter said, "You didn't do any business?"

"One look and I could tell there wouldn't be enough money in the till to make it worth the risk. We'd have that deputy on our tail before we could clear town. Probably the sheriff too, and no tellin' how many townfolk. We'll have to give up the luxuries and get by on what we've got till we get to where they're havin' that feud. Our luck will change there, you just wait."

Scooter tried to recall what luxuries they had had. Offhand, he could not remember any.

When they reached the edge of town he said, "I'm a Jonah to you, Pa."

"How do you figure that?"

"You heard him. They're lookin' for a man and a boy travelin' together. If you was by yourself, they wouldn't look at you twice. The next place we come to, they might not be as easy to fool as that deputy was."

"We ain't splittin' up, if that's what you're gettin' at. We already been apart way too long. Anyhow, where would you go?"

"Back to the Ranger camp. They're good to me there."

"They wouldn't be good to you no more. They know you was with me in Kerrville. Like as not they'd send you to one of them reformatories and keep you there till you're old enough to shave. I've heard stories. They'd feed you bread and water and put the whip to you every day."

Scooter shuddered.

Lige said, "We'll take roundance on the towns from now on till we get to where we're goin'. Me and you are stickin' together. Father and son, like it was before I went off to work for the governor."

10

ONE OF THE BRACKETTS' BLACK FIELD HANDS sighted the two Rangers' approach and went running to the main house ahead of them. His frantic manner said he was on his way to give warning.

Rusty took that as a sign of trouble. "He acts like he's afraid of somethin'."

"Probably didn't recognize us."

The sight of strangers would not ordinarily arouse fear on the Brackett farm, though memories lingered of times during Reconstruction when Farley was having difficulties with carpetbag authorities. Seeing the visitors before the visitors saw him had been the difference between life and death.

"Got any hunches, Andy?" Though Rusty on occasion had played down Andy's hunches, he was aware that they proved correct often enough to be disturbing. It was as if Andy had some supernatural power, though Rusty had not brought himself to accept that premise.

Andy said, "Maybe Farley has threatened to peel the

hide off of him if he lets somebody come without lettin' him know."

"That sounds like Farley."

Bethel stood on the porch, arms folded in an attitude of defiance until she recognized Andy and Rusty. She hurried down to meet them, her eyes anxious. "Lord, I've prayed for you-all to come."

Andy's pulse quickened. "Trouble?"

"Two days ago. A deputy sheriff showed up looking for Flora Landon."

"Did he find her?"

"Yes. He dragged her away, him and five others. He took Farley too. Wouldn't listen to us trying to tell him he was still too hurt to ride."

A large bruise darkened her cheekbone. Andy demanded, "Who did that to you?"

"The deputy, when I tried to hold on to Farley. He was a big fellow. Pushed Mother off of the porch too. She's stove up so badly she can barely walk."

Andy's face heated. "That'd be Big'un Hopper. What about the old man, Flora's daddy?"

"He was out in the field. They missed him. He slipped away as soon as the posse was gone. Probably went to tell Jayce Landon."

Andy dismounted for a closer look at Bethel. He touched her cheek. "Are you sure you're all right? Nothin' worse than that bruise?"

She reached up and pressed her hand against his. "Nothing that won't heal. Except I'm still mad enough to chop that big deputy into little chunks and feed him to the hogs. I'm worried about what they might be doing to my brother. They accused him of helping with the jailbreak."

"Big'un has accused me too, but he's a liar. He knows me and Farley had nothin' to do with that."

"Just the same, I'm afraid. They treated Farley rough. They knew he was wounded, but they didn't care. That deputy seemed to take pleasure in hurtin' him."

Andy's antipathy for Farley Brackett mattered little now. Farley was a fellow Ranger. "What're we goin' to do about it, Rusty?"

"By rights that's a decision the captain ought to make, or at least the sergeant."

"They're not here. So what would you do if you had to make the decision?"

Rusty said, "The Rangers have always taken care of their own."

"The longer we wait, the more time they've got to torment Farley. And Flora Landon."

Rusty had one reservation. "Don't forget that the law over there would like to jail you too."

"Just let Big'un try. He'll see hell from the bottom side."

Bethel agreed to send a field hand to town to find the sergeant and advise him that Andy and Rusty had proceeded on their own volition. She asked, "Do you know how you're going to handle this?"

Rusty said, "Like Rangers always handle things: straight-ahead on."

Andy had no quarrel with that.

ANDY POINTED DOWN THE street toward the courthouse. "The jail is on the other side. Hard to see it from here." He drew his pistol to be certain it was fully loaded.

Rusty said, "I'd leave that thing in the holster, was I you. It's always better to try and talk your way through. There's time enough later to shoot your way out."

Andy holstered the weapon, but only after inserting a cartridge in the chamber he customarily left empty for safety.

Rusty warned, "Remember, we're here on our own. We don't have authorization from the captain, or even Sergeant Holloway."

"Any reason we have to tell anybody that?"

"None at all. We might even lie a little if it helps."

Andy could not see that they were attracting any particular attention as they rode down the hoof-scuffed street, stirring a little dust with their passage. The few people they encountered had no reason to know they were Rangers. Neither wore a badge, for the state had not yet adopted an official design. Some Rangers fashioned their own, most often from Mexican silver pesos. Neither Andy nor Rusty had chosen to do so. Silver was hard to come by.

The stable keeper stood outside the big doors of the livery barn. Recognition made his jaw sag. He started to raise his hand in greeting but withdrew the gesture before it was completed.

Rusty asked, "Friend of yours?"

Andy explained that the hostler seemed to be neutral in the Hopper-Landon feud, accepting business from both sides. "He was some help to me and Farley, but nobody saw it except us. I suspect he'd duck in his hole like a prairie dog if things started to pop around him."

"I notice a lot of the store signs have got the name Hopper on them. I haven't seen a one that said Landon."

"There's considerable more Hoppers than Landons. That's why the Hoppers have control of the county. Dick Landon was right to join the Rangers and get away from here. If I was a Landon I'd leave too."

"There's not much logical about a feud. Family pride gets tangled up in it, and hate twists people to where they can't see straight."

"I don't understand that. I guess it's because I don't belong to a family. Not a white family, anyway."

Rusty's face pinched with a momentary sadness. "Neither do I. But maybe that helps me understand it better. I'd give all I've got to be part of a family."

Andy knew Rusty was thinking of the Monahans, especially the lost Josie. He said, "We've got one another."

Rusty nodded. "Two orphans thrown together by the luck of the draw. That's not quite the same." He forced a half smile. "But it's the best we've got."

Andy tensed as the jail came into view. "How about we barge in there like we had the whole Ranger force behind us? Catch them standin' on their left foot."

Rusty made no argument. "You've been here before and know the layout. You do the talkin' and I'll follow your lead."

Andy had long been used to following Rusty. It struck him as strange now for Rusty to be the follower.

I can't keep leaning on Rusty all of my life, he thought. But there was still much he did not know. It would be easy to make a costly mistake. He had made several in the course of growing up, mistakes that had brought trouble to others as well as to himself.

Well, if I make a mistake again, it won't be for standing back.

He did not knock on the jail door. Finding it unlocked, he pushed it open and stepped inside. Sheriff Truscott sat at a desk. Startled, he dropped papers he had been reading and jumped to his feet. Andy made several strides, stopping so close that he could have reached across the desk and grabbed the sheriff by his shirt. Truscott was not wearing his pistol. It and its belt and holster lay at the edge of the desk. He made no move to reach them.

Andy summoned the strongest voice he had. "You don't need that gun. We're Rangers, and we're here on official business."

The lawman seemed slow to gather his wits. "I know you. You and your partner Brackett was the ones helped my prisoner get aloose."

"We had nothin' to do with that. I think you know it. Now you've got Farley Brackett locked up here on false charges. This is Rusty Shannon. Him and me, we've come to get Farley."

"That's easy said."

"Either we leave here with him or you'll have the state adjutant general and his headquarters Rangers down here. You'll feel like you been tromped by a buffalo herd."

Truscott's face reddened as he struggled for a reply. "Everybody and his damned dog has been tryin' to tell me what to do lately."

Andy had bitten off a big chunk with his bluff, but there was no backing down now. "What do you say, Sheriff? Do you turn him loose or do we go in and take him?"

Big'un Hopper walked in from the back room where the cells were. "What in the hell's goin' on out here?"

Truscott pointed his chin at Andy and Rusty. "These men are Rangers."

Big'un grunted. "I know them. That young one anyway." He pointed at Andy. "I can spot a Ranger half a mile away. Further sometimes."

Truscott said, "They've come for Brackett."

Big'un's jaw dropped. "You better not let them have him. Uncle Judd would bellow like a bull."

Judd. Andy remembered that was the judge's given name. Judd Hopper had survived the hazards of the vendetta to become patriarch of the clan.

Truscott turned on Big'un with sarcasm. "Maybe your Uncle Judd would like to come talk to these Rangers. They claim to have the state law behind them."

"Us Hoppers are the law here."

"Here, maybe, but nowheres else. You want Austin sendin' a force down here to poke around? Me and you and your uncle Judd would likely wind up in the penitentiary. And some of your other kin, besides."

"I say we ought to secede from the state of Texas like Texas done from the Union."

Truscott shook his head impatiently. "Big'un, I wish you was twice as smart and half as loud."

Rusty spoke for the first time. "You remember what happened to that other secession. Texas lost."

The deputy seemed to swell up to a couple of sizes larger. "I don't see but two of you."

Rusty said, "We're Rangers. Two is enough."

Truscott looked away from the big deputy. "I guess we can give up the Ranger. We still got Jayce's woman."

Big'un said, "And givin' her three meals a day at county expense. You know what I favor givin' her." He turned into the light. Andy noticed a ragged cut and discoloration around his right eye.

The sheriff snapped, "I told you to stay out of her cell. She gave you just what you had comin'."

"Yeah, but I'd have given her somethin' too if you hadn't come in there raisin' hell. I'd show her again why they call me Big'un."

Truscott's eyes betrayed concern as he glanced at Andy and Rusty. "Damn you, Big'un, keep talkin' and some folks in this town will peel your hide with a horsewhip. Won't matter if you *are* a Hopper."

Andy had an ugly mental image of Big'un forcing himself on Flora Landon, or trying to. Fighting down his anger, he demanded, "Now, what about Farley Brackett?"

The sheriff gave Hopper a go-to-hell look. "Go on, tattle to Uncle Judd, but I don't care to have the Texas Rangers on my neck. I'm givin' them Brackett."

Big'un scowled. "You'd better hold on to that woman. We ain't done with her."

"Don't you be tryin' to tell me what to do, even if you are the judge's pet nephew. Yes, we'll keep her for now. I'm spreadin' the word that I'm willin' to trade. If Jayce Landon will come and surrender himself, I'll let his wife go."

Big'un's square jaw dropped. "You wouldn't do that."

"Damn right I'd do it. We ain't all lost our sense of decency."

Big'un glared. "You're a poor excuse for a Hopper."

"I ain't a Hopper at all. I made the mistake of mar-ryin' one, but my name is still Truscott. And I'm still the sheriff of this county."

"We'll fix that, come next election."

Andy told the sheriff, "Looks like you need to move to some county where there ain't any Hoppers."

"I've thought about it. A lot." Truscott jerked his head as a signal to Andy and Rusty. "Come on back."

A set of keys lay on top of the desk. Big'un grabbed them to keep them from Truscott. "If I was runnin' this office, a lot of things would be different."

Truscott jerked the keys from Big'un's hand. "You ain't, no matter how many times you kiss Uncle Judd's ass." He unlocked the door to the cell block. "Brackett, you got company."

A blanket hung in front of one cell. Andy realized it was a concession to Flora Landon's privacy. The builders of the jail had not considered female prison-ers. From behind the blanket came a woman's angry voice. "Oscar Truscott, if you let Big'un in this cell again I swear I'll kill him. Even if you hang me for it."

Truscott said, "I've told you I'm sorry, Flora. If he ever tries it again I'm liable to kill him myself."

Rusty vented his anger. "A man who would abuse a helpless woman ought to be shot. Or at least tarred, feathered, and run out of the county on a rail."

Andy suspected Rusty was thinking about Josie Monahan.

The sheriff said, "Whatever else you might say about Flora, you can't call her helpless. She fights like a cornered wildcat."

Rusty added, "Big'un ought to be *in* jail instead of

helpin' run it. I don't see how you can keep him as a deputy."

"The judge don't give me no choice. I have to try and keep peace in the family. Most of the Hoppers think Flora deserves anything that happens to her. I've thought about shuckin' the whole business and leavin' here for good."

From inside another cell came Farley's grumpy voice: "I'd be willin' to pay for your train ticket."

Farley stood hunched, one hand gripping a bar to steady himself. He seemed not to see well. "Who's that out yonder? If it's Big'un come to beat on me again . . ."

Truscott said, "It's a couple of Rangers, fixin' to take you out of jail. And out of the county, I hope."

Farley squinted to recognize Andy and Rusty. "Badger Boy, you took your sweet time gettin' here."

Farley's face was bruised and skinned, one eye swollen almost shut. Andy turned angrily on the sheriff. "How could you let somebody do that to him?"

"Like I said, I don't call all the shots. I can't be here all the time."

Farley's good eye seemed afire. "You don't try any too hard. When that good woman was hollerin' her head off, you was awful slow in comin'."

"She took pretty good care of herself."

"But if she'd been a weaker woman, Big'un would've got what he went in there for."

Truscott unlocked Farley's cell and pulled the iron door open. Its hinges squealed. "Come on out. You're leavin'."

Farley was unsteady but waved off Andy's instinctive move to help him. "They ain't managed to cripple me yet." He held one hand to his ribs, where he had taken the bullet.

Andy demanded of Truscott, "Have you had a doctor come and look at him?"

"Once, when we first got him here. He gave old Doc such a cussin' that he won't come back."

Farley muttered, "Damned quack done me more harm than good. Like to've killed me, pokin' with his fingers. Then Big'un come and tried to finish the job."

In the outer office, Big'un watched darkly as the sheriff took Farley's belongings from a desk drawer. They amounted to little: a pocketknife, a few coins, a leather wallet. Farley looked in the wallet and grunted, "Empty."

Truscott shrugged. "There's people in and out of here all the time. I can't watch everybody."

Farley turned to Andy and Rusty. "Oscar stays out of the office a right smart, like he don't want to know everything that's goin' on. And what does go on around here would gag a buzzard." He gave Big'un a blistering look.

Big'un declared, "If it was up to me you'd stay in yonder and rot."

Farley pointedly ignored him. "I had a six-shooter. I ain't leavin' this place without it."

Reluctantly Truscott opened another drawer and withdrew a pistol, belt, and holster. "It's empty. Leave it that way as long as you're in this county."

Farley strapped the belt around his waist. He checked the pistol and found it empty of cartridges as the sheriff had said. He took a step toward Big'un. "If this was loaded I'd shoot you right now."

"You might try. Once."

"Even unloaded, it's heavy enough to make a hell of a weapon. If I wasn't inclined to be peaceful I'd hit you up beside the head with it, like this." He swung the pistol so quickly that Big'un had no time to dodge. The heavy barrel struck just behind the deputy's temple. Big'un went to his knees.

Farley said, "It's a good thing I'm of a forgivin' nature. If I wasn't, I'd hit you again, like this." He swung the pistol and knocked Big'un to the floor. He gave the sheriff a challenging look. "Any charges?"

Truscott made a poor effort to hide a smile. "I reckon not. But get out of here before he comes around."

Andy and Rusty hustled Farley outside. Rusty said, "If you'd hit him one more time you'd probably be up for murder."

"He deserved it. What a roastin' he's got comin' when the devil gets ahold of him. And the sooner the better."

Andy asked, "Do you think you're strong enough to ride?"

"I'm strong enough, but I ain't goin' nowhere. I'm stayin' right here till I see that poor woman set loose."

Andy said, "That 'poor woman' sounded pretty strong to me."

"Not strong enough to keep beatin' off the likes of Big'un. She took him by surprise the first time. Next time won't be as easy."

"I heard the sheriff tell him not to try it again."

"Oscar and Big'un hate one another's guts, but Oscar ain't goin' to stay and face him in a showdown. He'd leave town before he'd stand up to Judge Hopper and the rest of his kinfolks."

Andy said, "This Uncle Judd must be a ring-tailed panther."

Farley said, "He came into the jail once and looked me over like I was a beef bein' dragged to the slaughter. I could see why folks are scared of him. Even Big'un."

"But they're kin."

"Big'un has got plenty to be scared of besides Judd Hopper. When the Landons hear what he tried to do to Flora, he'll be lucky to see another sunrise. I'm stayin' here and make sure the word gets out."

Rusty said, "The Rangers aren't supposed to get tangled up in personal feuds unless there's a killin'."

Farley's lips pinched together. "There'll *be* a killin'. It'll be Big'un's."

They took their horses to the livery barn. The hostler seemed hesitant at first to accept them but softened when Rusty offered him money. "Havin' you-all in my wagon yard is like standin' in a storm with a lightnin' rod in my hand." He focused his interest on Farley. "I figured if you ever came out of that jail it'd be feet first. Big'un was braggin' that he'd see to it."

Farley said, "Big'un ain't seein' anything real clear right now."

The hostler seemed to pick up on Farley's implication. "The Landons would give you a medal if you was to put Big'un's lights out. Even a Hopper or two might chip in."

"I didn't put his lights out. I just turned the wick down a ways."

"That'll tickle a lot of people who ain't even kin to the Landons." The man paused, reflecting. "It ain't fair to put all the blame on Big'un, though. Jayce shot his brother Ned. You wouldn't believe it, lookin' at Big'un now, but as a young'un he was the runt of the litter. Other boys picked on him all the time. It's no wonder he got mean. Once he started comin' into his growth, he got over bein' a runt but he never got over bein' mean."

Andy said, "I suppose he paid back the boys that had picked on him?"

"He's still doin' it. One of them was Oscar Truscott."

Farley gave the hostler a minute's speculative study. "I don't suppose you're the type that spreads gossip."

"Not me. Gossip is a sin."

"If the Landons was to hear what I'm about to tell you, there's no tellin' what they might do." He proceeded to describe Big'un's attempted assault on Flora Landon.

The stableman listened with rapt interest, his eyes wide. He shook his head and clucked in sympathy for the woman. "Nobody likes Big'un very much, not even some of his kin. This would sure rip his britches if it was to get out."

"I'm tellin' you in strict confidence."

"It won't go no further."

The stableman led the horses away to turn them loose in a corral. Farley made a grim smile. "By sundown the story will be all over town and halfway across the county."

Andy said, "It's like you painted a target on Big'un."

"Right between his eyes."

11

LIGE TENNYSON SURVEYED THE SMALL TOWN FROM a bend in the road a quarter mile away. He looked as if he had ordered whiskey and been given milk. "I'm disappointed. I thought Hopper's Crossing would be a lot bigger than this."

Scooter echoed his misgivings. "Don't look like enough of a place for people to fight a feud over."

"They ain't fightin' it over just the town. Once there's been blood spilt, a feud don't have to be over anything else in particular, just blood. Other reasons don't count anymore."

"You really think they'll pay you to fight for one side or the other?"

"It's been nothin' but amateurs so far. I figured somebody'd be willin' to hire a professional. At least I thought so till I saw how puny a town they've got. Well, I'll ride on in and look things over. Worst come to worst, I can always visit the bank, if they've got one.

But there may not be twenty dollars of real money in the whole shebang."

"Want me to come with you, Pa?"

"No, you shade up in them trees yonder and wait for me. The laws are still lookin' for a man and a boy travelin' together. It's better if you stay out here where it's safe and don't cause no notice."

Scooter accepted without argument. His father had demonstrated early on this trip how suddenly he could explode into a rage, though his temper usually cooled as rapidly as it flared.

Lige removed his feet from the stirrups and stretched his legs without dismounting. The long ride had stiffened him. "Be a good boy and maybe I can bring you some candy."

"I'd be tickled, Pa."

Lige looked back once and was pleased to see that Scooter had ridden that paddle-footed old horse into the shade and had dismounted to rest and wait, as he had been told. He smiled and thought how lucky he was to have such a good and obedient son. During his years of incarceration he had worried a lot about what would become of the motherless boy. He had not left him in the best of hands, letting him fall in with the no-accounts Arliss and Brewster, but he had had little choice. He had feared that the authorities would put Scooter into some bleak orphan's home if he stayed around where they would notice him.

That was the way with government, always messing in where nobody had invited it, he thought. Life would be a lot less complicated if there wasn't some law to get in a man's way every time he tried to turn a dollar or do something that pleasured him.

A good boy deserved a better horse. Lige had it in mind that when they left here and started up toward Indian territory he would watch for a better mount and do a little quiet trading. It was a father's duty to provide for his son. Nobody was apt to think enough of one horse to trail them all the way to Red River and beyond.

The town was as inconsequential close up as it had appeared from a distance. The residential area consisted of no more than a dozen houses, most built of rough-sawed pine lumber. The main street, actually only a wide wagon road, had a handful of business buildings: a general store, a cotton gin, a blacksmith shop, a church, a livery barn with several log corrals behind it. He noticed right away that there was no bank.

Scooter had been right. It was not worth fighting over.

He stopped in front of the general store and tied his horse to a hitching rail strung between two posts, its rawhide strips almost rotted through. A mongrel dog lying in the shade of the storefront made a halfhearted effort to get up and move out of the way, then settled back down. Lige had to step over him.

A couple of elderly loafers sat on a bench, watching him with a curiosity that told him the town did not have so many visitors that they went unnoticed.

He remarked, "Not too busy around here today. I thought Hopper's Crossing would be a livelier place."

An elderly man with a long gray beard and a cane said, "Hopper's Crossing is. But this is Landon's Flat. Hopper's Crossing is about six miles further up the road."

Lige felt relieved. Maybe the trip hadn't been a waste after all. "My mistake. I didn't know this place was here."

"Neither do many other people. That's the trouble. Now, if we'd won that fight over the courthouse . . ."

The other man looked as if he had just bitten down on a sour persimmon. "Spilt milk, Homer. No use hashin' over somethin' that happened a long time ago."

The man named Homer reacted with impatience. "There's plenty others still hashin' it over. That's what the feud is supposed to be about, even if most folks have forgot."

Mention of the feud brought Lige to full attention. "What do you mean?"

The sour-faced one said, "Been thirty-forty years ago. There was an election to decide which place was goin' to be the county seat. See that big empty lot over yonder?" He pointed an arthritis-twisted finger. "That was goin' to be our courthouse square. But them crooks over in Hopper's Crossing voted more than once and throwed in their horses and dogs. Stole the courthouse from us, is what they did. Us Landons put up a squawk, and the shootin' started. There's more of them Hoppers than there is of us, and they own most of the money."

Lige saw his chance. "Maybe what you-all need is a real gunfighter, somebody who knows what needs doin' and how to do it."

"A man like that would cost a lot. Like I told you, most of the money is over in Hopper's Crossing with their names on it. Bein' the county seat, their town prospered while ours . . . well, you can see for yourself."

Lige's first reaction was sympathy, but his practical side did not tolerate it for long. He hadn't come all this way to donate his services. He had come for the best reason he knew of: money.

He asked, "If you was to want to shoot the top man of that Hopper bunch, who would it be?"

The two old men looked at each other. The sour one said, "Judge Judd Hopper is the head of the clan. But if it was me doin' it, I think I'd shoot Big'un Hopper first. The judge runs the family, but Big'un is the one he sends out to do the dirty work. He enjoys his job."

"Where would a man find Big'un Hopper, if he was of a mind to look?"

"He's a deputy under Sheriff Oscar Truscott. He fiddles to the judge's tune, though. He don't pay much attention to Oscar, nor anybody else besides old Judd. Come to a showdown, he might not listen to Judd either. He's built like a bull and got a head like one."

Lige said, "Sounds to me like he'd be the one to kill, all right." But he was thinking Big'un would be the one to see about a gun-toting job. It was evident if he was to make any real money out of this situation, it would have to come from the Hoppers. Teaming up with the Landons would be like fishing in a dry hole.

He was about out of tobacco, and he had promised Scooter some candy. He remembered how much he had liked candy when he was a boy and how seldom he ever had any. Life was going to be better for his son than it had been for him, no matter what Lige had to do to make it happen.

Always in the back of his mind when he entered a place like this general store was the feasibility of emptying its cash box. He dismissed the idea in this case. From the looks of things he wouldn't get much more than tobacco money. He would stir up all the John

Laws within a hundred miles and almost certainly spoil his chance of profiting from the Hopper-Landon feud. If prison had taught him nothing else, it had taught him patience.

The clerk seemed grateful for even so small a sale. Lige thanked him and turned back toward the door, thinking that Scooter was the only one who profited much from this trip. At least he would be getting some candy. On reflection Lige realized the knowledge he had picked up was likely to be of good use. At least he knew not to waste his time with the Landons. He would try the Hoppers instead. Failing that, the Hoppers' town must have a bank to hold all that money.

The two loafers had not moved from their place on the bench. Homer said, "Didn't take you long to do business."

Lige said, "Ain't much business to be done around here. That dog looks about as busy as anybody in town."

Like the old loafers, the dog had not moved.

Scooter waited in the shade of the trees as he had been told. Lige handed him the sack of candy. "Don't eat all of that at once. It'll make you sick at your stomach. Good things need to be stretched out so you enjoy them longer."

"Thanks, Pa." Scooter took a piece of hard candy from the sack. He held it up and stared appreciatively at it for a minute before he put it in his mouth. He talked around the candy. "I don't reckon you saw a bank?"

"Takes money for a place to have a bank. This wasn't the town I thought it was. We'll do better in the next one."

"We goin' there today?"

Lige looked up at the sun. "We still got some day-light ahead of us. Ain't no use wastin' it."

He set his horse into an easy trot. Scooter followed, crunching the candy with his teeth. The sound made Lige's skin tingle. His own tobacco-worn teeth would crumble if he put them through that torture.

He said, "I sure wish we could give these horses a good bait of oats. They've earned it, bringin' us this far."

The candy made Scooter's words sound garbled. "Oats cost money, don't they, Pa?"

"We'll have money when we get through with our business here. Them old fellers back yonder told me the Hoppers have done right good. I figure they'll be willin' to fork over for gettin' some of the Landons out of their way."

"You'd kill them people, Pa?"

"You've got to look at it from my side, son. Them people don't mean nothin' to us. They're goin' to kill one another anyway. I don't see nothin' wrong if I push things a little. I'm bettin' the Hoppers would be glad to keep their hands clean by turnin' their dirty washin' over to somebody else. Wouldn't be nothin' the law could do to them, and me and you would be long gone."

"Them Landons are liable to shoot back."

"The bigger the risk, the bigger the gain. Even mar-ryin' an Indian woman and gettin' head-right land, we'll need some start-up money in the territory."

Scooter asked, "You reckon you'll make a good farmer, Pa? Been a long time since you done much of it."

"I growed up with my hands shaped like a plow handle. It's a good life."

He had not always thought so. Years ago he had decided that harvesting banks and prosperous storekeepers was better than picking cotton. Graying hair and arthritis now draped a nostalgic curtain over fading memories of a sore back and bleeding fingers.

They stopped in a stand of timber half a mile from Hopper's Crossing. "We'll make camp here. We've got the river for water and plenty of deadfall wood for a cook fire. Ain't nobody liable to pay us much mind."

Scooter asked uneasily, "You goin' to visit the bank, Pa?"

"Maybe later, when I'm done with the other business. Right now I'm goin' in to stable my horse awhile and get myself a haircut. I want to find out what direction the wind blows."

Scooter did not understand about the wind. It was coming out of the south. He could tell that without having to ask anybody.

Lige said, "Ain't no place better than a barbershop or a livery stable to find out what's goin' on in a town. I want to learn more about that feud and be sure who to talk to about offerin' my services."

Scooter seemed resigned to being left alone. "I'll keep out of sight, like before."

"I'm sorry, son, but once we get up into the territory, there won't be no need for you to hide anymore. There won't be no Texas law up there. We'll ride together, proud as two peacocks in the sunshine."

Lige sought out the livery barn first. The stable hand met him at the open doors of the barn.

"Want to put your horse up for the night?"

"I won't be stayin' that long, but I'd like him to have a bucket of oats. He's been rode a long ways, and he's kind of drawed."

"So are you," the stable hand said. "If you're hungry there's a pretty good eatin' place up the street yonder, toward the courthouse. How far have you come? Where'd you start from?"

"Over east." That was the opposite of the truth, but somebody toting a badge might come along and ask questions of the liveryman.

Lige figured he had come to the right place. This man looked like a talker, and Lige had come to listen.

LIGE WAS FAIRLY SURE he recognized Big'un Hopper as the deputy sheriff walked out of the jailhouse. He had the stableman's description and his own memory of the lawman who visited the Ranger camp on the San Saba. Hopper was one of the largest men Lige had ever seen. He had a bandage wrapped around his head, a present from an angry Ranger, the stableman had said. Lige approached him warily, for he could not be sure how seriously Hopper took his responsibilities as a lawman.

"I expect you'd be Big'un Hopper."

From Lige's viewpoint the deputy towered like the cupola atop the courthouse. He outweighed Lige by at least a hundred pounds. Big'un took a belligerent stance. "I don't know you. Give me a reason why I ought to even talk to you."

"I think I could be of service."

"I don't need no ditches dug nor fields plowed, and

we generally got a prisoner or two to sweep out the jailhouse."

"Them things ain't my specialty anyway. I do most of my work with this." He dropped a hand to the butt of his pistol. "I hear you Hoppers have got enemies."

Hopper showed a flicker of cautious interest. "Even if we do, what business is it of yours?"

"I could handle them for you at so much per head. All you'd have to do would be to point them out. I'd lay them out. Wouldn't be nothin' the law could hang on your family because I ain't no kin to any of you."

Hopper's interest grew. "Let's go in the jailhouse yonder and talk about it."

The thought of entering a jail gave Lige a chill. "If it's all the same to you, I'd rather we went someplace else. Someplace where nobody would see or hear us."

Hopper pointed to a small frame building with peeling red paint. "The blacksmith is shoein' horses out of town. His shop is private enough if you don't mind a horse or two."

The place smelled of iron and burned coal. Lige walked through it, checking the horse stalls, then peering out the back door to be sure no one was near enough to overhear the conversation.

Hopper asked, "Sayin' I was to agree to somethin', how do I know you could do the job? You don't look like no notorious gunfighter to me. I don't even know your name."

"For now, just call me Bill Smith."

Hopper seemed amused. "Smith? We've entertained a lot of your kinfolks in that jail yonder, one time and another."

"If I was to tell you my real name you'd recognize it.

But I don't think I ought to, seein' that badge you're wearin'."

"This badge ain't tattooed on my skin. I know when to look the other way." Hopper's face twisted in a minute's silent study. "I'll give you a chance, but I don't want you seen with me or any other Hoppers. I don't want folks to make any connection."

"I don't care to have too many people see me anyway. I expect there's a reward out. They might get notions."

"I know an old farmhouse nobody is livin' in. You can stay there. When I've got somethin' lined up, I'll come and talk to you."

"I'll be needin' some supplies for me and my boy."

"Boy?" Hopper's eyebrows went up.

"My son. He's travelin' with me."

For a moment Hopper seemed to reconsider. "That's an extra witness. It's a complication I hadn't figured for." A calculating light came into his eyes. "Travelin' with a boy. Seems to me I've seen a flier." He snapped his fingers. "Timson. Wanted for bank robbery."

Lige corrected him. "Tennyson. At least you know a little about my reputation."

Hopper smiled as if he had just drawn four aces. "I believe you'll work out perfect." He drew some bills from his pocket. "This ought to tide you over for a week or two. Now here's how you get out to the place." He squatted on his heels and drew a map in the sandy floor.

Hopper left the shop first. Lige waited a bit so no casual observer was likely to realize they had been together. He moved to the shop door, then took two fast steps backward into the shadows. Surprise quickened his pulse. He could hardly believe what he saw: the two Rangers named Rusty and Andy and a third man who limped along, hunched over as if hurt.

Involuntarily he held his breath until the burning in his lungs forced him to expel it.

How in the hell could they have tracked us so far?

He felt trapped. He had been confident he had shaken off pursuit. Now here were these damned Rangers, so close he could hit them with a rock. He retreated to the back of the shop, where the shadows were darkest, and watched as the three passed the front door. He barely dared breathe. For a fleeting moment he entertained the notion of shooting them while they weren't looking. With a little luck he might get all three before they had time to realize what was happening.

But he dismissed the idea. Back-shooting had never been his style. Anyway, chances were that at least one would survive long enough to put a bullet in him. What would Scooter do then? The boy would be lost if his father failed to show up. Lige gradually calmed and tried to think rationally.

There was no question of staying in town to buy supplies. He had to get out of this place as quickly as he could without letting the Rangers see him. Perhaps they were not after him in the first place. Perhaps something else had brought them here, far from their camp on the San Saba. If that was the case, they would not be expecting to see him. He intended to make certain they did not.

He had tied his horse behind the bank. He did not know why he had chosen that spot except that something in his nature always seemed to draw him to banks. He eased back to the front door so he could watch the Rangers. He saw them enter the livery stable and disappear into its darkness. He went out through the back door of the blacksmith shop and hurried to his horse. He left town in a slow trot to avoid attracting attention. He looked over his shoulder until Hopper's Crossing was well behind him, then set his horse into a lope.

It was a point of pride for Lige that his son watched his surroundings closely. He seemed to see everything that went on around him. Scooter walked out a little way to meet his father.

"Thought you was fixin' to get a haircut."

"Changed my mind. Didn't get supplies, either. I saw a couple of your Ranger friends, Andy and Rusty."

Scooter's eyes opened wide. "They after us?"

"Could be, or maybe we've just fallen into a run of bad luck. I didn't stay around to ask them."

"What'll we do, Pa?"

"We'll ride back to that last town and buy what we need. Then we'll go to a farm a feller told me about. He said it's a good place to stay out of sight till I'm called on to do a job."

The farmhouse was about as Big'un had described it, no better and no worse. It appeared not to have had permanent tenants for several years. Broken shingles on the roof would let water leak into the house when rain fell. A front windowpane was broken.

Scooter eyed the place with misgivings. "It'll take a week to clean this place up."

"We may not be here a week. At least this place is mostly in the open. We can see anybody who comes this way."

"You lookin' for somebody to come after us?"

"With the Rangers, you never know."

But Lige was worried not only about the Rangers. He did not entirely trust Big'un Hopper. The odds were that the man had been on the level about hiring him for a job. But after all, he *was* a deputy sheriff. He had recognized Lige and remembered he was wanted for bank robbery. Perhaps he was simply setting Lige up so he could claim the reward, if any was offered.

Well, Lige Tennyson had not lived this long by trusting to luck. He had learned long ago that those who keep a hole card and watch out for themselves are usually the luckiest.

"We'll fool them. They'll expect us to be in the house. But we'll camp in the barn back yonder. If the wrong people come, we can ride out the back and be in the timber before they know what happened."

12

ANDY THOUGHT THE DOCTOR WAS GOING TO SLAM the door in their faces when he saw Farley Brackett. He stood with hands pressed against the jamb on both sides, blocking the doorway. He was a little gray-bearded man with rolled-up sleeves and an apron stained by old blood specks that never washed out. He looked as if he had just smelled a skunk.

He said, "Last time I treated that man he cussed me like a mule skinner. If he's not dying, take him to somebody else."

Andy said, "His wound is tryin' to heal, but we don't like the color around the edges. We'd take it as a favor if you'd look at him."

Reluctantly the doctor drew back from the door. "First cussword I hear out of him, I'll put a twitch on his nose the way I'd do an unruly horse."

Farley growled, "I told you he's just a horse doctor."

Andy said, "Be watchful what you say. He might decide he needs to cut on you, and I'll bet he could make it hurt."

The doctor said, "Your damned right I can. How did this disagreeable son of a bitch ever get to be a Ranger?"

Andy decided it might be wise to let Farley answer that for himself, but Farley had nothing to say except, "Let's get on with it."

He took off his shirt and shed the long underwear from his arms and shoulders. The doctor peered closely at the healing wound, then poked it with the tip of his finger. Farley shouted, and the doctor grinned.

"A little angry around the edges," he said, "but it's coming along. I wouldn't worry about it."

Farley said, "Of course you wouldn't. It ain't yours."

Andy asked, "Do you think he can ride?"

"He can if he's willing to put up with a lot of hurt and the risk of bleeding again. If it was me I'd wait a few days before I started off on any long trip back to wherever it is you-all come from."

Farley pulled up his underwear and put on his shirt. He moved gingerly, trying to minimize the pain.

Andy asked, "What do we owe you, Doctor?"

"I've got a special deal for Rangers since it's their duty to protect us even if they have to shoot us to do it. My services are free the first time. After that it's regular rates. A man dumb enough to get shot a second time doesn't deserve any favors from me."

"Thanks. Maybe we can send you some payin' customers."

"You already have, the night you two knuckleheads faced that mob in front of an empty jailhouse."

Andy tried to help Farley down the front step, but Farley motioned irritably for him to back off. "Don't treat me like I'm crippled. If whoever shot me is watchin', I want him to know that he didn't do but half a job."

"What if he tries to finish it?"

"I'm hopin' he does. I'd like to return the favor."

Rusty had not gone with them to the doctor's house. He had talked little during the time they had been in Hopper's Crossing. His gaze was often vacant, his thoughts seemingly far away. His concern over Farley's wound had been that of one Ranger for another, not one of personal friendship. His relationship with Farley had been uneasy since the time Farley's transgressions against Reconstruction authorities had brought trouble to Rusty's door.

He was brushing his horse when Andy and Farley entered the stable. He gave Farley only a fleeting glance, and he asked no questions. "I'm thinkin' about goin' on back to the San Saba," he said. "The captain's probably wonderin' what's become of us."

Andy said, "The doctor says it might be better if Farley doesn't ride just yet."

"He stands a good chance of gettin' shot again in this place. If he doesn't want to go stay with his mother and sister, he can batch at my farm till he's healed up better. I doubt that the Hoppers would want him bad enough to hunt him down over there."

Farley said, "I'm in no hurry to leave here. I want to see Big'un get what's comin' to him."

Rusty gave him a grim look. "Suit yourself, but it's time me and Andy was leavin'."

Farley lay down on a steel cot the liveryman had dragged out for him. "If the captain complains, tell him he can fire me."

Andy pointed out, "Without bein' a Ranger you'd have no authority to enforce the law."

"The law ain't enforced much here anyway."

Late in the afternoon the stableman came into the building and stopped to blink until his eyes adjusted to the dim light. He looked behind him before he approached the three Rangers. "I ain't gettin' myself mixed up in you-all's troubles, but I got a message for you."

Andy took the lead. "What about?"

The stableman looked back again. He lowered his voice. "Walter Landon came to my house. Said he was speakin' for his brother Jayce. He heard about the sheriff's promise to let Flora Landon go if Jayce would turn himself in."

Farley sat up on the edge of the cot. Pain from the quick movement made him wince. "Anything to get her out of that jail and away from Big'un."

Rusty asked, "What's this got to do with us?"

"You Rangers delivered Jayce here in the first place. He'd like you-all to be the ones to do it again."

Rusty said, "He wouldn't need us to deliver him. He could just deliver himself."

"He knows one or another of them Hoppers would kill him before he ever saw the inside of the jailhouse. But if you-all were guardin' him, they might not try."

Andy said, "Maybe they would and maybe they wouldn't. If they didn't, they'd just wait till he was in jail, then break in like they tried to do the last time."

"At least his wife would be free. If he got killed before he went into the jail, Oscar Truscott might not feel like he had to live up to his promise about Flora."

Andy frowned. "Jayce seems to've made up his mind he's goin' to get killed one way or another."

Rusty's eyes were cold. "After all, he committed murder." Since Josie's death he had lost sympathy for criminals who had blood on their hands. He had that much in common with Farley.

Andy argued, "In a way he's still our responsibility. It was Rangers who caught him and Rangers who brought him here."

Farley said, "He's set to hang anyway. A good, quick bullet would be better than chokin' at the end of a rope."

Andy turned back to the stableman. "How do we go about meetin' up with Jayce?"

"After dark a couple of his kinfolks will come in the back way lookin' for you. Be saddled and ready. They don't want you bringin' any guns."

Rusty said, "We're not goin' anyplace without guns."

"You'll have to talk that over with them, not me. I'm just deliverin' the message."

Andy looked at Rusty. "You and me. Farley's not in shape to be ridin' anywhere."

Farley said, "Like hell." He rose to his feet but sat down again, sucking in a sharp breath and bringing his hand up to the wound. "It's just as well. I don't want to look at Jayce, anyhow, after what he's put his good woman through."

Rusty asked, "Can we trust these Landons?"

The stableman considered. "Their word is good. Their only bad failin' is that they like to kill Hoppers. It's brought a right smart of grief down on them."

Rusty said, "It's our job to bring Jayce in, not make deals with him. But I suppose it won't do any harm to talk."

The stableman looked behind him. "If anybody asks, I had nothin' to do with this. Wouldn't be healthy for me to get on the Hoppers' bad side."

Andy and Rusty delayed saddling their horses until full dark in case some Hopper might be keeping an eye on them. They waited inside the barn's back door. After a time Andy heard a gate latch move. From outside, a voice spoke just above a whisper.

"Rangers? You-all in there?"

Andy looked to Rusty to answer, for he was senior. Rusty said, "We're here. Who are you?"

"Walter Landon, but that don't matter. Are you ready for a ride?"

"We've been waitin' for you." Rusty opened the back door and led his horse out. Andy followed. He saw two men, though in the darkness he could not make out their faces.

Rusty asked, "Where's Jayce Landon?"

Walter Landon's voice was young. "Not far. We'd rather you left those guns here."

"The guns go or we don't."

Landon yielded with a shrug. "Then give us your word you won't do anything against Jayce till he's had a chance to talk with you."

"That's fair enough. Lead out."

They rode about an hour. Andy realized the two men led them in a zigzag pattern to confuse them should they try to retrace their path in the daylight. But he had a good sense of direction. He knew they traveled generally northwestward.

A dark farmhouse loomed ahead. Landon hooted in the manner of an owl. From the house came an answer. No real owl would have been fooled, Andy thought.

Nor would any Comanche, even given their dread of owls.

Landon warned, "Don't neither of you make any suspicious moves. Jayce is mighty edgy."

Andy did not doubt that Jayce had a rifle or six-shooter trained on them. It did not seem probable that he would have summoned Andy and Rusty out here only to kill them. Nevertheless, Andy felt cold.

He saw a movement on the dark porch and heard a voice he recognized as Jayce's. "Get down and tie your horses, Rangers. We'll parley out here. The house is hot and dark, and I don't favor lightin' no lamp. You sure none of the Hoppers followed you?"

Walter said, "We were careful."

Jayce asked Andy, "How's your head? Too bad I had to club you that time, but I needed to try and get away."

"The swellin's long gone."

"Where's the Ranger that gave me a beatin' for it?"

"Farley Brackett is laid up. Took a bullet tryin' to keep a mob from breakin' into jail and killin' you. We didn't know you'd already lit a shuck."

Jayce showed no sign that he felt any guilt, or any sympathy for Farley. He turned to Rusty. "Don't believe I know you. You *are* a Ranger, ain't you?"

Rusty made no effort at sounding friendly. "Name's Shannon. I've been a Ranger off and on since before the war. The *other* war."

"Damned poor way to make a livin', but I guess everybody has got to be somethin'."

"What do you consider yourself to be?"

"A Landon first, then a Texan. I shot Yankees durin' the war, but I was fightin' Hoppers when I was a kid."

"The last killin' you did wasn't any fair fight."

"We didn't always fight the Yankees fair, either. Main thing was to win. Polite gentlemen generally die first."

Andy could see the exchange drifting from the subject at hand. He said, "We didn't come here to talk about who's to blame. We're supposed to talk about you tradin' places with your wife in jail."

Jayce's voice hardened. "I heard about Big'un and her. I've got to get her out of there, whatever it costs."

Walter argued, "Givin' yourself up is an awful price to pay, even for Flora. You know how long you'll last in that jail. And even if you lived till the trial, Judge Hopper would see you hang before the sun went down."

Jayce shook his head. "I don't see no other way."

Rusty said, "There might be one. What do you-all think of Sheriff Truscott?"

Jayce's voice was sharp. "He's a Hopper-in-law, but he's a cut above the others. He's about as fair as you'll find amongst that tribe."

Rusty nodded. "That's the impression I got. On the way out here I've been thinkin' about a deal we might put to him. We'd turn you in to the law but in another county."

"This county or some other, it ain't apt to make a lot of difference in the long run."

"If we can get you a change of venue, you'll at least have a fair trial in some court besides Judge Hopper's."

"A change of venue won't save my neck. Ned Hopper was a son of a bitch, and I killed him. I ain't denyin' it. I'd holler it from the roof of the courthouse." Jayce stared off into the darkness, weighing Rusty's proposition. "You got a place in mind?"

"Sheriff Tom Blessing is a good friend of mine.

Whatever the outcome, he'll see to it that you're dealt a square hand."

Jayce stared into the darkness while he considered the proposition. "At least it'd be somebody besides a Hopper who put the rope around my neck." Jayce beckoned his kinsmen into the house. Andy could hear the low murmur of voices but could not make out what they were saying. When they returned to the porch Jayce said, "Go talk to Oscar Truscott. If he says yes, I'll surrender. Not to anybody else, just to you Rangers."

RUSTY TOLD TRUSCOTT THEY needed to talk to him in private. Truscott called to the jailer. He was not the same man who had been on duty the night of Jayce's escape. That unfortunate had prudently left town before daylight and had not been seen since. "Curly, go get yourself a drink. Maybe two of them. Don't be in a rush to come back."

The jailer gone, Truscott said, "I heard by the grapevine that you-all went out of town last night."

Rusty replied, "You must have eyes everywhere."

"I don't miss a lot."

"We had an interestin' visit with an acquaintance of yours."

"Jayce Landon? You didn't bring him in, though."

"No, but we worked out a deal for you." Rusty explained his idea about delivering Jayce to a more secure jail and seeking a change of venue.

Truscott frowned at first but gradually softened. "I know Tom Blessing. If he said it was fixin' to freeze on the Fourth of July, I'd carry my coat with me to the celebration."

"He'd take good care of your prisoner."

"I'm just wonderin' who'd take care of *me*. Things'd get ugly around here when Judge Hopper and Big'un and the rest got wind of what I'd done."

"If we handle it right, it'll be over with before they know."

"But I'd still be here afterward." Truscott mulled it over. His mustache began turning up in a tentative smile. "It'd probably lose me a wife, but she's took to sleepin' in another room anyhow, and her cookin' wouldn't tempt a hog." The smile broke into full bloom. "I'd love to see what it feels like to look the judge in the eye and tell him I'm through shinin' his boots. And I've wanted for a long time to poke Big'un in the eye with a sharp stick."

"When're you goin' to release Jayce's wife?"

"Right now, into your custody. She's been an albatross around my neck." Truscott reached into a drawer and withdrew a printed form. He dipped a pen into an inkwell and scribbled some lines. "Bring this back to me with Tom Blessing's signature on it, swearin' that he's got Jayce Landon locked up."

Rusty took the paper. "When it's all over you can catch up on your sleep."

"Not after the word gets out." Truscott led Rusty and Andy back to the cells. He said, "Gather your things, Flora. You're leavin'."

She remained hidden by the blanket that covered the front of her cell. Her voice was anxious. "What've you done to Jayce?"

"Ain't even seen him, but he's agreed to give himself up to these Rangers if I let you go."

She pulled the blanket aside, her eyes fearful. "You

know he's got no chance if he comes back in here. I ain't lettin' you trade me for him."

Truscott told her that Jayce would be jailed in another county. She chewed her lip. "I'd rather see him run off to Mexico or someplace."

Rusty said, "He wouldn't do that, not and leave you in here. He's that much of a man, at least."

She declared, "He's a better man than any I see here."

Truscott said, "You better git while the gittin's good, Flora."

"I'll go, but if I get a chance to help Jayce get away I'll damned sure take it."

The sheriff grunted. "I don't doubt that." He unlocked the door. "I'll leave the blanket up. Likely nobody'll miss you before mornin'."

Flora came out carrying a small canvas bag. Her hair was disheveled, her dress wrinkled from sleeping in it. Truscott walked ahead of her and blew out the lamp in the front office. "You-all better go out the back door." He opened it cautiously and peered out into the night. "Looks clear."

Flora paused. "Oscar, for a Hopper-in-law, you're a better man than I thought." Then she was out the door.

The sheriff warned Rusty and Andy, "You-all better keep a close eye on her. She meant what she said about helpin' Jayce get away."

Rusty said, "You've got to respect a loyal wife."

"Jayce never deserved her. I can't see why she chose him over his brother Dick. There's no figurin' women."

Andy had not expected Truscott to release Flora so quickly, so they had not brought an extra horse for her. Andy put her up into his saddle. "I'll go back to the stable and get Farley's horse. He won't be needin' it for a while."

Rusty said, "While you do that I'll get her out of town, to where Walter Landon said he'd be waitin'."

"I'll find you."

In the stable, Farley arose stiffly and sat on the edge of his cot. He watched by lamplight while Andy saddled up. "You stealin' another horse from me, Badger Boy?"

Farley never would give up needling him about Long Red, Andy thought. "Call in the law if you want to."

Farley shook his head. "I can guess why you need him. Tell her not to use spurs. He's liable to throw her off."

AT THE EDGE OF town Andy put Farley's horse into an easy lope. He caught up to Rusty and Flora before they reached the farmhouse where Jayce was supposed to be hiding.

Rusty asked, "Anybody see you?"

"Just Farley and the stable hand. They won't be talkin'."

Flora was still nervous about her husband. "This place where you're takin' Jayce, are you sure it's safe? Them Hoppers have got a long reach."

Rusty said, "If you're lookin' for an ironclad guarantee, there ain't any. But it'll be safer than that jail back yonder. There's not a better sheriff in Texas than Tom Blessing."

"From what I've seen of sheriffs, that ain't a strong recommendation."

"You've got to realize that savin' him from a

lynchin' doesn't change things for him in the long run. He hasn't got much of a future either way."

She squared her shoulders. "Maybe. We'll see about that the first time somebody gets careless."

Walter and a couple of other men stepped down from the porch to meet them in the yard. The house was dark, but Andy could see a rifle in Walter's hands.

"That you, Flora?"

"It's me. Where's Jayce at?"

A figure stepped out from a black corner of the porch. "Right here, darlin' girl. Come see Papa."

Flora did not wait to be helped down from the horse. She slid out of the saddle and hurried to the porch as Jayce stepped to the ground. They embraced, then Jayce pushed her off to arm's length to look her over. "Are you all right?"

"Why wouldn't I be all right?"

"I heard about Big'un. I wanted to kill him."

"Him bein' bigger just makes it easier to hit him where it hurts the worst. I laid it on him good."

Andy grinned, remembering the bruises and cuts on Big'un's face. He was probably bruised in other places where it didn't show.

Rusty was impatient. "We better be movin'. No tellin' how soon before the Hoppers'll find out she's gone."

Jayce said, "I can't figure Oscar Truscott lettin' you go so easy."

"He trusted the Rangers. Bad as I hate to say it, you and me have got to do the same."

Jayce turned to Rusty. "You'll let her ride along with us, won't you?"

Rusty nodded. "It won't be safe for her here, at least

till things cool off. Tom Blessing will see to it that nothin' happens to her."

Walter said, "Maybe some of us better ride along with you too."

Andy started to protest, but Rusty spoke up ahead of him. It seemed to Andy that he always did when something really important was at hand. "Andy and me are escort enough." Rusty's hand was on the butt of his six-shooter.

It would be easy for the Landons to overwhelm the two Rangers and set Jayce and Flora free. Andy suspected such a notion had prompted Landon's offer. Normal restrictions did not apply in family feuds. When survival was at stake, acts normally regarded as treachery were considered justified.

Flora told Walter, "I wish you'd let my daddy know that I've gone with Jayce."

"I'll see to it. We've got him hid. Big'un and his bunch might want to take it out on him when they see that they've lost you and Jayce both."

Andy saw no sign that any of the Landons followed as he and Rusty rode away with Jayce and Flora. But he slipped his pistol out of its holster and held it for the first couple of miles, just in case.

13

THE MORNING WAS FAR ALONG WHEN THEY RODE UP to the jail where Tom Blessing kept his office. Jayce surveyed the frame building with disapproval. "It don't look any stouter than the one over at Hopper's Crossing. At least that one's built of brick."

Rusty said, "They've talked for years about buildin' a better one, but the county's always short of money."

"Short or not, I'll bet the taxes ain't cheap."

"No, but there's still never enough money."

Andy looked toward the courthouse. It was his theory that the county's financial problems resulted mainly from leaky fingers. People normally tight with their own money were sometimes loose with other people's. In any case it made for interesting politics, each side promising to waste less than the other.

Tom looked up in surprise as Rusty and Andy ushered the Landons into his office. His expression showed that he recognized Jayce on sight.

Rusty said, "Brought you an early Christmas present. I know you didn't ask for it, but here it is."

Blessing studied Jayce with misgivings before looking back at Rusty. "You sure ain't Santy Claus. What do you want me to do with him?"

"Keep him away from the Hoppers till he can stand trial. And we'll need to get him a change of venue out of old Judge Hopper's jurisdiction."

"I guess I can take care of the first part. You'll need to talk to a lawyer about the other." He looked at Flora, a question in his eyes.

Rusty said, "This is Jayce's wife. We need a safe place for her too."

"This jail ain't really fixed up for a woman. Any charges against her?"

"Not unless she tries to help Jayce get away. Again."

Tom thought about it. "She'd be good company for my wife out at the farm."

Flora objected. "I want to stay in town, where I can be close to Jayce."

Tom shrugged. "You can put up at Mrs. Smith's boardin'house. But if the Hoppers was to come lookin', it wouldn't be hard for them to find you there."

Flora's jaw set grimly. "It'll be their own fault if they do. They don't know how good a shot I am."

Andy wondered what she intended to shoot them with. She'd had no weapon when she left Truscott's custody, though one of the Landons could have slipped one to her later, in the darkness. Andy had checked Jayce to be sure he was unarmed, but he had not felt comfortable about putting hands on Flora. He did not intend to do it now. Some things had to be taken on faith, or at least on hope.

Tom said, "I'll need help guardin' Jayce. Can't be here twenty-four hours myself, and I've only got one deputy. If the Hoppers was to come down on us in force, one man couldn't stop them."

Rusty said, "Me and Andy. He's more our prisoner than he is yours anyway. I'll wire the captain for permission."

Tom nodded. "I'm obliged." He touched a finger to a marked calendar behind his desk. "District judge is due to hold court here next week. I'd like to get Jayce on the docket as quick as I can. The sooner he's out of this jail, the better I'll feel."

Flora said, "If you-all would turn your backs for a minute or two, you wouldn't have to worry about guardin' Jayce. Him and me would be on our way to Mexico."

Rusty said, "I halfway wish we could, but that'd break our agreement with Sheriff Truscott."

Andy said, "And our oath as Rangers."

Jayce said, "Don't worry about it, darlin' girl. I ain't been hung yet. A lot can happen."

Tom frowned. "Don't be gettin' notions. It's been a long time since I shot a prisoner tryin' to escape. I didn't sleep for a week afterwards, but I done what I had to. I'd do it again."

Jayce's voice was full of irony. "I sure wouldn't want to cost you any sleep." He took Flora into his arms. "Us Landons have died of everything else, but there ain't none of us ever been hung. If things go my way, I'll send for you from Mexico. Or maybe South America. I hear it's mighty pretty down there. They pull fruit right off of the trees, and nobody has to work if they don't want to."

To Andy that sounded more like Preacher Webb's version of heaven. It seemed unlikely that Jayce Landon was going to end up in heaven, or anywhere close to it.

Tom got his keys and motioned toward the back room where the cells were. "Like I said, Rusty, you sure ain't no Santy Claus."

SHERIFF TRUSCOTT GLANCED UP from a paper he had just signed as Big'un Hopper entered the office. The sun was already two hours high. In the past Big'un's perpetual tardiness had irritated Truscott, but this morning it was welcome. He would have been even happier if Big'un had not shown up at all. The two men tolerated each other only because Judge Hopper forced them to.

Big'un snapped, "Is that all you got to do, sit there writin' letters?"

"Writin' reports is part of the job. Austin always wants to know what's goin' on here."

"When I get to be the sheriff I'll tell Austin to go to hell."

"What makes you think you'll ever be sheriff?"

Big'un headed toward the cells in back. Truscott said, "I've told you to stay away from Flora unless I'm with you."

Big'un snickered. "Afraid I'm goin' to give her what she's been needin'? If I get a notion to do that, it'll take more than you to stop me. Hell, I got the notion right now." He resumed his march toward the cells. Truscott reached into a drawer and withdrew a set of brass knuckles he had taken from a Dallas footpad who had not been half so tough as he thought he was.

Big'un came roaring back, face splotched with anger. "What've you done with her? Where's she at?"

Truscott almost smiled. "I ain't got the faintest notion. I traded her for Jayce, like I said I would."

"You're lyin'. Jayce ain't there either."

"I turned him back over to the Rangers. They've taken him out of the county to get a change of venue."

Not quite believing, Big'un said, "Uncle Judd wouldn't give you permission to do that."

"I know he wouldn't. So I didn't ask him."

Big'un made two long, angry steps toward the sheriff's desk. Truscott raised his hands defensively, showing the brass knuckles. Big'un saw them and stopped, but his face kept getting redder. A wail of rage rose in his throat.

Truscott said, "Careful, you're fixin' to bust a blood vessel. That seems to be a Hopper family trait."

"You had no right."

"I'm the sheriff."

"You won't be sheriff long, not when I tell Uncle Judd about this."

"I'm sheriff till the next election. After that, you and the judge can go to hell for all I care. The Hoppers and the Landons and the whole damned county too."

Big'un's eyes narrowed. "You may not live till election." He stamped out the door.

It would not be long before Judd Hopper came boiling into the office just as Big'un had. Truscott found it odd that he felt relief rather than dread. In the past he had never been able to face down the judge. The man's overpowering presence had always cowed him. But now that the fat was in the fire, he almost looked forward to the confrontation. This time he had nothing to lose. He had already resolved to give up his office when his term was finished. The judge could do nothing to hurt him.

As he expected, Judd Hopper flung the door open and strode in, Big'un just behind him. The judge demanded, "Is it true what my nephew's been tellin' me?"

Truscott was surprised by how calm he felt. "Big'un has got a reputation for abusin' the truth, but in this case I expect he told you the straight of it. I let the Rangers have Jayce."

The judge placed his palms flat on the desktop and leaned across toward Truscott. His breath was hot on the sheriff's face and reeked of chewing tobacco. "You know I wanted to try him in my own court."

"I doubt that it'll make much difference where he's tried. He's guilty, and he'll be sentenced to hang."

"But his crime was committed here."

"Against your kin. Any normal judge would recuse himself from the case if it involved his own family."

"I wanted to personally have the pleasure of tellin' him he's fixin' to hang by the neck until dead, dead, dead."

"Big'un and his cronies would see to it that he was shot or hung before he ever got to trial. They tried it the last time, only the bird had already flown."

The judge sputtered, struggling to raise more argument but seeing the futility of it. His face was crimson, and veins stood out on his temples. "You're through in this county, Oscar. I'll see to it."

"Ain't much you can do till election. After that you can have the whole shebang."

The judge gave Truscott a look that would wilt cactus, then spun on his heel, starting toward the door.

Big'un protested, "Ain't you goin' to do somethin', Uncle Judd?"

His uncle gave him no answer. Big'un followed him outside. Catching up, he said, "Looks to me like there ought to be somethin' you can do."

The judge's voice dripped sarcasm. "You want me to shoot him?"

"That ain't a bad idea. I've got half a mind to do it myself."

"If you do, you've got no mind at all. No Hopper can afford to shoot him. The state would have a dozen Rangers down here before you could spit."

Big'un thought about it. "What if somebody else done it, somebody who has nothin' to do with any of us Hoppers?"

The judge took a few more steps, then stopped, suddenly intrigued. "What do you mean, somebody else?"

"There was an old man—"

The judge raised a hand to stop him. "Don't tell me. I've got to stay clean. I don't want to know anything about it."

"All right. I'll wait a day or two till Oscar figures he's got us up a stump. Then don't be surprised at anything that happens."

The judge stared at him, torn between doubt and hope. "Nephew, you're not the brightest lamp in the window, but occasionally you think with your head instead of your fists. I hope this is one of those times."

"It is. You'll see."

Two days later Big'un made a show of rifling through the recent fugitive notices in the sheriff's office. He and Truscott had barely spoken since the confrontation with Judge Hopper. Now Truscott glanced up irritably from a report he was writing. "What're you lookin' for?"

"A telegram that came in here a while back. Described a man who robbed a bank out west."

"You think you've got a line on him?"

"Maybe. Feller told me about somebody he seen at the old Yancey farmhouse." He found the telegram and ran a stubby finger along the lines. "Sure enough sounds like the man, all right."

His interest piqued, Truscott took the telegram from Big'un's hand. "You certain this is him?"

"Can't be certain of nothin', but the description fits. The telegram mentions a reward. I thought I would ride out and at least take a look. I could use the money."

"If this is the right man, you'd probably get your head shot off. I'd best go with you."

Big'un feigned a protest. "I can handle it."

"Don't worry about the reward. It's all yours. But if this is the real bank robber it's liable to take two of us to bring him in."

"Suit yourself."

"I'll saddle up and meet you here in ten minutes. This report can wait till I get back."

Big'un smiled grimly as the sheriff walked outside.

"Hell, Oscar, you ain't comin' back."

SCOOTER TENNYSON SAT IN a rickety chair leaned back against the barn door, dozing in the warmth of the early-fall sun. He dreamed he was fishing in the San Saba River and Bo brought an ax from behind the kitchen tent, telling him to cut more wood.

He awakened with a start, remembering that he was supposed to keep watch while his father slept inside. Blinking the sleep from his eyes, he saw two horsemen approaching. He froze in panic for a moment, then rushed into the barn.

"Pa, wake up. Somebody's comin'."

Lige Tennyson was quickly on his feet, grabbing for his pistol. He hurried to the barn door. "They're almost on us. You was supposed to keep watch."

"I'm sorry, Pa."

"Sorry don't fix it." Lige squinted, then relaxed. "One of them is that deputy I told you about, Big'un Hopper. Reckon he's come to give me a job like he promised. But I didn't figure on him bringin' anybody else." He started to put away the pistol, then thought better of it. "You stay back out of sight just in case."

"All right, Pa."

Lige walked out into the open. He kept the pistol in his hand but lowered it so it would not appear to offer a threat.

Big'un eyed the pistol with suspicion, but his voice sounded jovial enough. "Howdy."

"How do, yourself."

The other man spoke. "Do you go by the name of Tennyson?"

"Sometimes. Depends on where I'm at and who I'm talkin' to. And who *am* I talkin' to?"

So quickly that Lige missed the move, Oscar Truscott drew a pistol and pointed it at Lige's belly. "I am the sheriff of this county. I am placin' you under arrest for bank robbery and attempted murder. Drop that pistol."

Lige let the weapon fall to his feet. Confused, he looked at Big'un. "What kind of a trick is this?"

"Not quite the kind it looks like." Big'un drew his own pistol. Lige saw murder in the man's eyes and braced himself for a bullet.

Instead of aiming at Lige, Big'un pointed the pistol toward Truscott. The sheriff blinked in confusion.

Big'un said, "Looks like election is comin' sooner than you thought, Oscar." He squeezed the trigger. Truscott jerked. His horse jumped as the sheriff slid down over its left side.

Truscott looked up in mortal pain. "For God's sake, Big'un."

"God ain't watchin', Oscar." Big'un leaned from the saddle and fired again.

Observing from the barn, Scooter froze in shock.

Lige said, "God amighty. What did you do that for?"

Big'un smiled grimly. "The county is fixin' to get a new sheriff. A bank-robbin' fugitive just killed this one."

Shaken, Lige said, "Me? I ain't fired a shot."

"Nobody'll believe that. He came to arrest you, and you shot him."

"You bottom-dealin' son of a bitch."

"I found out a long time ago that you do what you have to if you want to win." He raised the pistol to fire.

Scooter hurled a rock almost the size of his fist. It struck Big'un's horse on the chest. The animal reared and whirled away. Big'un involuntarily squeezed the trigger. The bullet smacked against the side of the barn.

Lige scooped up his own pistol and fired as Big'un

struggled to regain control of his mount. Big'un got off one more shot, then spurred hard to move out of range. Lige steadied his pistol and fired once more. He thought he might have grazed Big'un, but he was not certain.

Scooter stepped hesitantly toward the fallen sheriff. He wanted to throw up. The man's eyes were open. "I think he's alive, Pa. He's lookin' at me."

"No, son, he's halfway to either heaven or hell." Lige bent to close the lawman's eyes. "Like as not he was a good sheriff, but he sure picked a coyote for a deputy."

"What'll we do now, Pa?"

"Only one thing *to* do. We'll run like a rabbit."

"Where to?"

"There ain't nothin' but Texas all around us. Soon as that deputy gets to town and tells his story, every badge toter in the state will be huntin' for us. They'll shoot us down like hydrophoby dogs." For a moment Lige drifted toward despair. He blinked away tears. "They won't stop to ask your age."

Scooter's alarm intensified. He remembered seeing his father cry only once, when Scooter's mother had died.

Lige said, "I done you a bad wrong, son, bringin' you into this kind of a mess. Best thing I can do now is to send you back to your Ranger friends, where I found you."

"I don't know if I could find my way. I'm stayin' with you, Pa."

Lige's eyes were bleak. "When bullets get to flyin' they don't care who they hit. Man or boy, a bullet can't tell the difference."

"How far do you reckon it is up to the Cherokee country?"

"A long ways. There's probably fifty sheriffs between here and the Red River. That don't even count Rangers and town constables."

"We can travel in the dark of the night and hide durin' the daytime."

"That's the only thing to do. We'd better saddle up and get gone before that four-flusher comes back with a posse fired up to kill us both."

From the corner of his eye Scooter sensed a movement. Turning, he shouted, "Look out, Pa. He's comin' back."

A bullet thumped against the barn. Big'un had reversed direction and spurred toward them, firing as he came.

Cursing, Lige leveled his pistol. "Down, boy. Flat on the ground." He took two shots at the deputy.

Dropping to his knees, Scooter felt something strike his hip. It burned like a hot poker.

One of Lige's bullets grazed Big'un's horse. The animal squealed and broke into pitching. Big'un grabbed the saddlehorn and held on with both hands. He dropped the pistol. The bridle reins went flopping.

Lige tried to get him in his sights, but the horse's frenzied bucking made it impossible. Big'un managed to get hold of the reins and bring his mount under a measure of control. He turned toward town. The animal alternated between running and pitching. Lige took one more shot, but it was an empty gesture.

He said, "Get up, son. We got to go."

Scooter moaned. "Somethin's wrong, Pa. I can't get up."

Lige dropped to one knee, eyes fearful. "My God, he hit you."

Scooter looked down at his hip. He saw the blood and felt nausea wash over him. Though Lige was skinny as a log rail, he picked up his son and carried him to the old house's back porch as though he weighed nothing at all. "Slip them britches down, son. Let me take a look."

Scooter's hands were trembling. He could barely manipulate his belt buckle.

Lige asked, "Does it hurt bad?"

"It's startin' to. Mostly it burns."

Lige felt around the wound, then wiped his bloody fingers on one leg of his trousers. "Looks like the bullet went plumb through. Might've nicked the bone, though. I need to take you to a doctor."

"You can't go to town. Folks there would kill you in a minute."

"At least I've got to stop the bleedin'. Then we have to make a lot of tracks. You think you can ride?"

"I don't know. Maybe you ought to leave me here."

"And have that deputy kill you to shut your mouth? That's the reason he turned around and came back, hopin' to finish us both so we couldn't tell what we seen here."

"Would anybody believe us?"

"Not likely, but he can't take the chance. He's got to kill us."

He fetched a half-empty whiskey bottle from his blanket roll in the barn. "This is goin' to burn like the fires of hell. Holler if it helps."

Scooter hollered, but it did not help.

Misery in his eyes, Lige said, "Somewhere we'll

find somebody who can help you. Till then, you've got to hang on, boy."

BIG'UN HAD A DOZEN men with him, all Hoppers or Hopper kin. Approaching the farmhouse, Deputy Harp asked, "Hadn't we better go in slow and careful?"

Big'un kept his horse in a stiff trot. "That outlaw will be miles away from here by now. But we'll pick up his trail and ride him down like a lobo wolf, soon as we do right by poor old Oscar."

A wagon trailed a couple of hundred yards behind. It would take the sheriff's body back to town for proper services and burial.

Old Oscar ought to be grateful to me, Big'un thought, rubbing his sore arm where Lige's bullet had grazed it. I've made a hero out of him. Every Hopper woman in town will cry at his funeral, and some that aren't even kin.

Harp said, "Reckon why that robber picked this place to hide out?"

Big'un replied, "Like as not them Landons put him up to it. Probably had him hired to kill some of us and keep their own hands clean. But me and Oscar flushed him before he had time to do any such of a thing."

"Damned shame your horse went to pitchin' when you tried to protect Oscar. You could've finished that killer then and there."

Nobody had questioned Big'un's account about Tennyson shooting Truscott in cold blood and about Big'un's horse going into a panic at a critical moment. Horses were like that. "Don't worry, we'll get him sooner or later. But everybody better remember, we're up against a murderer who won't stop at nothin'. He won't give any mercy, and he's got no mercy comin' to him. Shoot to kill."

"What about the boy?"

"Just remember that he put a bullet in Oscar too. He's already ruined for life, travelin' with an outlaw daddy. He's probably carryin' the trace of a noose around his neck." He had heard it said that anyone destined to hang bore a faint birthmark that foretold his fate. Perhaps it was the mark of Cain that Big'un had heard preachers talk about. He had looked for it on his own throat and had been relieved not to find it.

Truscott lay where Big'un had left him except that he had been rolled over onto his back, his arms folded across his chest and his hat covering his face.

Harp said, "Odd, ain't it, that an outlaw would do such a thing for a sheriff?" He lifted the hat to look at Truscott's face. "Looks natural, Oscar does, like he's just asleep. You reckon he felt any pain?"

Big'un remembered the pleading look in Truscott's eyes before the second shot. "I doubt he ever knew what hit him, it happened so fast." Nevertheless, the memory made him shiver. He turned in the saddle to hide the emotion from the posse members. "Where the hell is that wagon?"

Harp stepped up close to the house. He said, "Did Oscar ever reach the porch?"

Big'un replied, "No, he fell right where he is now."

"Then you must've hit somebody. There's blood up here."

The stain had soaked into the dry old wood. Big'un studied it and felt a quick uplift. Maybe he had shot the old reprobate after all. He hoped it was a fatal wound.

The boy would soon be caught, wandering around by himself. Given any kind of chance, Big'un would see to it that he did not live long enough to testify about what had really happened.

One of the men had circled the house. He shouted, "I've found their trail."

Big'un rode out to look. The tracks headed north. "Funny they'd go that way. Was I them, I'd head for Mexico."

Harp suggested, "Maybe they figure on some of the Landons helpin' them. We ought to wipe out the whole damned litter, or at least run them out of the county."

Big'un was surprised at how well this whole affair had played into his hands. "But the first thing we got to do is catch these killers. Afterward we can deal with Jayce Landon. We'll do what we had figured to do when we had him in our jail."

"We don't know where the Rangers took him."

"There's still one Ranger in town, the one called Brackett. He'll know."

"He won't tell."

"Yes, he will. One way or another, he will."

14

SERGEANT HOLLOWAY HAD RETURNED TO THE SAN
Saba River camp. Rusty sent the captain a brief
wire explaining the situation and requesting permission for him and Andy to guard Jayce until the circuit
judge reached town. The captain wired back advising
that additional ranger help would be sent if requested.
Tom Blessing decided not to ask for it.

"Got to save the taxpayers' money where we can,"
he said. "Lots of them think we're stealin' it or
throwin' it away on luxuries."

Andy smiled. If the courthouse or jail contained any
luxuries, he had failed to see them. The place begged
for a coat of paint, and a piece of cardboard had been
tacked up where a windowpane was missing.

Flora was on her long daily visit to her husband. She
responded to Tom's comment. "Jayce'd feel better if
you would ask the captain to send brother Dick."

Rusty frowned. "Dick would take it hard, watchin'

Jayce tried for murder. We all know what the out-come'll be."

She said, "Havin' him here would be a comfort to Jayce. I'd feel better too."

Rusty gave in. "It's against my better judgment, but I'll wire the captain."

When Flora left, Andy told Rusty, "Somebody said Jayce and Dick both courted Flora."

"It's a shame she made the wrong choice."

"When Jayce is gone she'll have a second chance. Maybe she'll take it."

Rusty observed him quizzically. "I knew that Farley Brackett was some taken with her, but I didn't know you were too. She's ten years too old for you."

Andy's face warmed. "It's not that way at all. It's just that she's got a lot of gumption. You have to ad-mire that."

"You'd better admire her from a distance. She'd shoot you in a minute if it would save her husband."

"I'd call that gumption."

So far as Andy could tell, Rusty had shown no inter-est in Flora as a woman. He saw her only as a compli-cation in his effort to guard Jayce, to keep him from escaping and at the same time to protect him from his Hopper enemies. Rusty seemed too tied up in his grief over Josie Monahan to involve himself with another woman. Andy's subtle and sometimes not so subtle ef-forts to arouse his interest in Josie's sister Alice had bumped against a stone wall of resistance.

Every time Andy went to the cells he felt Jayce's eyes watching him, calculating, ready to seize any op-portunity for a break. Tom Blessing did not allow

Flora direct contact with her husband. She did her visiting from a cell ten feet away from Jayce's. She could not even hand him tobacco. Either Tom or Rusty would examine it first, then pass it to Jayce.

Anyone who took a meal tray to Jayce had to leave his pistol in the front office and slide the tray through a wide slot in the cell door. Before anyone entered the cell to empty the slop jar or sweep out, Jayce had first to shove his arms out with a bar between them and submit to being handcuffed.

Andy said, "Tom's carryin' things to an extreme."

Rusty replied, "By the time you put in as many years as he has, you'll know not to get careless with the likes of Jayce Landon. He'll grab any chance, and he'll be willin' to kill anybody who stands in his way. So would Flora, I'm thinkin'."

Andy found it hard to imagine Flora killing anyone, even to save Jayce. But he took care not to get close enough that she might grab his pistol.

FARLEY BRACKETT'S ARRIVAL TOOK Andy by surprise. His face was bruised and swollen, cut in half a dozen places. He attempted to dismount by himself but fell to hands and knees. His startled horse jerked free and ran several yards before turning to look back.

Andy rushed to help. Though he had never liked the dour Ranger, he felt outrage at seeing him so badly battered. He lifted Farley to his feet and held him to keep him from falling again. He said, "You look like you've been drug at the end of a rope."

Farley's lips were swollen and cut. His speech was distorted. "Where's Rusty? Got to see Rusty."

"He's inside. Hang on to me. I'll get you there."

Farley had difficulty in keeping his legs under him. With Andy's support he labored up the step and through the door. Rusty sat at Tom's desk, writing a report for the captain. Tom lay napping on a cot, one arm over his face to shield his eyes from the light. He had stood watch for half the previous night. Awakening, he pushed up onto his elbow. "What in the world . . ."

Rusty strode across the room to help. Tom arose from the cot and motioned for them to place Farley on it.

Rusty demanded, "Who did this to you?"

Farley cursed under his breath as he stretched out on the cot. "Big'un. Who else? There's hell to pay over at Hopper's Crossing. The Hoppers are tied up in a manhunt. But when they get done with that they'll be comin' for Jayce."

Rusty said, "They know where we brought him?"

"They do now. Big'un had him a set of brass knuckles. I didn't have the strength to give him much of a fight."

"Nobody could blame you for tellin' him."

"I didn't tell him nothin', but the little feller that runs the livery stable spilled it all. He had heard you-all talk enough that he knew you brought Jayce over here."

"So you figure Big'un will be comin' after him?"

"As sure as New Year's follows Christmas. I ought to've killed him when I had the chance. I will yet."

"Better not. Remember, he's a deputy sheriff."

Farley cautiously ran his fingers over some of the angry cuts on his face. "Worse than that. He's the actin' sheriff now by order of Judge Hopper."

Farley explained about Truscott's murder. "Accordin' to Big'un, it was old man Tennyson and his boy that done it. He put out an order to kill them both on sight."

Andy felt his heart sink. "Scooter?"

"Big'un said him and the sheriff went out to make an arrest. The old man and his boy shot it out with them."

Andy declared, "Scooter wouldn't do such a thing."

"It don't matter whether he did or not. Big'un put out the word to take no chances, to shoot the both of them on sight."

Andy felt a chill. "He must be lyin'."

"Like as not, but most of Hopper's Crossing believes him. They're huntin' high and low, like a pack of coyotes. I wouldn't bet a Confederate dollar on the daddy or the boy either one livin' to get away."

Andy turned to Rusty in anguish. "We've got to do somethin'."

"Lige Tennyson picked his own road."

"I doubt that Scooter had any say in the matter."

"We wouldn't have any idea where to look for them. Anyway, it's our assignment to guard Jayce."

For the moment Andy hated Jayce Landon and Lige Tennyson both. Most of all he hated Big'un Hopper, responsible for their having to guard Jayce and for the shoot-to-kill admonition that put Scooter in jeopardy.

Flora called from the back room. "You-all come and let me out of this cell."

Farley pushed up onto his elbows. "You-all got that good woman under arrest?"

Rusty said, "We're tryin' to make sure she stays good." He explained the conditions under which she was allowed to visit her husband. "She passed a gun to him once. We don't want her doin' it again."

Farley eased. "I didn't know anybody figured that out besides me."

Andy said, "You think you're the only one around here that's got any brains?"

Tom released Flora from her cell and followed her out into the office. The sight of Farley's battered face stirred her to indignation. "I don't suppose he fell off of a horse."

Farley said, "It wasn't a horse that done this to me. It was a jackass."

"Turn Jayce loose for a few days, and I promise you Big'un won't trouble anybody again."

Rusty said, "I'm sore tempted, but how could we know Jayce wouldn't head south for Mexico?"

"You could hold me here in his place. He'd turn himself in again like he did before."

"Maybe. Maybe not. Jayce knows Tom Blessing wouldn't mistreat you like Big'un did. And Tom couldn't hold you for long since there's no charges against you."

She argued, "No tellin' who-all Big'un is liable to stomp on before he's through. What Hopper's Crossing needs is a few funerals, startin' with Big'un and his uncle Judd. Give Jayce a chance and he'll see to it."

Farley said, "Once I get my strength back, I'd be glad to see to it myself."

SCOOTER SWAYED FROM ONE side to the other in the saddle. Lige said, "Stay awake, son. You don't want to fall and start the bleedin' again. It's taken too long to get it stopped in the first place."

But he realized Scooter was not simply falling asleep. Fevering, he teetered along the brink of unconsciousness.

"I've got to find help for you, and damned soon."

Because the bullet had passed through, he had hoped his son would be able to keep riding until they put a lot more distance behind them. But instead of starting the healing process, the wound was getting uglier, and Scooter's fever was rising. Lige's hopes for escape had all but vanished. At first he had circled around a few farmhouses, fearing word had gone out that he had killed the sheriff. Now that he made up his mind to accept the risk, he had ridden for miles without seeing a house.

He had only a general idea where he and Scooter were. He hoped they had crossed into another county, where Big'un would have less influence. He had started north, hoping to throw off or at least delay pursuit, then had turned westward where there would be fewer settlements, fewer people to witness their flight. That, however, complicated his search for someone to help Scooter. He had given up the notion of riding only in the dark of night. He traveled boldly in the daylight.

At last he saw a small cabin. Smoke drifted from the chimney. "Hold on, son. Maybe these folks can help you."

He heard the sound of an ax, then saw an old black man chopping wood behind the cabin. Disappointment left a sour taste in his mouth. "Damned little help we'll get here."

The old man straightened and leaned on the ax

while he rubbed his sleeve across his eyes in an effort to wipe away the sweat and sharpen his vision. Then he came limping out to meet Lige and the boy. "That young'un looks to be in a bad way."

"He's in need of help. Any white folks livin' close by?"

"Not close enough by the looks of him. There's the Shannon place over yonderway, but nobody's home. And there's Old Man Fowler Gaskin. You wouldn't take a stray dog to him."

"What about town?"

"It's a right smart of a ways. Too far for the boy to keep ridin' horseback, I'm afraid, and I ain't got a wagon. Bring him in the house. I'll see if there's somethin' I can do for him."

Lige had always considered it gospel truth that black folks were supposed to be subservient. He took the old man's blackness as an indication that the cabin was probably filthy and infested with vermin. The thought of taking Scooter in there repelled him. Yet he saw no choice.

He said, "I'm goin' to need hot water to clean him up."

"That won't take long. I got plenty of firewood, and there's water in the well."

The cabin's single room was bedroom and kitchen all together. Lige was pleasantly surprised to see that the place was clean. He asked, "You got a woman, I suppose?"

"Never had no chance to get married."

"The place looks too neat not to have a woman in it."

"I used to belong to Mr. Isaac York. When he was sober he was particular about keepin' the place up. He wasn't sober much, but I got in the habit of sweepin' and scrubbin' for the times when he was."

Lige gave the cot a doubting look. He distrusted it but was in no position to be choosy. He gently placed Scooter on the top blanket and pulled down the bloody trousers. Sight of the wound made him sick to his stomach. "How about that hot water?"

"It'll be comin' in a minute. What happened to this boy?"

"It's best you don't know. Then you can't tell them anything."

"He's been shot, that's plain to see. And I'm guessin' you're the ones the Rangers told me about."

Lige's nerves tightened. "The Rangers? What did they tell you?"

"Told me about a man and a boy that robbed a bank out west someplace. I got no money in a bank here or anywheres else, so it don't scrape no skin off of my nose."

Defensively Lige said, "The boy had nothin' to do with it."

"It don't seem likely he would, him bein' so young."

"How often do the Rangers come by here?"

"Ain't seen one in a while. Rusty Shannon was the last to come by."

The name jarred Lige. "Rusty?"

"He's the neighbor I was tellin' you about. A hailstorm beat down his crops, so he's gone back to Rangerin' 'til spring-plantin' time."

Lige thought of his ride with Shannon and Andy to the San Saba River camp, where he'd picked up Scooter. The Ranger had seemed to be a man of dark moods. "I've met Shannon. He didn't have a whole lot to say."

"Hard times been doggin' his steps like a hungry

wolf. He was all set on marryin', but his woman got shot and killed. He's a booger against men that breaks the law."

"And boys too?"

"He's got a soft spot for hard-luck boys. I mind the time he caught a white boy ridin' with the Comanches. They had stole him when he was little. Rusty taken him in and treated him like a brother. First time I seen Andy he was about the size of your boy here. Turned into a fine young man."

"Andy? Would his last name be Pickard?"

"Sure would."

"He was kind to my boy, Scooter."

"I ain't surprised. It would be his way of payin' back for what-all Rusty done to help him."

Lige tried washing away the blood, but his stomach turned over. He had seen lots of bloodshed in his day, but this time was different. This was his son.

The black man offered, "I'll clean him up for you." He took the wet cloth, rinsed it, and began washing around the wound. "This looks bad. I wisht I had whiskey to pour in that bullet hole."

Lige thought he could use some whiskey himself. "We need to cauterize that wound. Else it's apt to go to gangrene."

The black man's face twisted. "Old Shanty couldn't do that to this boy. I know how much it hurts. One time Mr. Isaac got drunk and taken a notion that I ought to be branded like he branded his critters. It was a long time before I could sit in a chair."

"I'm his daddy. It's my place to do it. You got a butcher knife I can heat?"

Reluctantly Shanty fetched a knife from his crude

cabinet. "I'll hold him for you, but I'm shuttin' my eyes."

Scooter had been unconscious. He awakened screaming at the touch of the hot blade. With tears in his eyes Lige kept pressing against the wound until the smell of burning flesh became too much for him. He rushed out of the cabin and threw up.

He reentered after a few minutes. Shanty said, "The boy's unconscious again. He ain't feelin' nothin'. I rubbed some hog lard over the burn."

"Is there a doctor in town that we can trust?"

"Folks around here swear by Dr. Parsons."

"I'd be obliged if you would fetch him."

"Like as not I'll run into Sheriff Tom Blessing. What will I say?"

"I don't see why you'd have to say anything."

Shanty considered. "I never was no great shakes at lyin'. Folks see through me in a minute. But maybe Mr. Tom won't ask me nothin'."

"I hope not. Folks have already accused me of shootin' one sheriff. No tellin' how high they'd hang me if it was two."

THE DOCTOR SPENT AN hour with Scooter. Lige watched him intently, looking for some sign of what he was thinking, but Parsons had the blank expression of an expert poker player. When Lige could stand the strain no longer, he demanded, "What's his chances?"

The doctor's eyes made a silent accusation. "They'd be better if somebody competent had seen him sooner. He lost a lot of blood, and what he didn't lose is in some danger of blood poisoning."

Lige's eyes burned. "You sayin' I'm fixin' to lose him?"

"I'd be lying if I told you he's going to be fine. But he's young and generally healthy. He's got that much on his side. I would caution you against moving him for a few days."

"This ain't no place for him." Lige gave Shanty an apologetic look. "Sorry, but that's the way I see it."

The doctor beckoned Lige outside and said, "There's not a kinder-hearted man in this county than Shanty York. You're letting his color cancel out your better judgment."

"I can't overlook it, though. It's the way I was raised."

"It got a lot of good men killed during the big war. For this boy's sake I hope you'll put those notions aside. At least for a few days, until he's stronger and better able to move."

"Looks like I ain't got much choice."

Back inside, Lige found Scooter half-awake. He placed a gentle hand on the boy's shoulder. He told the doctor, "There's people lookin' for us. I'd rather we wasn't found."

"I knew who you were as soon as Shanty told me about you. Lawmen over half of the state are on the hunt. The claim is that you two shot the sheriff over at Hopper's Crossing."

"But it ain't true. It was the sheriff's own deputy done the shootin', and he shot my boy too."

Lige could not tell whether Parsons believed or disbelieved him. That poker face gave nothing away.

The doctor shrugged. "It's been a long time since anything good came out of that county. Almost any funeral over there could be considered community improvement. Do you know I am obliged by law to report any treatment I do on gunshot wounds?"

"I remember when private matters stayed private."

"It seems that the government pokes its nose into just about everything these days. But I might get so busy that I don't turn in my report for a while. People my age are apt to be forgetful at times."

"What do I owe you, Doctor?"

A knowing smile crossed Parsons's face. "Did you come by the money honestly?"

"Some folks might argue either way about that."

"Just drop a couple of dollars in the plate the next time you go to church."

"If Scooter comes out of this, I'll let him do it."

Lige and Shanty stood on the narrow front porch, watching the doctor's buggy raise dust on the town road. Lige asked, "You a Bible-readin' man?"

"I don't read it, exactly, but I listen to the Word anytime I get the chance."

"Do you reckon the Lord allows for a righteous killin'?"

"You thinkin' about that deputy sheriff?"

"He does lay heavy on my mind."

15

AN HOUR PAST DARK BIG'UN HOPPER RELUCTANTLY rode into town with a volunteer posse of six men. Horses and riders were so weary that they seemed barely able to hold their heads up. It had been another hard day's ride, and a futile one. Big'un had mistakenly thought it would be easy to track the fugitives and put so many holes in them that their bodies would not float.

His cousin Harp said, "It's like angels lifted them up and carried them away. Or maybe it was the devil. Don't seem like the angels would help them that killed Oscar Truscott."

They had certainly not done anything to help Big'un. He had wanted to continue the chase if it killed half the horses, but the exhausted posse members had threatened to rebel. Even Harp had argued their side. If they couldn't find the trail in the daylight, they sure as sin wouldn't find it in the dark, he said.

Big'un knew they were right, though he had verbally chastised them and even threatened to beat up Cousin Wilbur, who had been a chronic bellyacher all his life. He knew the longer the fugitives remained at large, the less likely he was to find them. He hoped that Lige Tennyson's wound was serious enough to make him go to ground somewhere. After that, the boy would be easy. Sure, some people would balk at shooting him, but Big'un had told everyone who would listen that the boy had participated in the killing of Oscar Truscott. Once a young wolf got the taste of blood, he argued, he was beyond taming. Best thing was to shoot him at the first opportunity.

So far as he could tell, no one had doubted his story. Not even a Landon had spoken out against him. But if Lige and his boy had a chance to tell their version often enough, doubts might begin to surface.

It must have been the devil's doing that he had not been able to kill them at the farmhouse the way he had intended.

As the posse began to break up, Big'un declared loudly, "I'll expect every one of you to be here and ready with fresh horses at first light. Bring enough grub to last you for three or four days."

He heard a lot of groaning and knew that half of them would not show up. Things had come to a pretty pass when a man could no longer count on loyalty from his kin.

After the others pulled away, Harp said, "You never did like Oscar in the first place. Looks like we ought to be takin' care of Jayce Landon instead of chasin' over hell and half of Texas lookin' for that old man and his boy. The truth be told, they done you a favor. They made you the sheriff."

"You gettin' cold feet, Harp?"

"No, but I'm gettin' an awful sore butt. You have any idea how far we've ridden?"

"We'll ride a thousand miles if we have to. Jayce ain't goin' nowhere. We'll get around to him, but we've got this other business to finish first."

Harp accepted, but not with any grace. "If you say so, but was I you, I'd be givin' that Tennyson a medal."

"You've got no sense of justice."

Harp started to turn away but stopped, considering. "You sure you ain't just makin' a show for Oscar's widow?"

Big'un exploded into rage. "What kind of a man do you think I am? She's blood kin."

"She's good-lookin'. I ain't seen nothin' yet that would make you back away from a good-lookin' woman."

Big'un was tempted to lay the barrel of his new pistol against the side of Harp's head. But Harp was a better tracker than Big'un. He needed him. Someday when all of this was over, he would teach Harp a whole new code of conduct.

As he rode by the darkened courthouse a familiar, gruff voice hailed him. Judge Hopper walked out and jerked his head in silent command. Big'un dismounted but had to hold on to his horse for a minute while his knees threatened to collapse from fatigue.

The judge's voice was impatient. "I gather that you had no luck."

"We had luck, all right. All bad."

"This is the third day you've been out on the chase. Don't you think that's enough?"

"It won't be enough till we get them."

"No tellin' how far they've traveled by now. Everybody in town knows you and Oscar didn't like one another. Some are beginnin' to ask why you've let yourself become obsessed with this hunt."

"I've got my reasons."

"And I can guess what they are. But if enough other people start to guess the same thing, you're liable to be in more trouble than you can handle."

"You sayin' I ought to quit the chase?"

"I'm sayin' they're probably in another jurisdiction by now. Let somebody else capture them."

"I can't. I've got to be the one that does it."

The judge stared solemnly at him. "I've seen some smart men convicted in my court, all because they got in too much of a hurry and were careless enough to leave witnesses behind. Good night, nephew."

Big'un watched his uncle walk away and become lost in the darkness. He gritted his teeth and slammed his palm against the seat of his saddle, startling the tired horse into jumping away from him.

At that moment he realized that his uncle had served notice in an oblique way. If Big'un got into trouble over Oscar Truscott, he was on his own. Judd Hopper's court would be of no help.

Damn you, Lige Tennyson, he thought. This is all your fault.

LIGE STOOD IN THE middle of Shanty's garden, chopping weeds. He had been a little put off at first by the notion of doing chores for a black man, but it was better than sitting around fretting over Scooter's still-raw wound. That little cabin seemed to shrink a bit more every day.

Shanty rode up from the river on his mule. Lige straightened and wiped sweat from his face onto his sleeve. "Find your hogs all right?"

"Not all of them. I got a notion Mr. Fowler Gaskin has been over this way."

"Damn, but I hate a thief. Somebody ought to ride over to Mr. Gaskin's and plant a load of buckshot where it'll remind him what the Gospel says."

"It won't be me. Only reason I keep a shotgun is to kill varmints."

"From what you've told me, Gaskin is the biggest varmint around here."

"The Book says judge not if you don't want to be judged your own self. Now and then I get tempted, but I can't speak my mind free like if I was white."

Lige had never given thought to the fact that blacks had to be extra careful in expressing themselves lest they anger those whites who would not hesitate to inflict punishment. Lincoln's Emancipation Proclamation had granted them freedom on paper. It had not freed them from the invisible chains.

Shanty asked, "You looked in on the boy?"

"A while ago. He was asleep. That's what he needs the most, but I don't know how much more he can get."

"How come?"

"A couple of riders came by. I stayed in the cabin where they couldn't see me. I couldn't help thinkin' they're part of a posse, huntin' me and my boy. We need to be movin' along."

"Scooter's at a ticklish stage in his healin'. He oughtn't to be on his feet, much less in a saddle."

"If people keep comin' by, we may not have no choice."

"You're all right if you stay inside. Most white folks who pass by here wouldn't go in my cabin if you was to offer them twenty dollars."

"I expect the reward on me is a lot more than twenty dollars."

Shanty squinted against the sun, then lifted his hat to shade his eyes. "Looks to me like we're fixin' to have some more company, Mr. Lige."

Lige took only a fleeting look. "Good thing you seen him. I didn't." Bending over as if that would make him less visible, he retreated to the cabin. Shanty tied the mule, then picked up the hoe and continued the work Lige had begun.

Long before he could see the man's face, Shanty knew the visitor was Fowler Gaskin. Like Shanty, he rode a saddled mule, though a poor one that showed its ribs. Gaskin had a way of hunching over that identified him as far as a man could see him. Shanty forced a false smile. "How do, Mr. Gaskin."

Gaskin took a look around before he replied. "Anybody here besides you?"

"Ain't hardly anybody ever stops at my place."

"You heard what happened?"

"Ain't much to hear around this little old farm."

Fowler sat up straighter, enjoying the feeling of importance that came from being the bearer of news. "Been a killin' over yonder a ways. Seems like a man and a boy was wanted for robbin' a bank, and when the sheriff went to arrest them they shot him."

Shanty feigned surprise. "Wasn't Tom Blessing, was it? I sure would miss Mr. Tom."

"Naw, it was over the county line, by Hopper's

Crossin'. Been a *re*ward posted. I wondered if you've seen anybody like that lately."

"Ain't seen hardly anybody at'all."

"I could sure use that *re*ward money." Gaskin looked hard at Shanty. "I seen a couple of strange horses grazin' out yonder a piece. Didn't know you had any horses."

Shanty began feeling nervous. He thought he saw suspicion in Gaskin's eyes. "Ain't mine. Strays followin' the river, I expect."

"If it was me, I wouldn't let nobody's strays be eatin' up my grass."

"Horses don't know nothin' about property lines. I figure somebody'll come along and claim them."

"Maybe so." Gaskin looked toward the cabin as if he expected to see someone. "Mind if I stop at your well and get a drink?" Normally he never asked; he just took.

"Help yourself." To refuse him would strengthen Gaskin's suspicion. Shanty had never refused him anything. He could only hope that Lige remained inside and kept quiet. He went on with his hoeing, but his worried gaze remained fixed on Gaskin.

Gaskin brought up a bucket of water on the windlass but took no more than a sip before dropping the bucket back into the well. He gave the cabin a long study. When he rode away he changed direction and kept looking back over his shoulder.

When he felt that Gaskin could no longer see him, Shanty laid down the hoe and went to the cabin, half trotting, half hopping on his arthritic legs. Lige came out onto the narrow porch to meet him. "Anybody we need to worry about?"

"It's past the worryin' part. That was Mr. Fowler Gaskin, and he looked like a dog that just found a bone."

Lige's eyes narrowed. "You didn't tell him nothin'?"

"Didn't have to. He seen your horses. I'm fair certain he figured it all out for hisself."

"That old mule of his don't look none too swift. I could catch up to him." Lige's eyes made Shanty feel cold.

Shanty said, "Ain't you already got trouble enough?"

Lige sobered. "Then me and my boy have got to get away from here before he comes back and brings some others with him."

"If you try to take Scooter very far, he ain't goin' to make it."

Lige's eyes showed fear. "I'm willin' to take my chances, but my boy . . .". The fear turned to anguish. "Ain't there no place safe for him?"

"The jail."

Lige stared as if he could not believe what he heard. "Jail?"

"Sheriff Tom Blessing's jail. Mr. Tom ain't goin' to let nobody touch Scooter or do him any hurt."

"My boy don't belong in jail. He ain't done nothin'. I'll admit I done the bank robbery like they said, but that was me, not him. He done his best to talk me out of it."

"I believe you, and I'll bet Mr. Tom will too. He'll see that Scooter gets the right doctorin'. He'll also see that nobody does him harm."

Lige wrestled with his doubts. "I've spent the biggest part of my life tryin' to stay out of jail. Puttin' that boy into one on purpose goes against everything I believe in."

"It'll be the savin' of him."

"You're probably right, bad as I hate to think so. But if I go with him I'll have gray whiskers down to my knees before I get out. If they don't hang me."

"I can take him. It'd be easier for you to keep hidin' out if you don't have the boy on your hands."

Lige nodded reluctantly. "I wouldn't go far. I'd want to be where I could sort of keep an eye on things."

Shanty considered. "Mr. Rusty's place. Him bein' a Ranger, I doubt as they'd do much lookin' around there. You could camp in the timber down on the river. If there was any news I could come and tell you."

Lige looked as if it would not take much to make him cry. "Ain't been but a little while since I got my boy back. It's a mean thing to think about us bein' apart again."

Shanty could only shrug. For this, he had no answer.

Scooter was too weak to get on his horse without help, and he bit his lip to keep from crying out in pain as his father lifted him into the saddle. Shanty said, "We'll stay in the timber as much as we can. It's a longer trip that way, but maybe we won't run into anybody."

Scooter's voice was almost too weak to be heard. "I'll be all right. Where are we goin'?"

Lige and Shanty had decided not to tell him until they had to. They knew he would resist the plan to separate him from his father. Shanty said, "To some good folks that'll take care of you."

It was dark by the time they reached the edge of town. Lige became agitated when he saw that a number of people were out on the street. "Why ain't they at home?" he demanded. "Even chickens know to go to roost come night."

Shanty said, "Maybe you better not go no further."

Lige turned to his son. "Shanty's takin' you on in. I'm goin' to have to quit you here."

Scooter was dismayed. "You're not stayin' with me?"

"It's for the best this way. But I ain't goin' far. Anything happens, I'll be here in a jiffy." He hugged his son, then looked away quickly, blinking. He cleared his throat and turned to Shanty. "I ain't never had much use for your people. Always thought they was shiftless and sticky-fingered. But you've done mighty fine by me and my boy. If there's ever anything you need . . ." He did not finish. He rode off into the darkness without looking back.

Scooter called after him, but his voice was soft and did not carry far.

Shanty said, "Hush, boy, you don't want the wrong people to hear you." He waited a minute, watching and listening. "Looks like there ain't nobody comin'. Let's go before somebody sees us."

"Where we goin'?"

"Told you while ago, to some good people who'll watch out for you."

As soon as he saw the jail, Scooter sensed the plan. He tried to turn his horse around, but Shanty caught the reins. "Hold on, boy. It's all right."

"You turnin' me in to the law?"

"Sheriff Tom Blessing ain't goin' to hurt you, and he ain't goin' to let nobody else do it. You can't keep runnin', the shape you're in."

"They'll try to make me tell where my daddy is at."

"You don't know, so you can't tell them much. Let me help you down. I'll take care of your horse later."

Though Scooter was not heavy, he was almost too much for Shanty. The old man sank halfway to his knees before setting the boy on the ground. "Hold on to me," he said. "I won't let you fall."

Shanty knocked on the door, then rubbed his knuckles, arthritis making them ache. In a minute someone opened the door slowly and cautiously. The muzzle of a pistol showed first. Then Andy Pickard poked a lamp out into the darkness.

"Shanty? What you doin' out this time of the night?"

"Brought you somebody."

Andy shouted, "Scooter!" He opened the door wide, looking past Shanty and the boy. "Got his daddy with you?"

"Just the boy. He's hurt."

Andy laid the lamp on the floor, then picked Scooter up and carried him inside. He laid him on a cot. "Better bar that door behind us, Shanty. Some folks from Hopper's Crossing have been hangin' around, lookin' for a chance to bust in."

"Nobody knew I was bringin' the boy here."

"It's not Scooter they've been after, not here at the jail." He explained that Jayce Landon was safely lodged in a cell.

Shanty said, "They're huntin' Scooter too. He witnessed a shootin'."

"So I've heard. They've got word out all over the country. They say his daddy murdered Sheriff Truscott."

"Scooter and his daddy tell it different. They say the sheriff's own deputy done it, then throwed the blame on Mr. Lige and the boy."

Andy absorbed that as he looked down at the youngster. "How'd Scooter get shot?"

"That deputy. He tried to kill the both of them so they couldn't tell what he'd done."

"Sounds like Big'un Hopper."

Scooter rasped, "That's him. That's what Pa called him."

Andy frowned. "If it was anybody else I'd find it hard to believe. But with Big'un, I'm not surprised at anything." He turned away. "I better go wake up Tom. He's been stayin' in the jail ever since we brought Jayce over here. Sleeps with one eye open."

Shanty said, "Come mornin' we better fetch the doctor. He treated the boy once, but he sure needs lookin' at again."

Andy blinked. "The doctor's already seen Scooter?"

"Once, out at my place."

"He didn't come and tell us about it."

Shanty headed off a smile. "I guess he ain't found the time. Doctors get awful busy."

"In some localities more than others."

Tom lay on a cot in an empty cell. He was already half awake when Andy went in to fetch him. He said, "I heard the door. I didn't hear any fight, so I supposed it wasn't any of the Hopper bunch bustin' in."

Andy explained about Scooter and his version of Truscott's death.

Tom said, "From what you-all have told me about this Big'un, maybe the boy's tellin' it straight. But we can't pass judgment. That's for a court to do."

"True enough, but we've got to give the boy protection."

"Sounds to me like he needed protection from his father."

"That's what I tried to tell the captain when he let Lige Tennyson take Scooter away with him."

"Where do you reckon the old man is now?"

"No tellin'."

"No matter. Our main job right now is to see that the Hoppers don't get to Jayce before he's had a chance to stand trial. If they want Lige Tennyson, they'll have to find him theirselves."

"From what Scooter and Shanty say, Big'un's liable to want Scooter as much as he wants Jayce."

"Let him come and try. Ain't nobody gettin' into my jail unless I put him there. Do you suppose anybody saw Shanty bring the boy in?"

"I think somebody is watchin' everything we do."

16

BIG'UN HOPPER WAS SO TIRED THAT WHEN HE TRIED to pull the saddle and blanket from his horse's back he dropped them. He expelled a long breath and reached down, then straightened, pressing his hand against his back in a futile effort to ease the pain.

He muttered to himself, "The hell with it. Let them lay." He slipped the bridle over the horse's ears and watched the animal turn toward the water trough. He was eager for a drink himself. It would be a mix of coffee and whiskey, light on the coffee.

Carrying a lantern, Harp walked out to the corral. "It's been dark for two hours. I thought you never was goin' to give it up and come in."

The words were not exactly critical, but Big'un took them that way. Most of his kin had been walking the long way around him the last few days, afraid he might bite their heads off. Or worse, badger them into joining his posse to hunt for Lige Tennyson and his brat. He said, "If the rest of you won't go with me, I'll keep goin' by myself. I won't quit till I get them."

Harp hung the lantern on a nail. "You can quit huntin' for the boy, at least. We know where he's at."

Big'un stiffened. "Keep talkin'."

"He's over yonder in Tom Blessing's jailhouse."

Big'un swore. "How do you know?"

"You recollect that you put Cousin Bim to watchin' the jail so we'd know if they tried to smuggle Jayce out of there? He seen an old darky bring the boy in."

"How did he know it was the right boy?"

"He hung around close and listened to the talk. It was the Tennyson kid, all right, and he was wounded."

"Who would've wounded him?"

"I reckon you did. We found blood on the porch, remember? You thought you had shot the old man, but it looks like you hit the boy instead."

It took Big'un a minute to absorb that. He had aimed at Lige, but hitting a target from a running horse was always highly chancy. Until he saw the blood-stains he had not thought he'd hit anyone. "Anybody see anything of the boy's daddy?"

"No, but it ain't likely he'd go far without knowin' his son was goin' to be all right. I figure he's hidin' close by." Harp's voice dropped. "And he's apt to be killin' mad. Was I you I'd be keepin' four walls around me and no windows. That broad back of yours makes a good target."

Big'un shivered at the thought of a bullet smashing between his shoulder blades, severing his spine and setting him afire. It could happen if Tennyson was the crack shot he had claimed to be.

Harp said, "If we could just figure some way to smoke him out . . ."

Big'un said, "You told me an old darky brought the boy in. Know who he was?"

"Bim never heard his name, but I've been thinkin' about that old man Gaskin. He said he had a notion where Tennyson and the boy was at. Wondered how much we'd pay for the information and if we'd let him have some of it in advance."

"I remember. Everybody said he was just a lyin' old drunk always lookin' to get money without havin' to work for it. I gave him a cussin' and sent him on his way."

"Maybe you cussed him too soon. It just come to me that he said he thought they was hidin' out with a darky. Could've been the same one that brought the boy to town."

Big'un felt as if Harp had struck him. "You knew that and still you stood by and let me run Gaskin off?"

"Thinkin' ain't exactly my long suit. I leave most of that to you."

"Reckon you could find out where Gaskin lives? I'd get him to take us to that darky."

"He oughtn't to be hard to find. He's got a reputation."

"Then get at it. And next time somebody offers information, don't be so quick to run him off."

FOWLER GASKIN'S PLACE LOOKED about as Big'un expected. "I never could understand how some people can live in a pig sty. He ain't crippled, is he?"

Harp said, "From what I heard, the only thing crippled about him is his ambition."

Gaskin's garden was badly in need of attention. Big'un indulged in a moment's revulsion at the many signs of neglect. Not seeing the old man, he hollered in the direction of the leaning cabin, "Gaskin, come out here." In a lower voice he added, "Before the whole thing falls down around you."

Gaskin ventured as far as the doorway, peering at the visitors through pinched eyes. "Who's that hollerin'?"

"Come out here. I want to talk to you."

Gaskin reached back inside the door and brought out a shotgun. Big'un tensed, wondering if the old reprobate had the guts to fire it. Gaskin said, "I remember you. You talked awful mean to me. I got no business with you now."

Big'un pushed his horse forward and wrested the shotgun from Gaskin's weak and trembling hands. "Yes, you do. You said you knew where we could find Lige Tennyson."

"I said I *thought* I knew, and you cussed me out like I was a nigger. I don't let nobody treat me thataway."

Big'un asked, "How much would it take to make you change your mind?"

Gaskin's anger subsided. "A sight more than I asked you the last time."

"How do we know Tennyson is still there?"

"You don't. But if he's gone, I'll cut the price to half."

Big'un reached down and grabbed a handful of Gaskin's shirt. He yanked the old man up against the horse. "You greedy old robber, I'll pay you what I figure the information is worth, and not a dollar more."

Gaskin cried, "You wouldn't treat me thisaway if my boys was still here. They died fightin' for the South."

"That war is over, old man. We've got a new one now." He gave Gaskin a push that almost made him fall backward. "Go saddle your horse. You're takin' us to that darky."

Gaskin whined, "I ain't got a horse. All I got is a pokey old mule."

"That'll do. Saddle him or ride bareback, I don't care which."

Looking back in anxiety, Gaskin trotted awkwardly toward the barn. Big'un tossed the shotgun through the cabin's open door and heard it clatter on the floor. He said, "I ought to shoot the old rascal on general principles."

Harp said, "I doubt that many folks would show up for the funeral."

Gaskin led the saddled mule from the corral. He had regained a little of his bluster, but not much. "I'll be tellin' Tom Blessing about this. He don't let people come into his county and mistreat the voters."

"Stop talkin'. Get on that mule and ride."

BIG'UN WAS A LITTLE surprised by the neatness of Shanty's little farm. The garden and the field had been hoed. The crops looked healthy, in contrast to Gaskin's. He said, "I thought this place belonged to a darky."

Gaskin said, "It does. Mine used to look like this before I got down in my back."

He must have been down in his back for a long time, Big'un thought. It took years for a place to get as run down as Gaskin's.

Shanty was standing in front of a small frame shed,

brushing a mule's back. He tried for a smile but could not mask his uneasiness.

Big'un asked Gaskin, "Is this the man who harbored Tennyson and the boy?"

"I'd bet a thousand dollars."

"You never saw a thousand dollars." Big'un turned to Shanty. "We know you took the Tennyson boy to town. Where's his daddy?"

Shanty considered a minute before he offered any reply. "I ain't got no idee."

Big'un assumed the old man was lying. He swung his quirt, striking Shanty across the shoulder. "I ain't got the patience to play games with you, boy. Where's he at?"

Shanty rubbed the burning shoulder. "I swear, mister, I don't know."

Big'un lashed him again. "That ain't the answer I want to hear. Try again."

Shanty's body shook, but he stood his ground. "I can't tell you what I don't know."

"He was with you. He's bound to've told you somethin'."

"He didn't tell me nothin'. Said it was better for me not to know."

Gaskin's courage had improved. He said, "These old darkys will lie to you every time. Give me that quirt and I'll put the fear of God into him."

Big'un suspected Gaskin was afraid he might not get his money if Shanty did not tell his tormentors what they wanted to hear. "Back away, Gaskin, before I use the quirt on *you*." He struck Shanty across the back. The old man flinched and choked off a cry.

Big'un said, "I'll bet you got aplenty of whip scars

on you, old man. You'll have a bunch more if you don't talk."

Shanty drew up into a knot. "I been tellin' you the truth. That's all I can do."

Big'un raised the quirt again. Harp caught his arm. "You're fixin' to kill him. You don't want another killin' on your conscience."

Big'un's chin dropped. "What do you mean, *another* killin'?"

Harp's eyes narrowed. "I expect you know what I mean."

"Who you been listenin' to? Somebody been makin' talk?"

Harp's face twisted. "There's several wonderin' why you want that old man and his boy so bad, seein' as they eliminated Oscar Truscott and got you the sheriff's job."

Big'un's eyes smoldered. "Is that them talkin', or is it just you?"

Harp raised both hands in a gesture of surrender. "I ain't doubtin' you a particle. I'm with you all the way. I'm just tellin' you what some folks are sayin'."

"Don't you be listenin' to people who make idle talk. You just listen to me."

"I am, Big'un, I am."

Gaskin understood none of the conversation. He watched, frustrated. "Are you quittin'? You just fixin' to ride away without him tellin' you what you came to find out?"

Harp glared at him. "Looks to me like he's told all he knows. There's no use beatin' a dead horse."

Gaskin got down from his mule. "He ain't dead yet.

I'll make him talk." Shanty drew his arms in tightly as Gaskin moved toward him.

Big'un pushed his horse between the two men. "I told you, Gaskin. Get back on your mule." He raised the quirt for emphasis.

Gaskin backed away. "I done my part. You owe me."

Big'un felt like quirting Gaskin, but instead, he dug a silver dollar from his pocket. He tossed it to the ground in front of the man.

Gaskin picked up the coin and flushed in anger. "A dollar? Is this all, just one dollar?"

"It's a dollar more than you're worth. If you don't want it, I'll take it back."

Gaskin put the coin in his pocket.

Big'un shook the quirt at him. "Now get away from here before I give you what you really got comin'." To Harp he said, "I hate a man who would betray his neighbor for money. Even a nigger neighbor."

Hunched in pain, Shanty watched as Gaskin got a hand-hold on the mule's ragged mane and pulled himself up. He said, "Mr. Fowler, my old dog died, but I'm fixin' to get me another one."

Gaskin snarled, "Your old dog was worthless. What you want another one for?"

"So that if you ever come messin' around my place again, I can sic him on you."

Gaskin's face colored. He turned to Big'un and Harp. "You-all goin' to let a nigger talk to a white man that way?"

Big'un said in disgust, "I don't see no white man."

* * *

IN THE MIDST OF Big'un's frustration an idea began struggling to break free. *Smoke him out,* Harp had suggested. Harp was about to speak, but Big'un raised a hand to stop him, to keep him from interrupting his thoughts before the idea was fully hatched. He asked, "They still got the same old jailhouse?"

"Not much ever changes over there."

"I spent a night in that place once, years ago. They said I was drunk and disorderly."

Harp grinned. "Was you?"

"I expect so. Ain't been back in that town since. I decided not to give them any more of my business."

"It's their loss, then."

Big'un cast a glance over his shoulder to be sure Gaskin wasn't following to plead for more money. The old reprobate had put the reluctant mule into a long trot toward home. "How many people they got standin' guard at the jail durin' the night?"

"Generally a night watchman patrollin' the street outside. Three Rangers and the sheriff sleep inside. A deputy usually goes home."

Big'un rubbed his chin while he let his imagination run free. "Ought not to be hard to take care of the watchman. A couple of guns at the front door and one or two at the back could keep anybody who's inside from comin' out."

"What good will it do you if they stay inside? You couldn't get at them."

"That old jail is mostly built out of lumber. Say a fire was to start along the outside wall. That thing would go up fast, and if them on the inside couldn't get out—well, wouldn't that be a shame?"

Harp stared slack-jawed, awed by Big'un's audacity.

Big'un said, "First I'd like to know just what's goin'
on in that place. I need a man to see inside. I want you to
find me somebody who'll do anything for fifty dollars."

"There's aplenty of them around."

"This has to be somebody Jayce nor nobody else in
that jail would recognize. Somebody who wouldn't
mind gettin' a little drunk and disorderly and spendin'
a night or two in the hoosegow. But somebody we can
rely on."

"That's some combination."

"Find him."

"You're goin' to a lot of trouble just to get rid of
Jayce Landon."

"That boy too. Let somethin' happen to him and like
as not his old daddy would come runnin'. All I need is
one clear shot. Now let's go where I can get me a bottle of whiskey. I got some thinkin' to do."

17

USED TO BEING IN RUSTY SHANNON'S SHADOW, ANDY was pleased at Rusty's attitude. He seemed to be leaning Andy's way in regard to Scooter.

Tom Blessing was still trying to make up his mind. He said, "The boy's fevered. Maybe he really saw what he says happened, or maybe it's the fever made him think he did. No jury is goin' to take his word against a lawman's."

Andy argued, "Even a *good* lawman goes bad once in a while, and Big'un's been a counterfeit from the start."

"I've known some lawmen who were bad to start with. Others learned it on their own. But I can't believe anything as cold-blooded as the boy tells about."

Rusty put in, "Whether it's real or he imagined it, Scooter's better off in here till everything settles into place. If Big'un did kill Truscott, he'll be lookin' to silence the boy. If it was Lige that did it, he'll probably stay around close so he can know what's happenin' to Scooter. That gives us a better chance to catch him."

Scooter lay on a steel cot in one of the cells. The iron-barred door was left open, for he was not technically a prisoner. Flora sat on the edge of the cot, keeping a damp cloth on the boy's head. She had all but adopted Scooter as soon as she first saw him. She had never had a child of her own. Andy doubted that this was for lack of trying on Jayce's part.

Jayce feigned jealousy. From his cell he shouted, "Darlin' girl, you're payin' more attention to that boy than to your poor old neglected husband."

Flora tried to sound sarcastic. "He's younger, he's better-lookin', and he's got nothin' on his conscience."

"He will have by the time he gets a little older. Show me somebody who's got nothin' on his conscience and I'll show you somebody who's spent his life asleep."

Listening, Andy conceded to himself that his own conscience sometimes troubled him when he had time to pay attention to it. In his first years back in the white man's world after his time among the Comanches, he had given those who befriended him plenty of reason to wonder if they should have left him where he was. He had caused anxiety for Rusty in particular. Looking back, he could well understand how Rusty might have given up on him, especially when he threatened to run away and rejoin the Comanches. Instead, Rusty had taken him back to the Indians at considerable danger to himself. Andy had found it impossible to remain in that other world, though even now he still grieved over having lost his place in it. He sometimes questioned if he belonged in this one either.

The hard truth was that he did not fit comfortably in either world, white or red.

Jayce Landon had talked Tom into bringing a couple of forked tree branches to his cell so he could fashion a set of crutches for Scooter. He had promised, "I ain't fixin' to hit anybody over the head with them. The boy needs to be gettin' up and movin' around some. He'll need help with his walkin'."

Now he had a pile of wood shavings in the cell. He had trimmed away the bark and smoothed the surface with a pocketknife borrowed from Tom. He said, "These things'll need some cloth wrappin' to see that they don't rub sores under his arms. Otherwise, they're finished."

Tom said, "If they're finished, I'll thank you to give me back that knife." He extended his hand.

Jayce acted embarrassed. He handed the knife back through the bars. "Sorry. I almost forgot."

Andy knew Jayce had not forgotten anything, but he had hoped the sheriff would. Tom Blessing seldom forgot anything important.

Flora said, "I'll finish them up." She started back toward Jayce's cell, but Tom stopped her. He had never allowed her within reaching distance of her husband. He knew about her slipping a derringer to Jayce in the Hopper's Crossing jail.

He said, "I'll bring the crutches to you. Slide them out here, Jayce." Almost apologetically he added, "I appreciate what you two are doin' for the boy, but I can't afford much trust. Given the slightest chance I think you'd be out of here like a turpentined cat."

Jayce shrugged. "I told you that when I first came."

Flora wrapped cotton cloth around the top of the

crutches as padding. "Feel like givin' them a try, Scooter?"

The boy turned himself around and cautiously put one foot on the floor. He had to use both hands to get the other leg into place. His face twisted with pain. Andy hurried to help him. "Does it hurt?"

Scooter grimaced. "Sure it hurts. But lift me up and see if I can fit them things under my arms." He was wobbly. Andy kept hold of him so he would not fall.

Scooter said, "I feel like I'm goin' down flat on my face. A little dizzy too."

"Don't be in a hurry. It'll take you a while to get the knack." He remembered a time long ago when a horse fall had left him with a broken leg. The crutches at first had seemed bent on bringing him down.

Tom asked, "Rusty, what did you find out about that bunch of riders who came to town this mornin'?"

Rusty said, "They were just Mexican traders bringin' a string of half-broke horses to sell to the farmers hereabouts. There wasn't a Hopper amongst them."

Tom said, "Strangers worry me, but the merchants wouldn't abide me turnin' them back at the edge of town. Visitors bring in money."

"It wouldn't be hard for a bunch of the Hoppers to slip into town at night. They'd love to get a clean shot at Jayce."

"That's why I put him in a cell that ain't got a window in it. As long as he stays there he's as safe as in church. Then after the judge gets here . . ." Tom did not finish. He did not have to.

Andy frowned. Flora did not deserve to be reminded constantly that her husband had an appointment with a rope. He said, "I need some fresh air. I think I'll go take me a little walk around town."

Rusty warned, "Keep watchin' over your shoulder. I wouldn't put it past the Hoppers to grab one of us and try to make a swap for Jayce."

Andy had not thought of that. He realized he should have. Rusty was usually a step ahead of him. Sometimes he despaired of ever catching up. He said, "If that happened, what would you do?"

Rusty said, "We're responsible for keepin' Jayce from harm till he's had his day in court. If it meant havin' to sacrifice one of us, that's what we're paid for. It's part of bein' a Ranger."

Tom nodded in silent agreement.

Their logic disturbed Andy. Jayce Landon was an admitted murderer. A death sentence was almost certain. To trade the life of a Ranger—any Ranger—to let Jayce live a couple of weeks longer seemed beyond reason. Andy deferred to the judgment of Rusty and Tom but retained his skepticism.

"I'll be careful," he promised.

Tom said, "Before you go, would you mind lettin' that drunk out of his cell? I expect two nights in there have sobered him up good."

The man had raised a ruckus in a saloon where things were usually so quiet the place could almost be taken for a Sunday school. Not wanting the burden of extra prisoners during this time of potential trouble, Tom had tried to let him off with a warning. At that point the drunk had thrown a chair through a glass window, and Tom no longer had a choice. Property must be respected, whether saloon or church house.

Andy unlocked the cell and beckoned with his

thumb. "You've had enough free meals. Sheriff says he doesn't want to see anything but the backside of you leavin' town."

The man picked up his hat. He had brought nothing else in with him. He rubbed his chin. "I sure do need a shave."

"Go get it in some other town."

Andy followed him out into the sunshine. The former prisoner blinked against the brightness and looked up and down the street. "Where'd you-all put my horse?"

"In a corral at the wagon yard."

"Hope he got fed better than I did."

In a minute he was gone.

The weather was still warm, but with each passing day the sun edged a little farther to the south. The smell of fall was in the air for a while in early morning, though summer still ruled later in the day. Andy wondered how winter's cold would affect Scooter's healing.

Farley Brackett sat on the jail step, whittling a scrap piece of pine down to a pile of shavings that littered the ground at his feet. The cuts and bruises on his face were healing. "Where you headed, Badger Boy?"

"Just takin' a look around."

"What're you lookin' for?"

"I don't know, exactly."

"If you don't know what you're lookin' for, how you goin' to know it when you see it?"

Annoyed, Andy said, "Maybe you ought to go with me and help me look."

"Can't. I'm guardin' the front door. If you get yourself into any trouble, Badger Boy, you'll have to fight your own way out."

Andy could accept advice, even criticism, from Rusty or Tom, but he drew the line at Farley. "You just watch me."

"Oh, I'll be watchin' you, all right. But don't expect me to come runnin'. Last time I did that I got myself shot."

Andy never expected anything pleasant to come from Farley, and he was rarely disappointed. He wanted to think of a good retort, but none came, so he did not try for the last word. He walked through an open gate in the fence that surrounded the courthouse and jail. He stopped a minute to look up and down the dirt street. Before many more days it would be bustling as farmers in mule-drawn wagons began hauling the first of their cotton crop to town for ginning. Farm families with fresh money in their pockets would be crowding in to buy clothes and other necessities for the coming winter.

Right now the street was quiet. It looked about the same as he had known it during the years since his return from Comancheria except that the town had grown. He saw nothing to be concerned about.

He spotted a farmer he knew and walked over to talk with him. The farmer shook Andy's hand, then looked across toward the jail. He said, "I hear you-all have got a dangerous man locked up, and you're afraid somebody may come and try to bust him out."

"Some people would like to. We're prepared for them."

"Just the same, I ain't lettin' my family come to town till everything is over with. I wouldn't want them to get in the way of a shootin' scrape. Or maybe you can guarantee me that there won't be one."

"I can't even guarantee that the sun will rise and set tomorrow the same as it always has."

The farmer grunted. "I hope the judge shows up pretty soon and gets this mess over with. My wife is bustin' to come to town and see what's new over at the mercantile."

Andy admitted, "It won't be a bad idea to hold her at home a little while longer."

"Maybe you-all better send for some more Rangers."

"There's already three of us, and only one jailbreak to worry about. The head office in Austin figures three is probably two Rangers too many."

"You ought to take up farmin', Andy. All you got to worry about is drought, flood, hail, grasshoppers, and low prices."

Andy walked on down the street with no particular mission in mind except to look for something or somebody that seemed out of place. He peered into the mercantile store and saw no one except the storekeeper and a woman customer. He stepped through the door of a saloon and glanced over the half dozen men there. All the faces were familiar except one, and he looked like a drummer peddling his wares. The saloon was more than just a place for drinking. It was a public service of sorts, a social center where men could meet and swap news and views, a trading site for discussing deals and shaking hands on them. More horses and mules and cotton bales had been sold there than at the livery barn or the gin.

The barkeeper said, "Come on in. No use standin' there blockin' the door."

"Just lookin' for somebody." Andy went back outside, remembering what Farley had said. He did not know who he was looking for. How would he know him when he saw him?

Down at the livery stable, toward the end of the street, a man sat in a straight chair leaned back against the door. Andy at first took him to be the proprietor but after a closer look realized he did not know the man. Yet the face seemed vaguely familiar.

"Howdy," Andy said, trying to remember.

The man stared back, his eyes not friendly. He did not speak.

Andy said, "Seems like I ought to know you." He remembered now. "Your name would be Hopper, wouldn't it?"

"Might be."

"A while back me and Farley Brackett were on our way to deliver Jayce Landon to the sheriff at Hopper's Crossing. You were with a bunch that tried to stop us."

The man's tone was insolent. "That might be too."

"So what're you doin' here?"

"I've got to be somewhere."

"Not here unless you've got business. What's your business?"

"I've got a wife who bitches at me all the time. I come over here now and then to get drunk without her knowin' about it. Any law against that?"

He did not look drunk. Andy thought he could guess Hopper's real reason. He said, "I think you better move on out of town."

"Look, Ranger, I'm spendin' good money here, and I come by it honest. If I've broke any laws, tell me. If I ain't, then leave me the hell alone."

Andy was losing the argument and knew it. He had no grounds for running Hopper out of town. If he did so anyway, he might be subject to legal action. If he did not, and somebody got hurt, he would be blamed for not acting when he had the chance. It was enough to make him wonder why he had chosen to be a Ranger.

For a moment he considered going back to the jail and asking Rusty what he should do. But he had leaned on Rusty far too many times. Sooner or later he had to begin deciding such matters for himself.

He warned, "Watch yourself."

Hopper replied, "I always do. And them that's around me."

Andy returned to the jail. Farley still sat on the step. He had a new piece of wood to whittle on. The earlier one lay scattered in curled shavings on the ground.

Andy said, "I'll bet you didn't know we're bein' watched."

"I know. Bim Hopper's sittin' over yonder at the stable. He's spied on us for several days."

"You knew about him all that time?"

"Spotted him as soon as he showed up. I got to know Bim pretty good when Big'un and his bunch drug me away from my mother's place. He's got mean eyes, and fists hard as a pine knot."

"What are we goin' to do about him?" Andy instantly regretted asking advice, especially from Farley.

Farley said, "I'm waitin' for him to make a wrong move so I can shoot his ear off, or maybe his big toe. Somethin' he'll remember me by."

"He says he's in town to get drunk."

"He ain't been drunk since he came here. He's watchin' for us to let our guard down so him and his cousins can storm the jail and drag Jayce out."

Andy did not admit it, but his thinking ran the same as Farley's.

Farley said, "I hope they try. It'll be the best fight I've been in since I shot hell out of the state police."

Andy was disgusted. "This ain't some kind of entertainment show. There could be dead men layin' out in the street."

"The world could get along just fine without some of them Hoppers. They're a nest of vipers."

"They might not be the only ones killed."

"Have you taken a good look at that old jail? It ain't pretty, but it's bull stout. A whole regiment couldn't bust in without they had a cannon."

Andy was not pacified, but arguing with Farley was like trying to converse with a fence post. He went on up and entered the jail.

Rusty asked, "See anything?"

"There's a man watchin' us from over at the stable."

"Yeah, a cousin to Big'un Hopper. We've been keepin' an eye on him."

"How come you didn't tell me about it?"

Rusty smiled. "We thought we'd see how long it took you to spot him yourself."

Testing me, Andy thought, irritated. Like I was a new recruit.

After consideration he realized the description fit. He stood small against experienced lawmen like Rusty and Tom, even Farley. But he said, "Hadn't we ought to run him off?"

"It's better we leave him where we can watch what he's up to. The time to worry is when we *can't* see him."

Andy went to the window and looked up and down

the street again. In a minute he said, "There's one thing you didn't know."

"What?" Rusty asked.

"That drunk we just let out of jail. He's over yonder talkin' to Bim Hopper."

Rusty and Tom both moved quickly to the window. Tom swore, "Well, I'll be damned. Looks like we've had a spy in our midst."

Rusty nodded. "Looks like."

18

BIG'UN HOPPER LOOKED BACK TO BE SURE NOBODY had deserted him. He had twisted arms to the breaking point to get the six men who accompanied him on this punitive expedition. It would not take much of a scare to send most of them scurrying back to Hopper's Crossing. The only ones he felt he could depend upon were cousins Harp and Bim. Even those would bear some watching.

The wagon jolted along behind with several cans of coal oil he had brought. He could not afford to buy it locally because he would be remembered and the finger of blame would be pointed straight at him.

At dusk they were within half a mile of town. "Let's pull over into them trees yonder," he said. "We'll wait till the dark of the moon."

Cousin Wilbur pulled his horse in beside Big'un's. "The closer we get, the less I like this whole notion. I'm in favor of us gettin' Jayce, but there's other people in that jailhouse too. We could be charged with murderin' them all."

"Not unless we get caught. They can suspicion all they want, but suspicion don't hold no water in court. Anyway, I told all of you what we were goin' to do. I ain't lettin' you back out now."

"Accordin' to Bim there's a kid in that jail. What about him?"

"Remember, he's an outlaw's boy, and he was in on the killin' of Oscar Truscott. He's probably got the mark of a noose around his neck anyway."

"I still don't like it."

Big'un grabbed his cousin's shirt just below the throat and shook the man harshly. "Any more of that talk and I'll see that you walk all the way home."

He was much larger and stronger than his kinsmen. They might grumble, but when the voices quieted down Big'un was confident he would still prevail. He softened his tone. "Uncle Judd gave us a warrant for Jayce's arrest."

Harp asked, "Does Uncle Judd's jurisdiction reach over into another county's jailhouse?"

"He's a judge, ain't he?" Big'un trusted that none of them understood the limitations of Judd Hopper's jurisdiction. They knew all there was to know about mules and horses, cows and plows, but the intricacies of law were a mystery to them.

Wilbur frowned, considering the matter. "If Uncle Judd approves, I reckon it's all right."

Actually, Big'un had told his uncle only that they were going after Jayce. The judge had not let him explain. He had said, "I do not want to know anything about this. Then I can truthfully swear that I do not know what was done or who was responsible."

Big'un had thought it wise not to tell the judge that Jayce might be only one of the casualties, that others might include a couple or three Rangers and possibly even a sheriff. The old man could get downright unreasonable about anything that might bring state investigators in to snoop around. He had some skeletons of his own that were not buried deeply enough for comfort.

Big'un stretched out on the ground to rest while he waited for darkness. He tried not to sleep, fearing part of his crew might quietly slip away. He had some kinfolks who weren't worth killing, but now and then they were useful to him.

If all of the Confederate Army was like them, he thought, it's no wonder the damn Yankees whipped us.

He had not gone to war himself. The judge had pulled political strings to shield as many Hoppers as possible from conscription, arranging for Landon men to take up the slack. That served the demands of patriotism and reduced the enemy's numbers as well.

He waited until the stars were in full array, then prodded his kinsmen into reluctant motion. "The sooner we get the job done, the better chance we'll have to get out of this county before daylight. There won't be nobody able to identify us."

By the time they reached the first houses at the edge of town Big'un saw that he had lost two of his helpers in the darkness.

Harp said, "It's Wilbur and his no-account brother-in-law. We ought to've left them at home."

Big'un cursed. "When I get through with Wilbur . . ."

He looked fiercely at those who remained. "If the rest of you have got any idea of quittin', put it out of your mind. I'll shoot the next man who turns back." He knew he would not, but it was important that they believed he would. When his temper was up, even the town dogs knew to slink away.

Only a few of the houses showed lamplight. Most folks had gone to bed. Things were working out according to plan. If he and his helpers got the job done quickly they should encounter little trouble from local citizens.

The courthouse and the adjoining old jail were like an island in the center of an open lot surrounded by a wooden fence that sagged in a couple of places. Big'un motioned for the driver to stop the wagon. They could carry the cans of coal oil from here. But first he had to locate and eliminate the watchman who patrolled the streets and periodically circled the courthouse. He waited a few minutes until he saw a man walking along the fronts of the buildings along the square, trying the doors to be certain they were locked.

Few people here were likely to recognize Big'un, but as a precaution he pulled his neckerchief up to cover his face. He stepped into the dark open space between two stores and flattened himself against a wall. He listened to the watchman's footsteps on the wooden sidewalk. As the shadowy figure crossed the opening, Big'un moved out behind him and clubbed him with the barrel of his six-shooter. He struck a second time to be sure the man remained out of action for a while. He dragged the limp body into the darkness between the buildings and left it.

He returned to where the others waited beside the wagon. "The watchman is out of the way. Now let's pull the wagon up to block the back door. Then their only way out is the front."

It took a little pushing and maneuvering to position the wagon over the single step so that the door could not be opened far enough for anyone to pass through.

A man stepped around the corner of the jail and stopped abruptly, drawing a pistol. "What're you-all up to?"

Before Big'un could think of a reply, a dark figure appeared behind the intruder and slugged him.

Big'un said, "Good work, Bim. He like to've caught us before we was ready." He unhitched the team and motioned for one of the others to lead the mules away. Big'un lifted a can from the bed of the wagon. "Let's give them walls a good dose of coal oil."

A cousin who went by the nickname Jaybo argued, "The thought of somebody burnin' up in a fire gives me the shakes. We could use a rail for a batterin' ram and bust the door down."

Big'un resisted an impulse to hit him in the mouth. "Would you want to be the first one to rush in there with three or four guns aimed straight at your gut?"

"If you look at it that way . . ."

Big'un assumed the argument was finished. "Bim, you watch the back door so no citizen comes and sets them free. The rest of us will take the front. If they try to bust out we'll shoot them. If they don't they'll know what hell is like before they get there."

Harp said, "Folks'll come runnin' to fight the fire."

"A shot or two in their direction will turn them back. This oughtn't to take long, dry as that lumber is."

Big'un tossed a match at the base of the jail's rear wall. The flames quickly licked their way up to consume the coal oil. He trotted around the side and lighted a couple of places. He motioned for his helpers to join him a few feet from the front door. He started a fire there, then drew his pistol and waited. "This'll be like pottin' fish in a water bucket."

ANDY HAD TURNED IN early, but he was not having a restful night. The folded quilt that served in lieu of a mattress did little to hide the fact that beneath it lay wooden slats that got no softer no matter how he turned. Farley Brackett occasionally broke into fits of loud snoring.

Rusty did not snore, but now and then he spoke a few words in his sleep. One word Andy recognized was "Josie." Though Rusty never spoke of her anymore, Andy sensed that she was still much on his mind. A couple of women here in town looked a little like her from across the street. Andy had noticed that Rusty seemed momentarily startled each time one of them appeared.

He managed to doze off and on, but the spells were short-lived. He worried about what was to become of Scooter. The boy was able to walk without the crutches Jayce had fashioned for him, though the effort was awkward and caused him considerable pain.

Scooter's father was hiding out there somewhere. Of that, Andy was sure. As soon as the boy healed enough to travel, Lige Tennyson was likely to steal him away. And to what? An outlaw life, probably, and most likely a short one. Andy had been considering the possibility of beating Lige to the punch, of taking Scooter where his father would never find him. Andy would have to resign as a Ranger, but he would be willing to pay that price. He would never be able to compensate Rusty directly. If he could do for Scooter what Rusty had done for him, however, that would be repayment of a sort.

And where could he take the boy? The Ranger camp had served as a temporary shelter, but it could not offer what he needed over the long term. The Monahan family kept coming to mind. They were generous, open-handed people who once had all but adopted Andy as one of their own. Surely they would do the same for another boy badly in need of a stable home and a sense of direction. And they lived far to the northwest, up in the Fort Belknap country of west-central Texas. Lige would have no idea where to begin looking.

It had been Flora's habit to spend most of the day at the jail, caring for Scooter and talking to her husband through two sets of bars. She would retreat to the boardinghouse at suppertime, not returning until morning. Tonight, however, she knocked urgently on the front door shortly after dark. "It's Flora," she said. "I've got somethin' to tell you-all."

Andy waited to see if someone else would get up and find out what she wanted. Farley grumbled, "Badger Boy, go let her in."

Andy's cot was farthest from the door, but he knew he could not outwait Farley. He had gone to bed with his clothes on, all but his boots. He lifted the heavy crowbar that blocked the door. "Anybody out there besides you?" he asked Flora. He was mindful of the possibility that someone might use her to gain entry and free Jayce, or kill him.

"Nobody," she said. "But somebody may be comin'."

She stepped inside, and Andy closed and barred the door. She said, "Scooter's daddy just came to see me at the boardin'house."

"Old Lige? How did you come to know him?"

"He's never been far from town. He noticed me comin' and goin' from the jail, so he followed me to the boardin'house and introduced himself. Every day he comes and asks me about his boy. Tonight he saw somethin' he didn't like, and he asked me to give you-all a warnin'."

"About what?"

"He was camped in some timber just outside of town. A while before dark some men came with a wagon and stopped to rest awhile. Big'un Hopper was leadin' them. The old man doesn't know what they're up to, but it can't be anything good."

Rusty had left his cot and stood nearby, listening. "Where's Lige now?"

"Somewhere close, you can bet. He's worried on account of his boy."

One of Tom Blessing's temporary deputies had been sleeping in an open cell. He pulled on his boots and said, "I'll go take a look around."

Rusty said, "Much obliged. If you see or hear anything suspicious, give us a holler."

The deputy took a rifle from the office's gun rack. He said, "You-all want to bar the door behind me?"

Flora walked out with him. Andy set the crowbar in place.

Farley stretched out on his cot. "It'd take half the

Yankee army to bust these heavy doors open. I'm goin' back to sleep."

Scooter had listened quietly. He said, "That's my daddy she was talkin' about. Did she say he's here?"

Andy said, "Somewhere around. He ain't forgot you."

He wished Lige would.

ANDY HAD NO INTENTION of going back to sleep. Thinking he heard low voices outside, he left the cot and walked to the window. At first he saw nothing, for the night seemed pitch black. He stepped back and stumbled into a tin can filled with ashes, substituting for a cuspidor. It clattered and rolled across the floor.

Farley's gruff voice demanded, "Don't you know we're tryin' to sleep?"

"Sorry."

Farley recognized the voice. "I might've known it was you, Badger Boy. For God's sake, go back to bed."

Andy was about to when he saw a flickering light reflecting upon the ceiling. He swung back toward the window. "Fire!" he shouted. "There's a fire outside."

Farley said, "You're crazy." But he got up and looked for himself. "By God, Rusty, the place *is* on fire."

With that Rusty was on his feet too. He quickly pulled his boots on. Recognizing the possibility of trouble, he had been sleeping in his clothes, as had the others. Tom Blessing was also up from his cot.

Andy lifted the crowbar out of its brackets and dropped it to the floor. He pushed the front door partway open. Blistering flames leaped into his face, and he jerked back instinctively. A bullet struck the facing, followed by another, which thumped into the heaviest part of the door. He pulled the door shut.

Rusty said, "That Hopper bunch. They knew they couldn't break in. They're tryin' to burn us out."

Andy trotted to the back door. He could push it only a few inches before it bumped against something solid. The opening was too small to squeeze through. Someone outside fired a shot that splintered the frame. He said, "They got the back door blocked."

Farley strapped his gun belt around his waist. "Be damned if I'll stay here and burn."

Tom said, "The front door is the only way out, and they're waitin' for us there. But we've got no choice."

Rusty said, "Scooter can't make it on his own, and Jayce is locked in a cell. We can't leave him there to die."

Farley said, "They're goin' to hang him anyway."

Andy said, "I can carry Scooter."

Farley said, "If you let Jayce out he'll run like a scalded dog."

Rusty repeated, "We can't leave him to burn."

"He will anyway, soon as the devil gets ahold of him."

From behind his bars Jayce shouted, his voice on the edge of desperation, "Get me out of this trap."

Tom tossed his keys to Andy. "We'll take our chances on him. Turn him loose."

Eye-stinging smoke was already boiling up in the section that contained the cells. Jayce coughed heavily. Andy swung the cell door open and said, "You're on your honor."

Jayce made no response except to lower his head

and cough into his hands. Once he was out of the cell area he said, "Let me defend myself. Give me a gun."

Tom Blessing said, "You know we can't do that."

"I ain't goin' out there empty-handed." Jayce stepped to Tom's desk and opened a drawer. He withdrew a pistol and spun the cylinder to see if it was loaded. "Now, are we goin' out there, or are we goin' to roast like a beef on a spit?"

Rusty accepted the situation without argument. "We'll go out shootin' and make them duck their heads. Andy, you follow close with Scooter. We'll be between you and them. Maybe they won't even see you."

Andy felt guilt about letting others stand the greater risk, but he knew if the boy tried to hobble out on his own, he would not get far past the door.

Farley gave a rebel yell and flung the door open. His pistol blazed. Tom and Rusty and Jayce burst out just behind him, firing at shadows. Andy crouched low, carrying Scooter in his arms.

Andy had heard Rusty say that rapid fire did not have to be accurate so long as it made the enemy keep their heads down. The Rangers and Jayce had cleared the door and were halfway to the fence before the Hoppers regained their wits enough to fire back.

An angry voice shouted, "Shoot, you cowardly sons of bitches. Shoot."

Andy would bet a month's pay the voice belonged to Big'un.

Someone in the Hopper line cried out like a hurt dog.

In the center of the yard was a well with a windlass and a circular stone wall three feet high. Andy dropped behind it. "Flatten out, Scooter, and pull your legs in."

He peered over the rim of the well, seeking a target. He fired once to no apparent effect.

He could hear excited shouts from over in town. Aroused citizens were beginning to respond to the fire and the shooting.

The Hoppers had lost their advantage. Now with the blazing building behind them, their silhouettes became targets. Rusty fired, and Andy saw a man fall. Then Rusty went down. Andy's heart jumped, and he fired at the spot where he had seen a pistol flash.

A rifle opened up from just beyond the perimeter fence. Someone had joined the Rangers in their fight.

Even with the light from the fire, Andy could see no faces he could swear to in court. A large figure arose from a squatting position and ran hard, disappearing around the corner while bullets whispered around him. Andy was almost certain he had seen Big'un Hopper.

A plaintive voice cried, "We give up. Don't shoot no more."

Andy sensed that Rusty was out of the fight. He took it upon himself to shout, "Everybody hold your fire. You Hoppers, raise your hands and stand up where we can see you."

The voice said, "I'm the only one still able to stand. Don't shoot."

The man who had fired from the other side of the fence climbed over, rifle in his hand. He had a shuffling gait. Andy recognized Lige Tennyson. Lige called anxiously, "Scooter! Where you at, boy?"

"Pa?" Scooter pushed to his feet and leaned against the well to steady himself. "Is that you, Pa?"

"It's me. Are you all right? They didn't hit you?"

"No, sir. Andy wouldn't let them." Scooter and his

father hugged each other fiercely. Scooter cried, "What you doin' here, Pa? They'll put you in jail."

"I had to know if you're all right." A section of the jail wall fell inward. A shower of sparks lifted high into the air, then fell. "Don't look like they've got a jail to put me in."

Andy said, "You got here awful fast."

"I didn't have to come very far. Did Mrs. Landon deliver my message?"

"She did. But none of us expected fire."

The jail began caving in, sending waves of blistering heat rolling across the yard. The townspeople set up a bucket brigade. It was too late to save the jail, but they worked to keep the adjacent courthouse from catching fire.

Farley limped badly. In the flickering light of the flames Andy saw that one trousers leg was bloody. "Looks like you didn't dodge quick enough," he said.

"Like I keep tellin' you, Badger Boy, you're a damned jinx. Every time you're around, somethin' happens to me. You better take a look at Rusty. I think he's harder hit."

Rusty lay twisted on the ground, his right hand gripping a bleeding left shoulder. He swore under his breath, fighting against the pain.

Andy dropped to his knees beside him. "How bad is it?"

"Busted the shoulder, I think. Big'un done it before he turned and ran."

In a flash of anger Andy said, "I'll catch him. I'll make him wish he never got out of bed this mornin'."

"What about the Hoppers? Big'un was the only one I saw leave."

Andy made a quick survey. One Hopper was dead and one dying. Another had an arm bloody and dangling uselessly. The only one on his feet identified himself as Jaybo. The one with the bad arm refused to answer any questions beyond admitting that he was called Harp. He said, "I want a lawyer. And if I don't get a doctor, I'll bleed to death."

Andy knew that under these circumstances some Rangers would simply put another bullet into him. He was tempted. "The doctor'll see to Rusty first. He can look at you later if you're still alive."

"You'd let me sit here and die?"

Farley said angrily, "Why not? You'd've let us burn to death."

Jaybo whined, "I didn't want to come here in the first place, but Big'un—"

Harp hissed, "Shut up. Don't tell them a damned thing."

Andy said, "You're lucky you're not facin' a murder charge." He looked around. "Where's Jayce?" His eyes widened. "Anybody seen Jayce?"

His gaze swept the yard. For a moment he thought Jayce might have fallen to the Hoppers' guns.

Farley put the obvious truth into words. "I told you. He's took to the tulies, just like I said he would."

A woman's voice cried, "Jayce!" Flora Landon held her long skirt up clear of the ground as she ran across the yard to the Rangers. "Did Jayce get out?"

Andy said, "He got out, and then he lit out."

It took her a moment to absorb what Andy said. She began laughing and crying at the same time. "He got away?"

Farley said, "Slicker than a greased pig."

Solemnly Andy told her, "You know we'll have to go after him again. He's still got a murder to answer for."

"A justified killin'."

"Murder is never justified."

"A good killin' isn't always murder." Flora looked around to see who might be able to overhear. She lowered her voice. "You know what Big'un tried to do to me in Oscar Truscott's jail?"

"I heard. They said he didn't get it done."

"But he *did* get it done once before. Him and his brother Ned caught me alone at home. I couldn't fight off two of them." She looked at the ground. "I was too ashamed to tell about it, but I was so bruised up that Jayce knew by lookin' at me. That's why he killed Ned. He'd've killed Big'un too, but you Rangers never gave him the chance."

Andy thought about it. "Then it's more than just the feud. Big'un has had an extra reason for wantin' to see Jayce dead."

Flora nodded. "As long as Jayce is alive, Big'un has to be afraid he'll get the same thing Ned got."

Andy mused, "I wonder if Big'un knows Jayce is on the loose again, and it's his own doin'."

Farley pulled his trousers leg up to examine his wound. "We ought to stand back and let Jayce have him. We could arrest Jayce later and charge him for two killin's instead of one."

Andy shook his head. "That wouldn't be accordin' to law."

"Law ain't always justice. There's some things they never wrote in that book."

Andy rarely found himself agreeing with Farley, but

in this instance he thought Farley made sense. The Comanches would never fret over piddling technicalities.

The doctor had come and was examining Rusty's wounded shoulder. "How does it feel?"

Rusty sucked in a painful breath. "It hurts, damn it! How do you think it feels?"

The doctor shouted, "Somebody bring a wagon. We've got to get this man over to my house."

The wounded Harp Hopper whimpered, "I'm bleedin' to death."

The doctor said without sympathy, "I'll probably have to take your arm off. Don't be in such a hurry to part with it."

Rusty looked up at Andy. "We have to see if we can find Big'un before Jayce does."

The doctor said, "You're not going to do anything, not for a while. That shoulder looks bad."

Rusty told Andy, "Then it's up to you and Farley."

"Farley's wounded too. Not as bad as you, but he won't be ridin' for a while."

Rusty fretted, "It's too much for you to handle by yourself."

Andy put on an air of confidence to cover his doubts. "I can do it. One thing bothers me, though. I can't charge him with murderin' Sheriff Truscott. The only witnesses were Scooter and his daddy. You've already said no court would take their testimony."

"But you can charge him with attempted murder of peace officers and with malicious destruction of this jailhouse. That should put him away for a few years."

Farley grunted. "Bury him six feet under and he'll never be a bother to anybody again."

Tom Blessing had been busy with the bucket brigade. The jail finally collapsed into a blistering-hot pile of charred wood and glowing coals. Only its two stone chimneys remained, standing like markers in a graveyard. When the courthouse was out of danger Tom walked over to join the Rangers. He checked on Rusty and Farley, then said, "Your prisoner sure made a mess out of my jail."

Rusty tried to smile but could not quite bring it off. "You've been wantin' a new one for a long time."

"I can already hear the taxpayers holler. They'll say the town is peaceful and we don't keep enough prisoners here to justify the cost."

"That'll change. The town's growin'."

Blessing mused, "It's just as well that Jayce got away. I have no jail to put him in now. The best I could do would be to chain him to a tree."

Flora protested, "He's a man, not an animal. He deserves a chance."

Andy said, "He had a chance, and he took it. You have any idea where he went?"

"I expect I do. Wherever Big'un goes, that's where Jayce'll go. If you want Big'un you'd better find him before Jayce does."

"I intend to try." Andy turned away from her. He found Lige standing beside the well, his arm around Scooter's shoulder. Andy said, "You know there's paper out on you."

"It'd be a wonder on earth if there wasn't. You fixin' to put me under arrest?"

Andy was aware that Lige's rifle had helped shorten the fight. "There's just one of me. I've got two wounded Rangers and two other fugitives to worry about. So far as I know the only legitimate charges against you are from Kerrville. Your take from that bank didn't amount to more than petty larceny."

"It sure wasn't what I expected. I never thought I'd be robbed by a bank teller."

"Do you suppose if I turned my back on you for a while you could disappear without causin' any commotion about it?"

"I'd bet you a hundred dollars on it, if I had that much."

"You have anyplace to go?"

"Maybe. Me and my boy talked about it some."

Scooter asked, "You takin' me with you, Pa?"

Lige bent down and hugged his son again. "I've done aplenty of thinkin'. You're a good boy. You've got a good future if you'll stay away from the likes of me. These Rangers can find a place for you where you'll grow up straight and strong and never see a jailhouse from the inside."

"Don't go without me, Pa."

"It's best this way. You may not see me again for a while, but if you ever need me I'll come runnin'. That's a promise."

Scooter cried, "I love you, Pa."

"And I . . . hell, son, you're a man almost. Men don't say things like that." He blinked a few times. "Men don't have to."

19

WALKING TOWARD THE COURTHOUSE, BIG'UN tipped his hat to Aunt Maudie, mother of his cousin Wilbur. Her lips pinched, and her eyes flashed resentment. He wondered what kind of story her son must have told her. Damn Wilbur anyway, for deserting when he was needed most!

The reception from his aunt shook him a little. He sensed that the one awaiting him from Uncle Judd might be worse. He paused at the open door to the judge's office, summoning courage. He had imagined the scene over and over during the ride home alone. He and his cousins had managed to burn the jailhouse, but so far as he had been able to tell they had not even touched Jayce Landon or the Tennyson kid. He had seen a Ranger go down. He did not know if he was killed. The only casualties he could swear to had been on the Hopper side.

His uncle's attitude was every bit as blistering as Big'un had envisioned. Judd Hopper pushed up behind his desk and scowled like a screeching hawk about to attack. "So you're back. Why aren't you dead?"

Big'un hunched a little, bringing his arms up as if to defend himself. He was not accustomed to having to explain anything. "I done the best I could. Things just didn't work out."

"You ran off and left two cousins dead, another wounded, and one taken prisoner. If that's the best you can do, you're not worth hanging with a secondhand rope."

Big'un puzzled, "How come you already know about it?"

"The telegraph, for one thing. The word's already gone out to Rangers and local sheriffs. They'll be on the lookout for you."

"I didn't think anybody would recognize me."

"It appears they did. And by now the cousins they took prisoner have probably spilled everything they know."

"I'm not sure who they caught. I hope it's not Jaybo. He hasn't got the guts of a jackrabbit."

The judge's eyebrows arched. "Then you shouldn't have taken him along. And the others who deserted you before the fight started, they came dragging into town during the night with their tails between their legs."

"Damned cowards. I ain't real proud of this family right now."

"And most of this family is not proud of you, taking your kin out on a fool's mission. Do you know which one got killed?"

"I seen a couple of them go down. I couldn't tell which they was."

"So you ran off and left them."

"The Rangers came out shootin', and everybody ducked. They even gave Jayce Landon a gun. Can you imagine that, givin' a gun to that killer? And then some of the people from town joined in. Wasn't nothin' left but to get out of there."

"So you abandoned your kin to face it alone."

"They was of damned little use anyway. I could've done better by myself."

The judge bit the tip from a cigar and spat it halfway across the room. He lighted the cigar, his severe gaze never leaving Big'un's face. "There's one more thing I learned from the telegraph. During the excitement, Jayce got away."

Big'un was slow to grasp the significance. "Then maybe I'll get another shot at him."

"More likely he'll get one at you. You tried to burn him to death. My guess is that he's already back here among his kin. And he'll be comin' to get you if you don't get him first."

Big'un shrugged off the warning. "There's more of us Hoppers than there is of the Landons. My kinfolks won't let him come that close."

"Don't depend on your kin. You've lorded it over them for years. Now this last wild sashay . . . Everybody around here is sick and tired of that old feud. You're on your own, Big'un."

The impact began to soak in. Big'un protested, "Mostly I've just done what you told me to. You're the one who wanted me wearin' a badge in the first place."

"That was when you were useful. Lately you've been like an anvil strapped on my back."

"So you've turned against me too?"

"The stink of this will reach all the way to Austin. The Rangers will be down here like a plague of locusts, and there's no telling what they may turn up."

"I could tell them aplenty if I was of a mind to."

"You won't if you've got a brain cell still working. You'll turn tail and travel as far as you can get before the Rangers catch up with you, or Jayce does." A small knot of fear began stirring in Big'un's stomach. It burned like acid. He considered making himself scarce for a while, maybe taking a vacation in Mexico. But travel could be dangerous. The Landons would be keeping a watch on him. Jayce might catch him somewhere out in the open. Big'un was not sure he could beat him in a fair fight.

He argued, "Travelin' takes money. I ain't got any. How about openin' that safe yonder and gettin' me some, say a thousand dollars?"

Judd exploded. "A thousand dollars? You're not worth two bits." He stood up and pointed toward the door. "Get out of my office before I shoot you myself and save Jayce the trouble."

Big'un looked at the steel safe standing in the corner. Many times he had seen his uncle open it, yet he had never had reason to watch closely enough to learn the combination. Now he wished he had been more observant.

Anger churned his stomach as he moved toward the door. "You'll wish you'd done better by me."

"I wish your mother had drowned you like a sick kitten the day you were born."

Big'un was not sure what he would do. He was sure about one thing he would *not* do; he would not leave here dead broke. Uncle Judd owed him, and somehow he was going to pay. But as long as Big'un hung around here in the open, he was in jeopardy. The safest place in town would be the jail. He could bar its door from inside, and nobody would get in unless he allowed it. Unlike Tom Blessing's, this jail was of brick construction, not easy to burn down. Surely the Rangers would catch Jayce within a few days and remove him as a threat.

But what if a jury failed to convict him? Then Jayce could stalk him at leisure. Someday when Big'un did not expect it a bullet could come from nowhere and cut him down.

He had seen juries do the unthinkable, but surely they would not in this case. Murder was murder. They would see that Jayce was hanged. They had to.

Walking down the hall, he encountered several county employees, none of them kin. He saw or imagined condemnation in their eyes. Stung, he crossed the street to a small dining room where he often took his meals. The place was operated by the widow Jones, whose husband had fallen out of a wagon and broken his neck after emptying too many whiskey bottles. She looked at Big'un as if he were a stray dog bringing in fleas. Everybody in town must know what happened, he thought.

He trusted that she liked money more than she disliked him. He said, "I'd like you to deliver me my meals over at the jail for a day or two."

She arched an eyebrow. "You figure bein' in jail will save you from Jayce Landon?"

His temper flared. If a man had said that to him he would have bloodied his knuckles. "You just fetch my meals. I'm not payin' for your opinion."

"This is goin' to cost you extra. And it'll have to be payment on delivery."

He understood her implication, that Jayce might find a way to get to him. She did not want him to die owing her money.

He said, "I'll pay you, but don't send nobody else. I won't be openin' the door to just anybody."

Stung by the unfriendly receptions, Big'un went into the jail. He locked the door with a heavy key, then put an iron bar in place. Some of the fear left him, but not all.

To himself he said, "Damn you, Jayce Landon. This is all your fault."

He sat in a chair and leaned back against the jail's office wall, staring at nothing in particular, trying to come up with an idea. There was no telling how long it might take the Rangers to get Jayce. Being shut up in here for days, even weeks, was too bitter to contemplate. His thoughts kept going back to his uncle's safe. The old man always kept a substantial amount of money locked in it. It should be enough to keep him a long time in Mexico.

Gradually he came up with a plan. It was so simple he was surprised it had taken him so long.

RUSTY LAY IN A bed in the doctor's house, his shoulder heavily wrapped. The doctor had drugged him to sleep. Standing over him, Andy thought he had never seen Rusty so pale, so helpless-looking. The doctor said, "He's one tough rooster. Others have tried to kill him, but they never got it done. He'll survive this time too."

"How many more can he take?"

"I hope he never takes any more. Every chance I get, I'm going to tell him to go home and stick to the plow."

Andy felt guilt. "I'm the one who talked him into goin' back to the Rangers after that hailstorm hit him. I wish I'd kept my mouth shut."

Farley sat in a chair across the room. His trousers leg had been cut away, and his wound wrapped almost as heavily as Rusty's. He said, "You never talked Rusty into anything he didn't want to do. He quit followin' advice a long time ago."

And *you* never started, Andy thought.

The doctor said, "Maybe when he's stronger you can take Rusty back to his farm."

"That's where he belongs."

"And maybe you can find a wife for him. He needs one."

"I've got one in mind," Andy said, thinking of Alice Monahan. "But Rusty will have to come around to it on his own." He straightened. "When he wakes up, tell him I'll be back soon as I can."

Farley said, "You're not very good at listenin' to advice either, but let me give you a little. Wire Austin to send you some help before you go pokin' around over in Hopper country."

"Can't lose the time. I expect Big'un has gone back over there, and Jayce is probably not far behind. May even be ahead of him."

"Wait awhile and you won't have to bring back but one. Or if you're really lucky they'll kill each other and you won't have to mess with either of them."

"That wouldn't be Rusty's way."

"It'd save the expense of one trial, maybe two. And

it might keep us from havin' to bury an Indian kid who's got more nerve than good sense. Gravestones come high these days." Farley saw that his argument fell on deaf ears. "Wait a couple of days and I'll go with you."

The doctor said, "Forget it, Brackett. You couldn't straddle a horse if they gave you a thousand dollars."

Andy said, "I appreciate you makin' the offer. I'll swing around and let your mother and your sister know what's happened to you."

Farley protested, "They'll just fret over me for no reason. I've had a horse hurt me worse than this, steppin' on my foot."

"They deserve to know."

Andy did not allow Farley time for more argument. He walked out into the cool of the early morning. The smell of smoke was still heavy in the air, stinging his nostrils.

He met Flora Landon walking up the street from the direction of the boardinghouse where she stayed. She said, "I was on my way to see about Rusty and Farley. How do they look this mornin'?"

"They won't be runnin' footraces for a while, but they'll live."

"I want to tell them how much I appreciate what they did. They could've left Jayce to burn. Instead they gave him a gun."

Andy started to tell her Jayce got the pistol for himself, but she was in a grateful mood. He saw nothing to be gained by disillusioning her. He asked, "Is Scooter takin' to the boardin'house all right?"

"He's still hurtin' over his daddy goin' away without him, but otherwise he's all right. Been on his best behavior. If me and Jayce had ever had a boy I'd want him to be like Scooter."

"I appreciate you lookin' after him. When we've put this trouble behind us I'll take him to some folks who will make a good home for him."

"I'd take him in myself except they burned my house down, and my husband is on the dodge. I suppose you'll be goin' after him?"

"I have to, but I'm goin' for Big'un first. I hope I can get to him before Jayce does."

"Why don't you let Jayce take care of the job for you?"

"Then he'd have two murder charges on him."

"They can't hang him but once."

"With the right judge and jury he might not hang at all for one killin'. But two of them . . ." Andy shook his head.

She said, "Be careful, then. Remember that those Hoppers aren't lookin' to make new friends."

"They won't catch me asleep."

"You've got a good reason to take care of yourself. You may not realize it, but that Bethel girl is stuck on you. She'd take it hard if somethin' bad was to happen."

Andy tried to laugh away her concern. "So would I."

HIS COURAGE ALMOST LEFT him as he approached the Brackett farm. For the tenth time since he had left town, he asked himself whether he should ride in or skirt around and proceed to Hopper's Crossing. His sense of duty prevailed. He owed it to Bethel and her mother to tell them what had happened to Farley.

It seemed that he never brought anything but bad

news to this place. The women had good cause to dread seeing him. He squared his shoulders and rode straight to the house. A shrieking peacock announced his approach.

Bethel appeared on the front porch, one hand shading her eyes. She anxiously searched Andy's face for a clue and asked, "Is it about Farley again?"

It was unlikely she had already heard. He wished he did not have to be the bearer of the news. "He's been shot."

She swallowed. "How bad?"

"Not as bad as it could've been. He was strong enough to give me a cussin' when I told him I was comin' here."

"He'll be cussin' when he draws his last breath." She made an effort at a smile, but it was stillborn.

Bethel's mother stepped through the door and joined her daughter. "What is it? Farley again?"

Andy tried to ease her mind as quickly as he could. "He'll be all right, Mrs. Brackett." He dismounted and moved closer to the porch.

Bethel said, "He's been shot again, Mama. I swear, he draws trouble like a magnet."

Andy told them, "Wasn't none of it his fault. It happened in the line of duty." He explained about the burning of the jail and its occupants' escape under fire. "Farley took a bullet in his leg. He'll be limpin' around for a while. But Rusty's the one to worry about. He got hit pretty hard."

"Where is Farley now?" Mrs. Brackett asked.

"At the doctor's house. Doc was sayin' he'd probably let him go to a boardin'house by tomorrow or next day."

Mrs. Brackett said, "He doesn't need to go to a boardinghouse. Bethel and I will take a wagon and fetch him home."

"He didn't even want me to come and let you know what happened. Didn't want you frettin'. Said he'd ride over here and tell you himself as soon as he could get on a horse."

Bethel said, "I wouldn't bet two bits on that. As soon as he felt like he could travel, he'd leave without lettin' us know. He's taken a fool notion that nobody cares about him."

Andy doubted that anybody other than immediate family cared much for Farley. Even they found him a trial. He went out of his way to ruffle those who might try to get close to him. He seemed to distrust friendship as if he knew it would not last. During the war it had not. He had lost too many friends, too much family.

Bethel said, "We appreciate you coming out to tell us."

Andy said, "It wasn't much out of my way. I'm goin' to Hopper's Crossing."

"You're after Jayce Landon, I suppose."

"Him and Big'un Hopper both. I figure where I find one I'll likely find the other."

Her eyes widened. "You're goin' by yourself?"

"There ain't but two of them."

Bethel grimaced. "That's about what Farley would say."

"There probably won't be but one if I don't find them myself before they find one another."

"If they shot each other it would stop a lot of misery for both families."

"That's just what Farley said."

"But you're goin' anyway."

"It's my job."

She blinked away a tear. "Someday they'll be haulin' you here like Farley, wounded or worse. Is your job worth that?"

"The only thing I know for sure is that I have to do it. Else I couldn't look Rusty and the rest of them in the face."

"If you get killed, do you think they'll cry over you?"

"I won't know about it one way or the other."

This time she let the tear roll down her cheek, unchecked. "*I'd* cry for you, Andy."

HE WAITED UNTIL DARK before riding in to Hopper's Crossing. From across the street he surveyed the jail, remembering the night he and Farley had taken it upon themselves to guard it against a mob, needlessly, as it turned out. Through a barred window he saw a faint glow as if a lamp's wick was turned down low. Looking around to see if anyone was watching, he dismounted and walked over for a closer look. He found that cotton cloth had been tacked up on the inside. It was thin enough to allow lamplight to show but heavy enough that Andy could not see through it.

He stood awhile, watching and wondering until someone cautiously lifted a corner of the cloth. Andy saw little more than one eye, but he was almost certain: Big'un was behind that crude curtain.

He did not know what to make of it. It seemed unlikely that Big'un had come back and resumed his sheriff's duties as if nothing had happened. Yet there he was. Andy flirted for a moment with the idea of try-

ing the door, but Big'un would be careful enough to
have locked and barred it. He remembered that it was
too strong for one man to break it down.

Hearing voices, he stepped into the darkness and
flattened himself against the jail wall. Boots trod heavily upon the wooden sidewalk, stopping at the jail
door. Someone demanded, "Big'un, open this door."

From inside came a familiar voice. "Who's out
there?"

"Your uncle Judd. I want to talk to you."

"You already done more talkin' than I want to listen
to. Unless you've brought me some money, that door
stays shut."

"The jail is county property. As county judge I'm
orderin' you to open up."

"For all I know, Jayce Landon is waitin' out there in
the dark. All he needs is for me to open this door and
give him a clean shot."

"Have you lost all your guts, boy?"

"Havin' guts is one thing. Bein' stupid is another.
You know Jayce won't give me a fightin' chance."

"And I know why. Just about everybody in town
knows." The judge cursed softly to the man who was
with him. "On account of Big'un, the Hopper name
doesn't mean what it used to around here. Before long
every dog in town will be hiking its leg at us."

The two men walked away, the judge still grumbling.

If the situation had not been so serious Andy might
have laughed at the irony of Big'un Hopper having
made himself, in effect, a prisoner in his own jail.

Knowing the effort would probably be futile, he
knocked on the door with the butt of his pistol.
"Big'un, open up."

Big'un hollered, "I told you, Uncle, I'm done talkin' to you."

"This is Andy Pickard. Texas Ranger. You're under arrest."

Big'un did not answer for a moment. "Arrest? Are you crazy? I'm in here, and you're out there. You ain't comin' in, and I ain't comin' out."

"Give up to me and I'll take you somewhere that Jayce can't get to you."

"I ain't afraid of Jayce."

"Looks to me like you are. Else you wouldn't have locked yourself up in there."

"Go to hell."

"I'm just tryin' to give you a chance."

"I'll make my own chances. Now git!"

Andy had not expected Big'un to surrender, at least not right away, but maybe this would get him to thinking. "If you decide you want my protection, send somebody to find me. I'll be around."

Andy thought that Big'un was not likely to go anywhere for a while, not until he was sick and tired of self-imposed imprisonment. He rode down to the livery stable. The hostler showed surprise. "You all by yourself, Ranger?"

"There isn't anybody else. The other two Rangers got wounded."

"I heard about that. Good news is a long time comin', but bad news spreads in a hurry. Which one are you after, Jayce or Big'un?"

"Both. I know where Big'un is at, for now. Got any idea where Jayce might be?"

The hostler shook his head. "I've got to live with both sides. Wouldn't want anybody accusin' me of bein' a gossip. But if it was me lookin', I'd say go where the Landons are the thickest. Maybe out to Walter Landon's farm."

"Have you seen Jayce yourself?"

The hostler let the question die unanswered. "You want me to put your horse up?"

"That was my first intention, but now I think I'll go to Walter Landon's."

"You'd better either sing out loud or tiptoe like you was walkin' on eggs. Them Landons don't appreciate surprises, and they are uncommon good shots." He paused, staring at Andy with some apprehension. "They ain't the kind that forgives easy. I'd rather you never told them you even talked with me."

"I'm not a gossip either."

There was probably not a bigger gossip in town than the stableman, but in this instance Andy felt that he would keep his mouth shut. He could not mention having seen Andy without being asked what they talked about. Andy had rather his return to Hopper's Crossing not be noised around before he had time to size up his options. He had not seen many so far.

He knew the way to Walter Landon's farm, though he lost it in the moonlight a couple of times where lesser wagon roads split off from the main one. As he began to discern lamplight in the front windows he wondered which of the hostler's recommendations he should choose: to ride in announcing himself or to sneak in and observe quietly.

His first instinct was to see before being seen, but three hound dogs took the decision out of his hands. As they began barking and trotted to meet him, the lamplight winked out. He suspected that one or more rifles or shotguns were aimed in his general direction. He shouted, "Hello, the house."

No one immediately shot at him, so he felt hopeful.

A voice answered, "Who's that out yonder?"

"Andy Pickard, Ranger. You-all remember me."

"Are you by yourself?" The voice sounded familiar, though he could not identify it.

"There's nobody but me." He rode up almost to the front porch, hoping the moon provided enough light that they could see he was alone. He raised his hands.

A match flared, and the lamp burned again. A man stepped out onto the porch. The light was at his back so Andy could not see the face. He thought he knew the man by his shape and his stance.

He said, "Howdy, Jayce."

He heard a chuckle. "Sorry, Andy. Come closer and look again."

Moving up, he recognized Jayce's Ranger brother. "Dick?" He recalled how much the Landon brothers resembled one another. At a distance it would be difficult to tell which was which. "I thought you were still in camp on the San Saba."

"I took a leave of absence to be at my brother's trial. But it seems like you-all can't hold on to Jayce long enough for him to get a shave."

"He had a close shave at the jail. We all did."

"I know. I'm grateful that you-all got him out."

Andy suspected Dick had heard about it from Jayce. "He took care of himself. I've got no credit comin'."

"So now you're here hopin' to take him back."

Andy nodded. "Him and Big'un Hopper both."

"Just you?"

"I'm all there is."

"It might get you killed."

Andy suggested, "You're still a Ranger. You could help me."

"I already turned my brother in once. It's weighed on my conscience ever since. I wouldn't do it again for anybody." Dick jerked his head toward the door. "Tie your horse and come on in. We're all friends here."

For the moment perhaps, but Andy knew that attitudes would change in a hurry if he tried to take Jayce back to jail. He wrapped the reins around a post and went up onto the porch. He asked, "Can you look me square in the eye and tell me Jayce ain't here?"

Dick smiled. "If I tell you where he ain't, you might figure out where he *is*. My duty as a Ranger is on leave till I go back to camp."

Andy stopped abruptly in the open door. Flora stood in the front room with a couple of men, one of them Walter Landon, and a woman he guessed was Walter's wife.

Dick said, "You know Flora, of course."

Getting over his initial surprise, Andy told her, "I'm bettin' Jayce himself brought you here."

She said, "I didn't need Jayce to show me the way. My home is just over the hill, what's left of it." It was the kind of answer that said neither yes nor no.

He said, "I thought you were takin' care of Scooter."

"Tom Blessing's wife took him out to their farm. Big'un wouldn't dare do him harm out there, even if he could find the place."

Dick said to Andy, "I didn't know you-all had the boy. What're you goin' to do with him?"

"When Rusty is ready to travel we intend to take Scooter up north to the Monahan family."

"I couldn't think of a better place for him. I know you and Rusty have shared some hard times with the Monahans, and some good times too."

"I've seen them go down bruised and bloody, but they always got up and went on with their lives."

"That's like us Landons." Dick rolled and lighted a cigarette, his eyes narrowed in thought. "You're takin' on too much of a load to tote by yourself. You'd best forget about catchin' Jayce. I'd be tickled to help you with Big'un, though."

Andy wondered if anyone had told Dick of the outrage Big'un and his brother Ned had forced on Flora. It was not his place to do so. Gunning for Big'un would be legal for Dick so long as he did it within his duty as a Ranger, but to do it for personal vengeance would outlaw him, as killing Ned Hopper had outlawed Jayce.

Dick asked, "Have you got a plan?"

"Not a trace. I'm hopin' somethin' will break in my direction."

Andy had a strong hunch Jayce was somewhere within shouting distance. He ventured a few probing questions that yielded him nothing. He realized that if he captured Jayce he would have to do it somewhere else. These people protected their own.

Dick said, "It's time to hit the soogans. I've been rollin' my blankets out here on the porch."

Andy took that as an oblique invitation to stay the night. It seemed a good idea if he was right about Jayce being near. Dick accompanied him to a corral, where he unsaddled his horse and turned him loose. He removed a blanket rolled and tied behind the cantle of his saddle. Back at the front porch he lay looking at the stars, crisp and sparkling in the chilled fall air. He caught the faint odor of Dick's cigarette.

He asked, "Why do you reckon it is that so many people can't find a way to live together? If they haven't got somethin' to fight about, they'll make up a reason. I'll bet you've got no notion how the feud started in the first place."

"I've always laid it on the stubbornness of the Hoppers, but I can't truthfully say they're more stubborn than us Landons. If one of us didn't start a fight, the other one would. I remember us young'uns jumpin' on the Hopper boys and fightin' when they hadn't even done anything to us."

"Maybe a Landon and a Hopper ought to marry one another. Things might get peaceful if everybody was kin."

Dick grunted dissent. "Things would just turn meaner. You ever watch a bunch of in-laws get together?"

Andy had never seen much of family life except among the Indians. There, just as in the white community, relationships could be fragile as glass. He said, "I get the idea that Big'un is the main one keepin' the feud stirred up."

"Him and his brother Ned. Ned's gone now, but Big'un is still a bad apple spoilin' the barrel. And behind Big'un is old Judge Hopper. He never gets his knuckles bloody, but he keeps stirrin' the pot. While everybody watches the fightin', he dips his hands into the county treasury."

"I'll bet if the Rangers got to lookin' around they could clean the judge's plow."

"Probably. But I can't put a halo around Jayce's head either. Even if he is my brother, I have to admit that he's done a lot to keep the fight goin'."

Andy thought before he asked, "Do you think Flora saw that side of him before she married?"

"I tried to tell her, but she wasn't ready to listen. After they went to the preacher it wasn't my place to tell her anything anymore. I tried to get Jayce to leave here when I did, to take her away from this part of the country and let the old fight die. But he didn't want to turn aloose. It had got in his blood like whiskey does for some people." He snubbed out his cigarette. "Flora deserves better than that."

ANDY HAD GUESSED WRONG. Big'un did not stay put.

Big'un was wary about going out the jail's front door, which faced the town's main business street. Even the back door could not be considered safe, but at least it was darker on that side of the courthouse square. Staying in the shadows as much as he could, he headed for the wagon yard. He had left his horse there in an open corral. He wished he could get his mount and go without the stableman seeing him, but that was not to be. The skinny hostler watched him saddling his horse and asked, "Where you goin' this time of the night, Big'un?"

"Vacation." Damn a man who asked personal questions, he thought. This nosy dickens's jaw would still be moving a week after they buried him.

"Ain't you afraid you'll run into a booger, travelin' in the dark?"

"The boogers we've got around here, they're even worse in the daylight."

Big'un tied his blankets and war bag on the saddle. As soon as he got his hands on a chunk of his uncle's money he would be gone. He was not sure how he would fit in Mexico, but if he liked it he might be a long time coming back. At least he wouldn't have to keep looking over his shoulder for that back-shooting Jayce Landon. And he would have a border between himself and the Rangers.

He reined his horse toward a quarry where workers cut building stones a few hundred yards from town. He had watched them use dynamite from a wooden shed. He had not learned much about handling dynamite beyond how to set a fuse and touch it off without blowing himself up. He figured that was enough in this case.

He had no idea how much he needed for the job, so he made a guess and tucked a box under his arm. It was about half full. He rode back to town and tied his horse to the fence behind the courthouse on the side opposite his uncle's office. Carrying the dynamite, he tried the back door and found it locked. He watched and listened before he drew his pistol and broke a pane. Reaching inside, he freed the lock. He waited and listened again until he was confident nobody had paid any attention to the sound of breaking glass.

The courthouse was almost pitch dark, but he had been to Uncle Judd's office so many times he could have found it in his sleep. He bumped into a desk on his way in, then felt his way along until he came to the safe. By feel more than by sight, he set the fuse and placed the stick back in the box with the others. He propped the box against the safe door, lighted the fuse, and moved out into the hallway to escape the blast.

The hallway was not far enough. The concussion lifted him off his feet and hurled him down the hall. His ears drummed with pain. Papers and pens and other small objects went flying. Windows shattered, and dust billowed like a dry fog.

Choking, he made his way back into what remained of his uncle's office. He saw a gaping hole in the outer wall. Glass crunching beneath his brogan shoes, he made his way to it and saw the safe lying outside. It was turned over, the door pressed against the ground. It would take several men to turn it.

Big'un did not know words strong enough to express his exasperation, but he tried all the ones he could think of. They didn't help. He could imagine his uncle Judd going into a mouth-foaming fit over this. Well, the money-grubbing old son of a bitch had it coming. It was his own fault.

Discretion told him he had better be moving before a curious crowd swarmed the damaged courthouse. He hurried out the back door and around the building. He feared the blast had frightened the horse into running away, but it was still straining against the tied reins. He patted it on the neck in an effort to calm it. As soon as he could get it to quit faunching around he mounted and set it into a long trot.

The stableman came running out through the barn's wide doors. He shouted, "What happened, Big'un?"

"Lightnin' strike." Big'un spurred his horse into a lope.

He had burned down a jailhouse and blown up a courthouse. Whatever might happen from now on, at least Hopper's Crossing would not soon forget him.

20

ANDY AWAKENED FROM A COLD HALF-SLEEP HE HAD endured most of the night. A bloodred sun was just beginning to rise. His muscles ached from the discomfort of lying on the porch's hard floor. He felt around for his pistol but could not find it.

Dick Landon had already rolled his blanket and placed it against the wall. He said, "Don't you worry about that six-shooter. You'll get it back when we figure it's safe."

"Safe for who?"

"All of us, includin' you."

Andy sensed the reason it had been taken. "What time did Jayce get here?"

"He was here all the time. Him and Flora slept out in the barn. They're in the kitchen now havin' breakfast. You hungry?"

"Think Jayce will trust me?"

"No, but as long as you're not heeled there won't be any trouble."

Andy pulled his boots on. The air had the crisp smell of fall but not yet of frost. If Rusty had not suffered from that hailstorm he would be harvesting his fields, not lying in the doctor's house badly shot up. Andy wondered what Rusty would think of him now, about to share breakfast with a fugitive on the fugitive's terms.

Andy looked at the blazing sunrise. "I've heard them say that a red sky at sunup means there's a storm comin'."

"Only if you get reckless."

Jayce stood in the door, looking calm and friendly. "Come in, Ranger, and let Flora pour you some coffee. Eggs and biscuits are about ready. Walter's family has done et."

Andy followed Dick through the door. He sneaked Dick's pistol out of its holster and stuck it into his boot while all attention was on Flora at the woodstove. She poured coffee into an enameled cup for Andy. He thanked her and turned to Jayce. He said, "I was hopin' you'd be halfway to Mexico by now. I wouldn't have to take you in."

Smiling at Andy's show of confidence, Jayce poured coffee into a saucer and blew across to cool it. "Sorry about your friend Rusty. Hell, I'm even a little sorry about that ornery Farley Brackett."

Andy wrapped his stiff fingers around the cup, enjoying its warmth. "You got away from that jailhouse fire awful quick."

"I saw Big'un light out. Thought I could catch him, but I lost him in the dark. I didn't see any point in stayin' around, so I borrowed some citizen's horse. I wish you'd take it back to him with my thanks."

"You can ride it back yourself when I take you in."

"You don't ever give up, do you?"

Dick Landon spoke. "It's the Indian in him. Did you know he was raised by the Comanches?"

"I ought to've figured."

Flora said, "As soon as I saw that Rusty and Farley were not goin' to die and I put Scooter in good hands, I followed my husband."

Jayce said, "I'd already told her that if I ever had a chance to get away I'd head for home. She'd know where to find me."

Both Jayce and Flora looked sleepy-eyed. Andy remarked, "After so much travelin', you-all appear sort of worn out."

The two smiled at each other. Jayce reached out to touch Flora's hand. "I take it you're not a married man."

Andy said, "Never been asked."

"When the time comes, be sure you get a girl like Flora. But not Flora herself. She's mine."

"You and her could still get away from here. There's not much I could do to stop you so long as your family has got me a prisoner."

"There's one job I ain't finished yet."

"Big'un?"

"He's done a lot of dirt to us Landons." Jayce's face tightened as he looked at his wife. "What kind of man would I be if I just let it go?"

"A live one, and free."

Andy saw something in Flora's eyes. He saw that he had reached her whether he had reached Jayce or not. She told Jayce, "If we stay here you know what'll happen. Big'un will find a way to shoot you in the back if

you don't get him first. And if you get him, the law will
give you a quick trial and then hang you. Either way,
I'll wind up bein' a widow. I want us to go somewhere
and start fresh."

"I can't forget what Big'un done to you."

"I can. Revenge isn't worth it. I'd rather have my
husband alive and at my side. The law will take care of
Big'un, or the devil will."

Jayce argued, "Maybe you've forgot that murder
charge against me, but the law hasn't."

Andy said, "That's Texas law. But you could go
someplace like Colorado or maybe California. They
never heard of Ned Hopper or you either."

He could see that Jayce was struggling. Jayce said,
"Before I go anywhere I'd like to have the personal
pleasure of sendin' Big'un to hell."

Andy had never quite grasped the concept of an
eternal fiery hell for sinful souls. It was not part of the
Comanche religion. "There's hell enough right here on
earth, Jayce. At the least we can send Big'un to the
penitentiary for a long stretch. At the best we might be
able to hang him for killin' Sheriff Truscott."

"I got a little inklin' of the real hell before we got
out of that burnin' jailhouse. That's the kind I favor
sendin' him to."

Andy pushed his plate away with half the bacon and
eggs uneaten. "Jayce, they'd drum me out of the
Rangers if they heard me say this. What if I was to turn
my back for a while, and you and Flora was to slip
away real quiet? I'd be so busy huntin' for Big'un that
I might not even miss you for three or four days."

Flora said, "He's offerin' us the best chance we'll

ever have, Jayce. We can get away from this awful old feud, away from Big'un and all the other Hoppers."

Dick said, "Listen to her, Jayce. Her and Andy are givin' you the best advice you'll ever hear."

Jayce looked across the table at Andy. "If I go, I want everybody to understand that it's for Flora and not because I'm scared of Big'un. I'd gladly meet him face-to-face, but he'd never do that. He'd lay in wait somewhere and bushwhack me."

Andy replied, "That's the way I see it. The longer you stay around here, the less chance you've got of seein' Christmas. If I was you two, I'd saddle up and git while the gittin's good."

Jayce said, "I'm bein' ganged up on. I guess I can't outargue you all."

Flora nodded at Jayce. He pushed back from the table. "Ain't got much to pack." Flora started to follow him out the door but stopped long enough to lean down and kiss Andy on the cheek.

Andy saw a wistful look in Dick's eyes as his gaze followed Flora out the door.

Dick said, "Andy, you've just violated a basic Ranger regulation. You've let a prisoner go."

"I never really took him prisoner." Andy reached down to draw Dick's pistol from his boot. He laid it on the table in front of him. "You can have your six-shooter back."

Dick dropped his hand and felt of his empty holster. "Well, I'll be damned." His eyes narrowed. "Would you really have used this?"

"I don't know. I'm glad I didn't have to find out."

Andy finished his coffee then walked outside, where

Dick watched his brother and Flora lead two horses out
of the corral. Dick said, "You've got me beat. I never
could talk Jayce into anything. All I could ever do was
wish him luck and cover his back when I could. I got
so tired of it that I had to leave."

Jayce pulled his saddle down from the plank fence.
As he picked up his blanket, he dropped suddenly to
one knee and grabbed his leg. Andy heard the crack of
a rifle. He saw a wisp of smoke in a patch of timber a
couple of hundred yards away.

Flora dropped her saddle and screamed, "He's
shot."

Andy and Dick ran toward the couple. With a shout
of rage Flora yanked a rifle from Jayce's saddle scabbard. She threw it to her shoulder and fired, then fired
again.

Dick shouted, "Come on, Andy, let's catch the son
of a bitch."

Andy paused for a swift look at Jayce. His trousers
leg was bloody. The wound was far from any vital
spot.

Dick grabbed Jayce's saddle and threw it on the
horse Jayce had been about to ride. Andy quickly
caught Flora's horse and put his own saddle on its
back. Dick was fifty yards ahead of him as Andy
mounted, but he soon caught up.

BIG'UN EXULTED FOR A moment when he saw Jayce go
down. Then he felt the breath of the first bullet as it
passed by his ear. He turned to grab his horse as the
second bullet struck. It was as if a sledgehammer had
hit him in the side. He went to his knees, almost losing

his hold on the reins. The air was knocked out of his lungs. He gasped desperately for breath. Each try felt as if someone were jabbing a knife into his side.

For a moment he went into a blind panic. My God, they've killed me, he thought. Slowly he began breathing, but with breath came feeling. The wound in his side began to hurt like nothing he had ever felt in his life. He knew he had some broken ribs, probably a punctured lung. He exerted a heavy effort struggling to his feet and drawing himself up against his horse. He made several tries before he was able to lift his left foot into the stirrup, then pull himself into the saddle. He leaned far forward and came near to falling off.

He grabbed the horn of the saddle and beat his heels against the horse's ribs, putting it into a long trot, then a lope. He tried to turn his head and look back, but dizziness overtook him. It threatened to make him lose his seat. He reasoned that some of the Landons must be coming behind him. They would have started their pursuit as soon as they could grab horses.

This was going to be a ride for life.

He wished now he had followed his plan to quit the Colorado River country and immediately head for Mexico. But he had feared that Jayce would follow him no matter where and how far he went. He had to eliminate Jayce before he could feel safe anywhere.

Now he had failed in that as he had failed with the jailhouse fire and with his attempt to blow Judd Hopper's safe open. Seemed like he couldn't do anything right anymore.

He wondered when his luck had started to sour. Maybe it was when he and Ned found Flora Landon at home alone. They had grabbed the opportunity to drag her back to her bedroom. He had always thought her one of the most provocative women he had ever seen. Taking her as he had should have been pleasurable, especially considering that she was the wife of a lifelong antagonist and this represented a victory of sorts. Instead, it had left him strangely unsatisfied. It also left him with bruises and abrasions that lingered long after the fleeting moment of pleasure.

The world went by him in a blur as he rode. With each stride, pain drove through him like a lance. Tasting blood, he rubbed his mouth and saw red smeared across the palm of his hand. He knew coughing up blood was a sign that life was ebbing away. He was bleeding to death.

He felt his hand loosen on the horn despite his effort to tighten his grip. He was conscious of slipping from the saddle. Striking the ground set off an explosion of agony as shattered ribs punched into a lung. He tasted dirt and tried to spit it out. He lacked strength to raise his head. Face against the ground, he managed a few more breaths until the dirt he inhaled choked him.

His last conscious thought was, "Damn you, Flora, this is all your fault. And you wasn't worth it."

DURING THE CHASE, ANDY and Dick had never come close enough to catch more than a glimpse of Big'un. They had to follow tracks, which slowed them. Andy said, "We don't even know for sure that it *is* Big'un."

Dick said, "Who else would've shot at Jayce? He could be anyplace out yonder, settin' up an ambush for us."

"I don't think he's a good shot. He just nicked Jayce in the leg."

Andy was first to see the saddled bay horse grazing peacefully where the grass still contained some green. Dick said, "That's Big'un's, all right. I've seen him ridin' it around the country."

At first Andy thought Dick might be right about Big'un setting up an ambush. Then he saw the still form of a man stretched in the grass. Wind rolled Big'un's hat along the ground and picked at the loose tail of his shirt. "That'd be him, I suppose."

Dick said, "Flora must've hit him." She was the only one who had fired in Big'un's direction.

Andy drew his pistol in case Big'un might be playing possum. Riding up close, however, he could tell that Big'un was dead. He dismounted and turned Big'un over onto his back. Much of the man's clothing was soaked in blood.

He said, "That's the way the hide hunters like to hit a buffalo, in the lung. Looks to me like he bled to death."

Dick got down for a look. "The slower the better. I hope he had time to consider all his sins."

Andy closed Big'un's half-open eyes. "He's been worried that Jayce was out to kill him. I wonder if he had any idea it was Flora who brought him down."

"Seems like justice to me, seein' what he did to her."

"All the same, this could cause her some trouble if she stays around here in Hopper country."

Dick shrugged. "Nothin' we can do about that. We've got to go to town and report what happened."

Andy considered. "Maybe not. What if Big'un just

disappeared and nobody ever knew what happened to him?"

Dick appeared intrigued.

Andy said, "We could tell them we lost his tracks. It should all seem natural enough. Big'un took his shot at Jayce and saw that it didn't kill him, so he quit the country. Lots of people drift away and are never heard from again. Everybody would figure after a while that he found him a safe place and decided to settle there for good."

"But what about his body?"

"All we need is a shovel."

Dick gave him a quizzical look. "That's crafty. Some of your Comanche raisin'?"

"I'm just thinkin' it would take care of several problems. If Jayce knew Big'un is dead he might decide not to leave. Then I'd have to arrest him and take him to trial. You know how that would likely come out, especially in this county."

Dick said, "I know a farmer who lives over the hill. He's not much for talkin', and he'd lend us a shovel without askin' questions. What about Big'un's horse?"

"We'll unsaddle him and turn him loose to find his way home. Folks'll figure Big'un caught a fresh horse and left for a better climate. With him and Jayce both gone, maybe the feud will die away."

They wrapped Big'un in his saddle blanket and buried him with his saddle and bridle. Andy watched the bay horse roll in the dirt then wander off, oblivious to the drama that had played out around him. Andy took a tree branch and smoothed the ground, hoping to hide the fact that it contained a grave. "It don't seem right without somebody sayin' some words over him."

Dick shook his head. "Wouldn't make any difference. He was beyond prayer a long time ago."

SCOOTER HELD THE WAGON team's reins, for his leg still pained him when he tried to sit on a horse. Rusty, his shoulder still bound, sat beside him on the wagon seat, restless eyes searching over the terrain. Andy rode horseback beside them, watching nervousness build in both Rusty and Scooter. The extra horses were tied on behind the wagon.

Rusty said, "The more I think about this, the more I get to wonderin' if it's right to burden the Monahans with me. I could heal all right in the Ranger camp."

Scooter asked, "What if they don't like me? And I don't know if I'll like them either." He still grieved over parting with his father.

Andy replied, "The Monahans wrote and told you-all to come, that they'd be glad to have you both. Anyway, Rusty, you've already been took off of the pay roster. Captain said anybody who's been shot up that much ought to retire before he gets himself killed. You've gotten to be a bad risk."

The captain had come near to taking Andy off of the roster too. "Look at your record," he had said. "You went off to transport a prisoner but lost him."

"It was the sheriff that lost him," Andy countered.

"Even so, he got caught a second time and you lost him again. Then there was the old bank robber, the boy's daddy. You had a chance to grab him but didn't.

And that jailhouse arsonist—you ought to've caught him but let him slip through your fingers. Lord knows where any of them are now. That is not a good record for a Ranger, even a green recruit."

Andy had said, "I'll bet I can learn better, sir."

"From what I've been told you showed initiative on several occasions. That is a point in your favor even if the results were not as we might have wanted. I'll give you another chance, but you are on probation, Private Pickard."

Andy had thanked him for his generosity and then accepted leave to take Rusty and the boy to the Mona-han family. Andy knew he had not followed the letter of the law, but he felt that he had served justice. That was the more important consideration.

A wheel dropped into a shallow hole and jolted the wagon. Scooter said, "Sorry, Rusty. I didn't see that one. I'll never make a teamster."

"You can make yourself into anything you want to be. You've just got to work hard at it."

"I'd like to be a Ranger someday, like you and Andy."

"You can do it if you want it bad enough. But by the time you get there things are liable to be considerable different. In my early days we mostly fought Indians. That's about come to an end. Now we're fightin' rob-bers and stock thieves, murderers, border jumpers, and the like. But we've got more to fight them with, like the telegraph. And they're startin' to build railroads across Texas. In a few years a Ranger will be able to put a horse on a train and take him halfway across the state in a day, then jump off ready for a chase. Show me the criminal who can beat that."

Andy said, "The way you talk, I think you'd still like to be a part of it."

Rusty shook his head. His hair that used to be red was rusty now, gray softening the color. "No, these last weeks convinced me it's time to hang up the six-shooter and take hold of a plow handle. This body has taken too many beatin's."

"The state will lose a good Ranger."

"But it'll gain a pretty good farmer."

A boy of about Scooter's size loped toward them on a paint horse, waving a misshapen felt hat over his head. He shouted, "Andy! Rusty!"

Andy pushed out a little in front to meet him. "Howdy, Billy. Still growin' too fast for your clothes, I see."

The boy rode up on Rusty's side of the wagon. "You been shot again? How many times does this make?"

"Too many," Rusty said, grinning. "How's all your folks?"

"Ready and anxious to see you."

Billy gave Scooter a critical scrutiny. "You the boy that's comin' to live with us?"

Scooter was ill at ease. "That's what everybody's tellin' me."

Billy considered for a bit. "I guess that'll be all right."

The Monahan homestead came into view. Billy said, "I'll lope on ahead and tell them to put supper in the stove."

Rusty leaned forward as if he could see the place better from the edge of his seat. "You'll like these folks when you get to know them, Scooter. They're the nearest thing to a family that I've got. I've seen happy days with them, and I've seen bitter tears."

"So I've heard," Scooter said.

Andy had told Scooter most of what he knew about the Monahans, about the tragedies they had suffered during the war because they had held to their Union sympathies, about their struggle to rebuild after the hostilities, about the loss of the patriarchs and the death of Josie Monahan, who was to have been Rusty's wife.

Rusty said, "The Monahans have been through more hell than most people ever ought to suffer. But they've always gotten up, squared their shoulders, and started again." His face went grim. "That's what we all have to do when trouble knocks us down. Else life will grind us into the ground."

"Like it did you when Josie was killed?"

Rusty looked at him sharply, then at Andy. "He told you about that, did he?"

Andy looked away, his face reddening. He had not considered that the guileless boy would say whatever popped into his mind.

Scooter said, "He told me Josie has a sister who's a lot like her."

Rusty's expression slowly mellowed. "Maybe a little bit."

The whole Monahan clan was waiting as the wagon pulled up to the house. Mother Clemmie, limping a little from lingering aftereffects of a stroke, led the greetings. She hugged Andy, then Rusty, taking care for the bandaged shoulder. She turned then to Scooter. "This is the boy you wrote about? I'm goin' to have to fatten him up some. Like he is, he won't hardly throw a shadow."

Andy shook hands with everybody who came up to greet him, then realized he had missed someone. Alice.

She and Rusty stood on the other side of the wagon. They had shaken hands, then neglected to turn loose.

Preacher Webb gave the blessing before supper, expressing special thanks for Rusty's survival and wishing a better future for the new boy who was to share the family's bed and board. Through supper Scooter and Billy kept eyeing each other nervously.

Afterward Webb sat down to read his Bible, though Andy was sure he already knew it by heart. Billy asked Scooter to go with him out to the barn. "We've got some new puppies. Maybe you can help me name them."

"I've never had a puppy," Scooter said.

"You can have one of these for your own if it likes you."

Andy stood at the window, watching the two boys start walking toward the barn, then break into a run. He turned back to help Clemmie and her married daughter Geneva clear the table. He said, "I'd best go look for Rusty."

Clemmie caught his arm. "I wouldn't disturb him right now, was I you."

Andy saw Rusty sitting on the front porch, talking to Alice. Clemmie smiled. So did Geneva. Clemmie asked, "How would you like some more of that cobbler pie, Andy?"

He said, "Sounds real good to me."

AFTERWORD

LIFE IN TEXAS WAS CHANGING RAPIDLY IN THE post–Civil War decade of the 1870s, the setting of this story. The long and much-resented federal occupation had ended. The disenfranchised former Confederates regained their vote, allowing them to elect state and local governments of their own choosing. They adopted a new constitution guaranteeing their individual rights.

The Texas Rangers organization had disintegrated during the war years and was abolished by the federally established postwar government. One of the first acts of newly elected governor Richard Coke in 1874 was to reorganize this force, which had first been called into service by colonizer Stephen F. Austin in 1823. Though a special frontier battalion stood watch at the outer edges of settlement, guarding against Indian incursion, a majority of the state's Rangers now concentrated on suppression of crime and violence.

A vigorous army campaign in the fall of 1874 drove

most Comanches, Kiowas, and other hostile Plains tribes to reservations. Buffalo hunters were systematically annihilating the vast shaggy herds, forcing the Indians into dependency on the government and opening the Plains for permanent white settlement. Apart from relatively small outbreaks, Indian trouble was over for most of the state. The Apaches continued to roam a few more years in far West Texas, but settlement there was sparse and remained so until most of the more productive Texas land was taken.

Law enforcement was the Rangers' main concern now, and the challenge was formidable. The war had left Texas threadbare. Veterans returned to find their families in deplorable straits, often losing land and home to opportunists who flocked in to reap where they had not sown. The excesses of corrupt officials had bred a widespread contempt for law and an acceptance of violence as a means to accomplish what might otherwise not be possible.

From its beginnings, Texas had been subject to savage feuds. In one case Sam Houston felt obliged to call out the army to quell a particularly bitter fight. Other feuds flared in the combative postwar climate and required response by the Rangers to cool them down.

The border with Mexico had bred racial conflict almost constantly since the Texas revolution and would continue to do so well into the twentieth century. Border jumpers were a major problem for the Rangers in the 1870s. Captain Leander McNelly once stacked the bodies of a dozen bandits in Brownsville's town square as an object lesson. However, the Rangers had never forgotten the Alamo and were prone at times to administer punishment to Mexicans simply for being Mexicans without regard to guilt or innocence.

Cattle drives to the northern railroads were bringing fresh money into an impoverished state. They increased the value of range cattle and encouraged rustling, sometimes on a massive scale. Rustling required physical labor, however. Robbing banks was easier.

The banking industry grew in response to Texas's gradual economic recovery. Banks became a prime target for robbery by organized gangs as well as ambitious individual entrepreneurs who might rationalize that they were simply carrying on the Civil War against Northern interests.

The Rangers embraced new technology to help them meet these challenges. The spread of the telegraph meant that word of a crime could be flashed instantly across the state. Texas railroads, though few and of a limited regional nature, were beginning to plan expansions that would revolutionize travel by the early part of the next decade. That would allow Rangers and other law officers rapid transportation no outlaw's horse could outrun.

A few people were already experimenting with Alexander Graham Bell's new invention. Shortly telephone lines would be spreading across Texas like spiderwebs. A Ranger in Fort Worth would soon be able to talk to one in El Paso and others in between. Such notable outlaws as Sam Bass and John Wesley Hardin, who earlier had been able to hit, then run for the brush, would soon find themselves hemmed in by wires and rails. They could still run, but it would be increasingly difficult to hide.